Craig Jones

2013, TWB Press
www.twbpress.com

Gem
Copyright 2013 by Craig Jones

Edited by Terry Wright

Cover Art by Terry Wright

ISBN 978-1-936991-64-8

Acknowledgements

To Claire and Shane for their undoubting support.

For Gemma James, who inspired (most) of who Gem
is...

And of course

For Terry and Bobette, Gem's #1 fans. Thanks for
believing

GEM – No Conspiracy

New York.

John Bradley barged past me and into our apartment. "Ladies, we have a problem." Usually such disrespect would have my gums throbbing, my teeth extending, and his blood all over my lips, but there was a look in his eyes I hadn't seen before.

He looks scared!

He turned to face me, wringing his hands. His top shirt button was undone, and his tie, usually so perfectly positioned, hung askew. Black stubble covered his chiselled chin and defined cheeks, and dark stormy shadows languished just below his eyes.

I closed the door, hoping my neighbours hadn't seen him storm in. They might call the cops.

Katrina is going to go ballistic that he's turned up unannounced!

"You'd better have a damn good reason for crashing my lair."

"Who knows about you?" he snapped, his lips twitchy and aggressive.

My gums ached to be split by my ferocious fangs. "Just us."

"Except for us, who knows?"

"Very few people," I replied, trying to remain calm. "Maria and Angel."

"Who else?" He gasped, and I thought he was actually going to fall to his knees on the floor and have a hissy fit right here.

He better not vomit on my new carpet. At fifty bucks a

yard...

I heard footsteps above me and knew within seconds Katrina would be making her way down the stairs.

This is going to get messy!

There had to be something I could say to calm Bradley down. "Our secret is safe."

"You're beautiful but so damned naïve, Gem," he said, his voice cracking. "After what I've seen tonight—"

"Gem," Katrina shouted from the top of the stairs. "What the hell is he doing here?" Her hands were jammed on her hips, and her right knee bent slightly. Damn she looked good in those short blue jean shorts.

Does she have any idea how hot she looks?

I was suddenly aware of how much we'd begun to mimic each other.

She glared at Bradley. "You have a lot of nerve—"

"Katrina!" he shouted. "What have you told your friends about us?"

She strutted down the stairs, blatantly ignoring him, and stood directly in front of me, a damnit-not-again look on her face. "We've got plans for tonight. You're not going out to kill someone. You promised!"

Bradley put his hand on her shoulder.

My vampire rage flared up.

No one touches my woman!

But then I saw the look on his face, the complete and utter desperation in those piercing eyes, and for the first time since he arrived in our lives, Bradley looked more than scared. He looked terrified to death.

I peeled his hand off Katrina's shoulder and placed my own conciliatory hand in its place. Her bare skin felt smooth and smouldering under my palm. "Nobody's going to ruin our night, babe."

Then I turned on Bradley. "I don't know what has gotten into you, but you have five seconds to tell us what is going on."

"Let me use your computer. I'll show you."

Moments later, Katrina and I flanked Bradley as he sat at my laptop, the one we almost died for, and he tapped a Web site into the browser.

www.twbpress.com

"What the hell is TWB Press?" Katrina asked. "Gem—"

"Just watch," Bradley implored.

The Web site booted up. It was an e-publishing site: horror, thrillers, science fiction.

"Look!" He scrolled down the page.

I suddenly felt a churning in the pit of my stomach as I recalled Bradley's earlier questions. Somebody did know about us, maybe the whole damn world.

"What the frick is going on?" I said, trying to keep my vampire blood pressure from blowing a gasket.

Katrina leaned forward and pushed Bradley out of the way to get a closer look at the screen. "Oh my god," she squeaked. "Gem! That's you!"

"That's what I saw in the mirror this morning." I was checking my gun, posing a little, okay, *I do that sometimes*, but somehow someone took my picture.

"There's more," Bradley said, elbowing his way in again. He clicked on my picture, it had my name on it and our motto, 'No Loose Ends' emblazoned across the bottom.

The picture grew bigger, and a brief description of my life appeared next to it.

**The New York underworld is no place for a lady...
but no one told Gem.**

Katrina's mouth hung agape.

A sick feeling in my belly spread throughout my body like I'd been shot in the heart with a silver bullet. I glanced down at Bradley. He actually looked a little relieved at having unburdened himself of this nightmare and proved he was not insane.

He clicked the mouse again. A new document appeared, pages of a book with the same picture of me looking at myself in the mirror. FREE Excerpt. Names appeared on the first page. Copyright by Craig Jones. Edited by Terry Wright. I wondered who the hell these people were.

Bradley flipped to the next page. A block of text came up. He butted his knuckles on the screen. "Read this."

Maloney looked around my room and nodded like he approved of the extravagance surrounding him: the inch-thick carpet with its diamond designs, the half moon flock of the wallpaper, and the antique furniture, polished to a museum quality shine. The two goons he brought with him flanked the door, equally impressed, I could tell by their dropped jaws and roving, wanton eyes. One of them set a briefcase on the floor beside him. Finally Maloney's eyes found me, and his expression turned from amazement to shock.

"I didn't expect you to be—"

"A vampire?" I asked, feeling the touch of a smile form on my lips.

"That's exactly how it began," I whispered. I would have shouted, but the breath had been sucked from my lungs.

Katrina pushed Bradley's hand off the mouse and began scanning ahead.

I shouted, "Katrina, no, please don't!"

But she found it; she read the part where Maloney first asked me to kill her. Of course I'd said no, but then he forced me to change my mind by threatening to kill Angel. A four-year-old little girl, damnit, Maloney had no couth whatsoever.

"I'm sorry you had to see that, Katrina."

Her chest hitched, and then she turned and sprinted from the room. I could hear her vomiting in the toilet.

"So you knew nothing about this biographer?" Bradley asked. "Craig Jones?"

"No, of course not."

"These two guys could take us all down, Gem. They know everything. What I've shown you is just the tip of iceberg. They know about Clayton, the botched job at the park, the dead woman, everything."

Katrina stepped back into the room. "Sorry about that. It's not every day you read about someone plotting your murder."

I stroked her arm gently and glared at Bradley. "Who the hell is this Jones guy, anyway?"

"Jones is from Wales," Bradley said, reading from a bio next to a photo of a scruffy-haired hunk.

"Where's that?" Katrina asked.

"Britain," I said.

"Some kind of tennis pro turned blabbermouth," he added.

"He's going on my hit list," I said, my fangs itching for his jugular.

"Then who is Terry Wright?"

"He's the editor," Bradley replied. "It's his Website. He's the ringleader."

"So he's pulling the strings?" I suggested.

"It's more like he's the Yoda to Jones' Luke Skywalker," Katrina offered.

Both Bradley and I looked at her, confused by her reference.

"Jones gets the scoop on us, then Wright hones the skills, trains him. They're working together."

"It's a conspiracy," Bradley said.

"So where's Wright?" I asked Bradley.

He brought up a photo of a well dressed man, hair going silver at the temples, smart-looking old guy. "Denver, Colorado."

I turned to Katrina. "Do you want to take a trip to the Rocky Mountains with me?"

"Oh. My. God," she said. "Are you going to kill Terry Wright?"

"He's on the top of my hit list, honey."

"Girls, girls," Bradley shouted. "He's probably heavily armed, heavily guarded."

I smiled "He won't even hear us coming."

Colorado

Slinking towards Terry Wright's front door, I felt my body change. Pheromones of murder pulsed through my undead heart. My perfectly manicured nails thickened and grew into talons. I felt the first stirrings of angst in my stomach. My gums split and my fangs extended. Sexual urges came to the fore, and images of Katrina writhing in our bed swamped my mind.

Focus, Gem. This is work.

The house was lit up, and the front door that I had every intention of smashing into matchsticks stood open. My vampire senses indicated that it was safe to enter, that I wasn't walking into a garlic trap.

I stepped inside, looked back at Katrina sitting in our hire car, and winked. I wanted her to feel at ease, to not worry, that we'd be all right after I finished draining this publisher's blood.

I need her to stay just where she is! In case I've underestimated Wright.

I closed the door behind me and stood silently in the hallway.

"Gem," a man's voice said. "Come in."

I almost jumped out of my perfectly smooth skin. How did he know I was here? How could he have been expecting me?

My vampire senses charged to full alert.

I followed the voice and walked into a study. Bookshelves lined the walls, floor to ceiling, 5000 strong, and posters of book signing events, The 13th Power everywhere.

Wright sat at a computer, his back to me.

My pupils dilated and my muscles tightened. I was ready to spring on him, drag him to the floor, and end his puppet master's life with a solid clamp of my jaw on his throat.

Terry Wright turned to face me, one hand still on the computer mouse, the other pressed flat to his chest. It looked like he was having trouble breathing. The old guy might die of a heart attack before I sucked him dry.

"Gads," he said. "You look just like Craig described you!"

I glanced past him at the computer screen where he'd been reading an email:

From: Craig Jones
Subject: Gem
The house was lit up, and the front door that I had every intention of smashing into matchsticks stood open.

What the hell?

Their conspiracy lay proven before me. They knew every move I was going to make before I did. The question was how did they do it, how did they know, and how much had they seen happen between Katrina and I...at night...when we're alone?

There was no way I could kill him before I learned the answers.

The computer pinged, announcing the arrival of an incoming email.

Terry's index finger twitched.

My muscles relaxed. As my anger faded to curiosity, my fangs withdrew back up into my gums, became teeth again, and my claws receded to beautifully manicured fingernails. I no longer wanted to tear Terry Wright limb from limb.

I read the words that appeared on the screen:

From: Craig Jones
Subject: Gem
Gem's anger faded and she no longer wanted to tear Terry Wright limb from limb.

"That's how it works," Wright said quietly, in a voice only a vampire could hear.

"But how do you do it?"

"I'm a publisher. I find writers and work with them to make their good stories great. Then I put them on the Internet for sale, worldwide. Craig sent me a story about a sexy vampire hit woman. I had no idea you'd turn out to be real."

The computer binged again.

From: Craig Jones
Subject: Gem
Gem shook her head. "I don't believe this."

I shook my head. "I don't believe this." My mouth fell open. I'd said everything that Craig had written.

How could I have been so wrong?

My brain filled with static. I couldn't think. Fear overwhelmed me.

Jones has been the real puppet master, all along! My *puppet master!*

Wright looked me up and down, *like most men do.* "Craig told me you were coming. I never thought you'd show up, but I wanted to meet you. And here you are, come to life."

Another email arrived.

From: Craig Jones
Subject: Gem
"You risked your life to meet me," Gem muttered.

I bit my lip, but the words muttered out anyway. "You risked your life to meet me."

Terry didn't bother to hide the smile that jumped onto his lips. "Sweetheart, I took out my own insurance." He tapped the hand that he held on his chest. "I'm wearing a crucifix under here, and if you attacked me, I was going to use it to stop you. I've read what happens to you if you see one of those bad boys."

Wright was right. He knew everything about me. He was in cahoots with the person who possessed the power to control me. My thought processes were like a plate of spaghetti.

"But you shouldn't want to hurt me. If it wasn't for me, you'd be history."

The computer beeped again.

From: Craig Jones
Subject: Gem
"Rubbish," Gem shouted.

I didn't fight it this time. "Rubbish," I shouted.

"When I first read about you, Gem was just one story. I suggested to Jones that he should write a series. It was me who kept you alive. And not just you." Wright paused and raised his brows, real cocky like. "But Katrina, too."

I raised my perfectly plucked eyebrows in response. "Katrina?"

"At the end of No Loose Ends, Craig made you kill Katrina. I made him rewrite the ending. I saved her, Gem. You owe me one for that."

My knees almost buckled.

I was meant to kill Katrina? Does Craig Jones have no heart?

I couldn't believe what I was hearing, what I had read in the emails Jones was sending Wright. The conspiracy had almost gone out of control. Terry Wright was my saviour.

I should ask Katrina to come in and thank him proper.

But my ire for Jones felt like a time-bomb ticking in my chest.

Another email:

From: Craig Jones
Subject: Gem
"So it's Jones I need to go after!" Gem said.

I shrugged. *Here it comes.* "So it's Jones I need to go after!" I said in a morose, monotone voice.

"You don't want to do that, either. If he dies, he stops writing. He stops writing and you will no longer exist."

No!

"And Katrina will no longer exist." Terry paused and respectfully lowered his head. "And Angel will no longer exist."

Jones has got me over a barrel.

The computer pinged again. I was beginning to hate that sound, and this time I didn't even bother to read the screen, I just let the words exit my stunned mouth.

"But my job relies on anonymity. If he's writing it down, then people are going to know what I'm doing. All they have to do is read the short stories."

"They'll think it's fiction," Terry said. "Simple as that. Come on, while Jones is knocking these stories out of the ball park, who's going to believe it's a real vampire bumping off New York's sleaze bags?"

I had no answer. Maybe Jones had a sudden case of writer's block.

But Wright was, once again, right. If I didn't cooperate, everyone I love will cease to exist. I was powerless against these guys.

I can't let anything happen to my girls.

An email arrived.

Jones suddenly had something for me to say. "So I go back home and forget this ever happened?"

"I advise it highly. But before you go, one more thing." He stood up and walked to the door. "Bobette!" he called.

A woman joined us in the study. She was wearing a gym kit like she'd just come back from instructing a Zumba class. She smiled at me like I was a celebrity.

"It's such a pleasure to meet you, Gem," she said. "I'm a big fan. I hope Katrina is well, and I'm so glad you didn't kill her."

"Your husband saved her life," I said with a slight bow of undying appreciation.

"I know," Bobette said. "That's all he ever talks about anymore, Gem, No Loose Ends. Gem, No Secrets. Gem. Gem. Gem. Now if you'll please excuse me, I'm missing American Idol, and I'm sure you have more bad guys to kill. It's been fun talking with you."

An email arrived.

"The pleasure is all mine. But now I have to go." I shook her hand, waved goodbye to Terry Wright, and left the way I came in.

"She's beautiful," I heard Bobette say behind me.

"Gotta hand it to Craig Jones," Terry replied. "He sure

knows how to pick 'em."

I enjoyed their conversation as I walked back towards the hire car and Katrina.

How the hell do I explain this to her?

I pulled the door closed with a clunk and tried to ignore Katrina's questioning glare.

"Well?" she asked. "Is he dead?"

"This is bigger than both of us, girl."

"You didn't kill him?"

"No. He's too valuable."

"So we're going after Craig Jones instead?"

"No. We're going home."

"But the conspiracy? How is Jones writing about us?"

"It's no conspiracy, Katrina. It's magic."

"So what do we do when we get back to New York?"

I sighed. "We wait to see what new adventures Craig Jones has in store for us."

GEM – No Loose Ends

The Deal

Can't a girl get any alone time?

Maloney stepped into my suite, looked around, and nodded like he approved of the extravagance surrounding him: the inch-thick carpet with its diamond designs, the half moon flock of the wallpaper, and the antique furniture, polished to a museum quality shine. The two goons he brought with him flanked the door, equally impressed, I could tell by their dropped jaws and roving, wanton eyes. One of them set a briefcase on the floor beside him.

Finally Maloney's eyes found me, and his expression turned from amazement to shock. "I didn't expect you to be—"

"A vampire?" A touch of a smile formed on my lips. I leaned back in the leather lounge chair I'd poised myself on, my black cocktail dress peeling up my tight thighs. His gaze traversed my favourite high-heeled boots, to my knees, jumped over the good stuff to my straight-combed black hair. I flicked it over my left shoulder and let it hang teasingly across my ample cleavage. To say I felt sexy would be an understatement.

"No," he said, the atmosphere between us thickening with distrust. "I know what you are."

I inhaled deeply on my cigarette.

So what if I'm a show off?

Tilting my chin up, I blew a perfectly formed smoke

ring toward him. It slowly circled its way across the room, glowing in the winter moonlight that beamed in through the window. "Then what did you expect me to be, Mister Maloney?"

He flicked his lighter to life and lit a foul-smelling Turkish brand cigarette someone must've told him was fashionable. "I didn't expect you to be so damn gorgeous."

"And is that a problem?"

"No. No. It's just that—"

"You have no problem hiring a vampire to do your dirty work, but a *damned* gorgeous woman vampire makes you question the reliability you're buying?"

He straightened the lapels of his jacket and refused to meet my stare. The suit, like his choice of cigarettes, stank of trying too hard to fit in with the Mob. He reeked of cheapness.

"Not at all. But a hit-woman with tits like those babies, *everybody* is going to see you coming!"

One of his goons let out a snort that was clearly a suppressed laugh. Maloney flashed him a look that, if I had been human, would have made my stomach tighten with fear.

"So you don't like my tits?"

"I was just surprised, is all. After everything I've heard about you, I expected an ugly bitch with muscles coming out her ears."

His accent was forced Bronx, but I'd bet he was no more than a generation off the immigrant boat from Dublin. With some clients, I'd leave the rich, velvet curtains that divided my lair in two sections wide open, so they could see my magnificent walnut coffin, set on its 24 carat gold dais, just so they understood the quality they were dealing with. But for this lowlife, Maloney, I was glad I hadn't bothered. He just wouldn't get it.

"Ugly bitch, huh. Don't judge a cover by its book, Mister Maloney, but I'm happy to hear my reputation isn't as pretty as I am."

"You're a killer. That's good enough for me."

I ground out my stub in the ashtray on the table next to my lounge chair and plucked another cigarette from its humidor. Before I had chance to strike a long wooden match, he relit his lighter and offered it to me.

Chivalry isn't dead, after all.

I nodded, his cue to approach me. As he stepped forward, I felt hungry for the blood pulsing through his veins but ignored my instincts and put my cigarette tip to the flame. A smile threatened to expose my thoughts as I admired the size of this guy, a big man but not fat. His body looked like he'd been cut out of wood, his jaw strong, his broad shoulders stretching the seams of his poorly tailored coat. He wasn't movie star good-looking, but he certainly had sex appeal. I couldn't lie to myself. There was something about him that made me ache for more than his blood.

"And what have you heard about me?" I probed, crossing my legs and running my free-hand fingers over my bare knee. I felt his eyes slide up my exposed thighs. The lust in his gaze told me he wanted to see more.

I may be a vampire, but every girl deserves a little flattery, right?

He exhaled, blowing smoke straight at me. "They say you're the best. That you make problems go away. You don't leave any loose ends." He sucked on his cigarette, and as the amber tip flared, the glow reflected off the sweat on his face.

I like to keep it hot in my lair.

"The problems you make go away don't come back, meaning my problem ain't gonna bob to the surface in the bay or wash up on Liberty Island where a bunch of tourists will scream and gawk at it."

"That's true," I whispered.

"So what do you say? You gonna kill her for me?"

I turned away from him and looked out of the window. My apartment, in a prime Manhattan location, overlooked Central Park. Clouds drifted over the moon, and the first wisps of snow were beginning to frost the treetops. The orange glow of the streetlamps that lined the path looked like upside-down snow cones, blurred in the thickening flurries.

"Depends. Who is she?"

"You don't need to know."

"Mister Maloney, you are going to have to tell me more. You say you've heard of me? Then you should know I don't take a job if there are drugs involved."

"No, not drugs." He blinked.

That blink told me not to believe him.

"My boss refers to you as Gem. Like the Hope Diamond, you know, he thinks you're priceless. What's you're real name?"

"Gem." I said it matter-of-factly in hopes of ending the issue.

My real name doesn't matter anymore.

Flattery was one thing, but he'd been trying to haze the issue, and I'd caught him on it. I made sure my eyes told him just that. His cheeks flamed with embarrassment. He inhaled on his cigarette, but the cheap brand had already burned out. As he lit it again, I noticed a gold band on the ring finger of his left hand.

I don't need my sixth sense to see where this one is going. Too bad for him. I don't do wives and mothers.

"I know you're expensive, and that ain't no problem because..." he turned to his goons, "...Jimmy, bring that briefcase over here."

The goon at the door bent over to retrieve the case at his feet.

"Don't!" I commanded with a pointed finger and noticed the scuffed condition of my fingernail.

I need to get a manicure tomorrow.

Jimmy froze in mid stoop. He didn't make eye contact with Maloney, just slowly straightened to his pointless sentry position.

"Don't insult me by showing off your money. I haven't agreed to accept the job."

"What's it gonna take?" Maloney dug a stained white handkerchief from an inside coat pocket and wiped the sweat from his eyes. "I know you don't do no job you don't believe in. Whatever the hell that means."

"It means I'm picky. I don't go around snuffing just anyone. The target has to be a mobster who is a clear and present danger to our organization. Our Mob. One of us, one of them, it doesn't matter. Is your wife a mobster, Mister Maloney?"

He shook his head.

"Then we are finished here. You're free to show yourself out."

The scowl on his face tells me he's never been spoken to by a woman in this way.

"She's my mistress, okay? My mistress."

"That settles it." I blew another smoke ring. "I should kill her just for her bad taste in men."

"My wife, since the kids left, you know, she's, not so much for the hanky panky, so I got me a little something on the side."

"Good for you. Why do you want her dead?"

"One night, I think she's asleep when one of my mob boys calls the hotel, and we make plans. Big plans."

I slowly uncrossed my legs and leaned forward, perching my elbows softly on my knees. I knew this would draw my dress up my thighs a little farther. I wanted him to think I was interested, in every way, just to keep his mind off balance. If he was going to slip up, now was the time. "What kind of plans?"

"Let's just say it's a new business opportunity." He dragged his lecherous gaze from my legs.

"Illegal arms trade?" I ventured.

"No guns. Damn it. You wanna hear this or not?"

I nodded and inhaled smoke.

"When I get off the phone, she's standing in the hallway, and though she swears she heard nothing, I see the lie in her eyes."

And I see the lie in his eyes too. He's not telling me everything. No doubt about it.

"Go on."

"So I tell my Bosses I think there's a leak, right? She might compromise our plans, and they tells me, either I deal with it myself, or they'll look after it for me. And I know that if they *look after it,* it won't be pretty. That's why I came to you."

I inhaled on my cigarette. "Dead is dead, what do you care how it's done?"

"I love her. There, okay, I said it out loud. I love her. I don't want her dead. But alive, she could rat us out to the cops, she could make a mint selling us out to another mob. I can't swear I trust her, so she's a liability, at least that's how the Bosses see it."

A sudden flash of clarity hit me like a board upside my head. I knew where he was taking this. The dirty rotten son of a bitch had a lot of nerve.

"But you...You can make her forget. You can..."

"Turn her?" I interjected.

"You can make her like you."

I hate it when I'm right.

"She won't remember what she heard."

"Or anything about who she was," I added, trying to keep my rising temper from showing. Maloney was just an idiot who didn't know what he was saying, what it meant to be turned, to be condemned to existing in an undead body."

"Then we can still be together," he went on. "I don't want to lose her."

I stubbed out my cigarette. "I'm not interested in

salvaging your love life, Mister Maloney. It's time for you to go." I stood and extended my hand toward the door.

Maloney made no effort to leave. "Don't be too hasty, Gem."

"I don't want the job." I maintained an amiable front. "It's that simple."

"I'm willing to pay you double your normal fee."

"I don't want your money, Mister Maloney. Now please go, before I insist like the ugly bitch I really am."

He smiled at me in a way that had undoubtedly broken a few hearts over the years. "All right, Gem, if you won't do it for me, and you won't do it for money..." he reached into his jacket, "...perhaps you'll do it..." and produced a photograph, "....for her," which he displayed like he'd just pulled the Ace in a poker tournament of champions.

I saw the picture, somewhat thankful it wasn't a gun, but the image tore into my heart sure as any silver-tipped bullet. Little girl, hugging a teddy bear, six years old, blond curls, Shirley Temple smile.

"Angel," I whispered. That was all the breath I could manage.

Questions reeled in my head. How did this creep get her picture? How did he even know she existed? The son of a bitch! "What are you trying to pull, Maloney?"

"You can't watch over her every minute."

He had me, and he knew it, the way his chest puffed out like a badass rooster.

Anger over took me, and with hardly an effort, I flung the table across the room with one hand. It tore through the curtain, impacted with a corner of my coffin and split in two, the crack of the wood as loud as a shotgun blast. Cigarettes flew from the humidor, and ashes blew into the air like a smoke bomb had exploded. With the curtains torn aside, my coffin sat there, exposed.

Like this piece of shit needs reminding what the fuck I am!

Maloney stumbled backwards and dropped the photograph. It floated to the carpet and landed face down. I ejected my ravenous fangs, my gums tearing and bleeding, they'd shot out so fast. "You dare to threaten her," I roared, my raging voice more masculine and demonic than I'd ever heard it before. Bloodlust flowed through my veins, blowtorch hot as I rose up on the balls of my feet, ready to spring for Maloney's throat.

His goons reached for their guns.

"Hold your fire, boys."

I could kill them all before their silver bullets took effect. One or two I could stand, maybe six, as pissed as I was. Hell, it would take a machine-gun's barrage to hurt me right now. Already my fingernails had transformed into talon-sharp claws, raring to rip flesh from bones.

Maloney jammed his palms at me. "Before you do something stupid, Gem, my Bosses know where she lives. If anything happens to me, the little girl gets it."

"I'll kill them too!" My fangs ached for Maloney's neck, and his goons' necks...

"You can't fight the whole mob, Gem. You better let us walk out of here, or one day you'll be sleeping in your box when my Bosses get to Angel. And it won't be pretty."

My breath hitched in my throat. He was right. I couldn't protect Angel every minute of every day. I'd need another set of eyes, someone I could trust to watch my back and help me keep her safe. No such person existed, not now, or ever had. Sooner or later, Angel would die at hands of the mob. Like her mother...

"Do what you're told, Gem. Nobody gets hurt."

Throttling down my attack, I realised there was no way I could win in the end. If I didn't turn his mistress, Angel's death would be my fault.

"What do you say?" Maloney asked, this time with a cocky edge to his words. "We got a deal now?"

Gem

The Deal Done

I could have kept walking on 59th Street, but instead, I took a right at the Pulitzer Fountain and headed down 5th. The snow had begun to fall steadily and was accumulating quickly in the gutters and on the sidewalks. Streams of taxi cabs sloshed their way down the road.

Angel.

She was all I could think about as the night around me turned chillier. The cold and damp air mirrored my dread for Angel and what Maloney or his Bosses would do to her if I failed to make this hit. We'd made a deal, all right, Maloney and I, but he'd made a mistake, trying to fuck me with his pants on. He wasn't going to get away with it, but right at this moment, I didn't know how I was going to fuck him back.

The city, even at this late hour, had a pulse. I could feel it everywhere I walked:

In the cold throat of the blond secretary being escorted by her boss.

In the strong neck of the cop directing traffic on Madison.

In the wrists of the newlyweds as they held hands, waiting for the cross sign to change to green.

I felt all of these feeding opportunities and more, yet I felt no urgency, no hunger. I had a job to do. For Angel.

I checked my Cartier wrist watch, nearly midnight, and lengthened my stride, my bare ankles not feeling the cold as my floor length mink coat rose up to accommodate my new speed. After Maloney had left, I'd picked out an appropriate dress. Sexy short, yes, of course, but for tonight's venue, more classy and upscale with lace and pearls.

Come midnight, Maloney was supposed to meet his mistress, Katrina, in the bar of the Waldorf-Astoria. If he wasn't there by half past, she was to make her way up to the room he had booked for them. She could open the bottle of Champagne there, waiting on ice, and slip into a nice warm bubble bath before he arrived. On this count I could not fault the man. He dressed like a fool, smoked like a grifter, but he knew how to treat a lady right.

He may have only booked her a sixth floor room, but it was still the Waldorf-Astoria.

Except, of course, Maloney had no intention of being anywhere near the place. Instead he'd arranged a substitute for his mistress, an unwelcome one.

Me.

As the Concierge opened the door, I slipped him a twenty and reviewed what Maloney had told me. She was a blonde, tall woman, and she would be wearing a camel coloured coat he'd bought her just the week before. I'd told him that was all I needed to know. After all, he'd unknowingly marked her with his distinct scent. In a roomful of camel-coated mistresses, I'd have sniffed her out in a second.

Those were the skills that the likes of Maloney usually paid over the odds for. Five grand up front. Five grand when the job was completed. And I was happy to take them any little trinket they wanted as proof the job was done.

I'd once carried a head through Chicago, torn a golden tooth out in Phili, and pulled off more wedding rings than Liz Taylor ever wore.

And all this schmuck wants is that expensive camel coloured coat.

I stepped into the bar and removed my mink in one easy motion. The Bell Hop was at my side in a second, and the garment was quickly in his care. My black cocktail dress was at least six inches shorter than any others in the room, and it drew the attention of a table full of businessmen, all overdressed, inebriated, and whooping their approval.

"Easy boys," I purred, taking a stool at the bar. I

placed my clutch bag on the marble surface.

The waiter slid a Cosmo in front of me. "From the gentlemen at the table over there."

I turned and nodded thanks to my businessmen fans, and then took a tiny sip. It gave me the second I needed to scan the room. I didn't spot Blondie anywhere.

Maybe she'd given up waiting for him and already went upstairs.

I hoped not and checked my watch again. Twenty past midnight.

If she did what she was told to do, she should still be here.

The door to the ladies' room opened, and the stink of stale Turkish cigarette smoke smacked me like a slap across my face.

And there she is, Katrina.

My mouth watered and my fangs slid out of my gums. Not from hunger, but from desire. She was blond and tall, all right, but leggy, as well. Her dress was as short as mine, hourglass shaped, low-cut, bare-shouldered, a blistering pink, and her shoes were a pair I would have chosen myself. She may have had bad taste in men, but Maloney's taste in women was most excellent.

She wore a watch but no other jewellery. Her make up was subtle but classy. She didn't look out of place in this ritzy setting. I almost forgot to breathe.

Her sultry eyes darted along the bar, towards the door, and back to the bar. She was looking for Maloney, I knew, but when her gaze landed on me, I smiled, hoping she could read into it what I meant.

I'm impressed. I'm interested. I'm turned on just looking at you.

But she just looked away, scanning barstools and tables for the wretched Mister Maloney.

I had to take a deep breath to get back on track. She was my target. I had a job to do, irregardless of my

feelings. If I didn't turn her, the mob Bosses would kill her.
I'm here for her own good, damnit.

And for Angel.

Katrina took a seat down the bar from me. That's when I saw the camel coloured coat. She had left it draped over her stool, and now she cradled it on her lap like a precious kitten.

Her fingertips tapped the bar in rhythm to strains of jazz that permeated the room. The bartender approached her. She shook her head, obviously turning down another drink. I sipped mine and watched her get to her feet. My heart beat jumped. The next few moments would require some highly sophisticated choreography. If I wasn't a vampire, I wouldn't be able to pull it off.

She glanced sadly towards the main entrance of the hotel and then pulled her coat over her shoulders. As she walked past me, I knew I would be doing her a favour tonight, but what a waste of beautiful flesh.

I waited until she stood in front of the bank of lifts, and then retrieved my bag and followed. Two of the younger businessmen spotted me, broke off from the pack at the drunkards' table, and halted my progress.

"Can we buy you another drink?" one ventured.

"Now, boys," I teased.

A lift door opened.

"I'll be back shortly. You can buy me a drink then."

While the other drunken businessmen whistled, egging these two on, I could see they would not be easily swayed.

"Just have a drink with us," the other man said. The oil in his hair made my nose twitch.

Katrina stepped into the lift.

"Like I said, later boys." I pressed for the lifts with more determination.

They grabbed my left arm. Stopped me. I almost dropped my bag.

"Don't make us look like idiots in front of our friends. Just..."

The door was closing.

I straightened the fingers of my right hand and jabbed my nails into the closest man's sternum. He buckled into my shoulder, gagging.

"Nobody touches me," I growled in his ear. To anyone around us, it looked as if we were having a tender moment, even as I grabbed the other man by the balls and yanked him into our lovely tryst. Both men were gasping. I hoped they could hear me. "When I let go, walk back to the table. Forget you've ever seen me. Got that?"

They whined like little boys.

I squeezed the balls harder. My vampire grip must've felt like a crushing steel vice.

"All right, all right." They let go of my arm.

I let go of the prick's balls.

Both men stepped away from me, a twin look of fear staring at me as they back-peddled towards the table.

Let's see them explain those bruises to their wives in the morning.

With a twirl, I hurried to the lifts, hoping beyond hope I'd make it upstairs before Katrina was safely put away in her room.

Another lift dinged its arrival. I rushed in through the still-opening doors and asked the operator for floor six. While on the way up, I pulled an old and empty purse from inside my clutch bag.

"Sixth floor," he announced, like I didn't already know.

I stepped out onto thick, luxurious carpet. Katrina was halfway down the corridor already. I would have to act quickly. I threw the purse along the floor and called amiably after her. "Miss! Oh, Miss? I think you've dropped something."

She stopped and turned. The coat was still slung over

her shoulders.

I tried to imagine this stunning creature lying naked next to Maloney. The pieces of that picture didn't fit.

"I'm sorry?" she asked. "What was that?"

I bent to scoop up the purse and held it out to her as I moved forward, a cat slinking up on a mouse. "Is this yours?"

She squinted at me and then at the purse. "No, no. That's not mine." She turned and withdrew her room key.

My gums tingled as my fangs pushed through. Even her voice made my vampire pheromones spill into my bloodstream, hot and lustful. "Are you sure?"

"Yes," she said as her door clicked open. "Maybe you should hand it in to reception."

My pupils dilated. I'd come close enough to her now, I could see her neck veins pulse.

"Of course. You're..." I slammed my elbow into her jaw. The snap of her teeth slamming together echoed along the empty corridor. She stumbled backwards into her room. The coat dislodged from her shoulders and fell to the floor, tripping her up. Before she had chance to catch her balance, I closed the door. As she fell onto the bed, my teeth were at her throat.

"Don't fight me."

"What do you want?" She gasped. "I have money—"

I bit her neck. My fangs sunk into her flesh easy as a warm muffin. Her pulse was racing, and that first swallow of blood was a red-hot gusher. The warmth spread through my body making me yearn for pleasures that would quench the unmistakeable heat between my thighs.

I felt her try to scream, but the pressure I put on her throat kept her quiet.

This is for your own damn good.

And Angel's.

I breathed through my nose between gulps. Her White Rose perfume inflamed my desire, not for blood, but for sex. I wanted her more than I've ever wanted anyone, and here I was sucking the life from her, turning her warm body stone cold in preparation for her transformation into an undead monster, like me. I killed for money. For the mob. I was their darkest agent. I was untouchable. Until now. Maloney was trying to change all that.

Why am I thinking of him right now?

I'd caught a whiff of his underlying stench, the foul stain he had left on this beautiful woman whose blood was now coursing down my throat. I could taste every drink she ever drank, every mouth she'd ever kissed, including Maloney's. I wanted to puke, but I guzzled on, not just for her sake, but Angel's, as well. I'd sworn an oath to keep her safe, a sacred pact with her mother as she lay dying in my arms that I would always protect her Angel. I wasn't about to break that vow now.

Katrina wasn't fighting me anymore. Her pulse became slow and weak. And as I drained her blood, I made sure to slop some all over Maloney's precious camel coloured coat.

The Deal Broken

The snowstorm had increased in intensity, so much so that I wished I'd worn my knee-high boots instead of these six-inch heels. Walking back to my place had become a trek through ankle deep snow. I carried the camel coloured coat over my shoulder with the blood stain folded inward. No sense advertising my latest meal. I hoped Maloney would choke on the damn coat.

Finally, I reached my apartment and unlocked the door. After kicking snow off my shoes, I stepped inside. My stomach felt instantly sick. My sense of smell swam in confusion, and I didn't know why. A blinding light suddenly burnt into my retinas. It took every bit of energy I had to lift my arms up in front of my eyes. Then I felt myself knocked toward the floor. Instinctively, I lashed out with balled fists, struck something solid, and then I hit the floor.

"She broke my arm," a man's voice shrieked. "My arm! My arm!"

I would have charged at the voice, if not for the blinding light in my eyes and my tethered sense of smell. And something had zapped my vampire strength.

A boot connected with my ribs, and I felt a bone snap inside my chest.

That hurt.

Before I had chance to defend myself, the boot smashed into my jaw. I think it was the same boot, I'm not sure, but there were at least two thugs in my lair, one screaming like a girl, and the other kicking the shit out of me.

I flipped over onto my back, and in the bright glow above me, dark shadows moved and hovered like menacing ghosts.

"That's enough, boys. Now back off."

Maloney!

The room dimmed and the pain in my eyes dulled. The odour of stale Turkish cigarette smoke now helped me focus. As I sat up, I brought my fingers to my lips. They came back smeared in blood.

My blood.

I looked around the room. Maloney and ten other suited mobsters surrounded me. Half of them held crucifixes, which they now pointed down at the floor.

So that's how they got me.

A crucifix was like a welding torch arc with the kick of a shotgun. I was powerless against one crucifix, crippled against five. "Why?" I muttered.

"I had to be sure you were under control before we had this conversation. It would take nothing for you to kill me..." he glanced at his goon buddies, "...all of us for that matter. Consider yourself handcuffed. It's for your safety and ours."

I should have known not to trust this fucker!

Before leaving the Waldorf-Astoria, I'd placed a call to Maloney on my cell phone, telling him to meet me at my apartment in half an hour. I had the proof he needed that the hit was made and told him to bring the rest of my money.

He plucked the camel coloured coat from the floor where I'd dropped it and brought it to his face, inhaling the sweet scent of the woman he wanted dead. When he took the coat away, his smiling face morphed to scorn. "What's this?" he shouted, pointing at the blood stain. "I told you not to ruin this coat!"

"Murder is a messy business," I managed to squeak out.

He scowled down at me. "You know how much this coat costs? Five grand. I can't give it to my wife in this condition."

"How good of you," I croaked. "Second hand coat for your wife. You think she's so stupid she won't smell the perfume in it?"

"White Rose," he said. "Same as my wife wears. That's not by accident. It's by design. You owe me five grand, bitch! But don't worry. I'll take it out of the final payment I owe you."

He threw the coat at me and charged across the room where he retrieved the briefcase he had left with me earlier.

The down payment on the hit!

He shook it in my direction. "And I'll be taking this as interest!" He stormed out of the room.

I tried to climb to my feet, but one of his goons raised a crucifix to my face, knocking me back down.

"Don't go after him," the goon warned. "Or you'll get worse than this."

"Like a wooden stake through your heart," another goon put in.

"Anything happens to Maloney, and the little girl gets whacked." Like a Blackjack dealer, he flipped a photo of Angel onto my chest. "Don't forget. We know where she lives."

"And this is for my arm, bitch." A boot slammed into my face again, kicking me into a deep dark well.

When I next opened my eyes I was alone. While I was out cold, my vampire body had started to heal. My rib was back in place and whole again. My lip was no longer split, and whatever that last kick had done to my jaw had been repaired. I struggled to my feet with a groan and staggered to the bathroom. The injuries may be healing, but I would still need to wash my blood off with soap and water.

Maloney had done his homework! He knew to smear garlic around the doorframes, the bathroom door and the front door, effectively sealing my fate.

Clever boy.

Although the use of garlic as a weapon against me was as pointless as a lead bullet, it did mess with my senses. No wonder they'd taken me by surprise. I couldn't smell them. And my sixth sense was short-circuited.

I entered the bathroom and washed my face.

But that'll happen just the once.

At the moment, *I* was the loose end that Maloney had failed to tie up. That blink when he'd lied to me about the drugs, the fact that he couldn't look me in the eye when he mentioned that so-called *business opportunity*: these things I had not forgotten. So I'd made me a backup plan. A fail safe. Now the lying scumbag was going to pay in full.

They should have killed me while they had the chance.

I dried my face and left my suite, pausing only long enough to pick up the ruined camel coloured coat on the way out.

The New Deal

I unlocked the hotel room door without a sound and

slipped inside the dark room. I could make out her shape on the bed, under the covers. Her toe wiggled, creating a tiny wave in the bedspread.

I paused, utterly silent, to hear her breathing, shallow and watery, like a kid sleeping with a snotty nose.

Satisfied she was alive, I folded the camel coloured coat over a chair and crossed the room with such stealth that even a fully awake guard dog would have mistaken me for a puff of wind. At her bedside now, I pulled the sheet away from the pillows.

Katrina was just where I had left her, in a room I'd booked on the eighth floor of the Waldorf-Astoria, after the attack, during the remorse, but before the guilt set in. I'd told the lift operator she was passed out drunk. In truth, I couldn't bring myself to kill her. Not for that lying son-of-a-bitch, Maloney. Not for the Mob. Not even for Angel, whom I would double my efforts to protect, like I would now protect Katrina. The Mob had fucked with the wrong vampire.

Her eyes fluttered as she tried to cling to consciousness. The puncture wound in her neck had wept a little, staining the pillowcase, but not so much as to arouse the suspicion of the maids.

A bloody nose would do worse.

And the stain could have been bigger if my saliva hadn't accelerated the healing process.

I switched on the bedside lamp and leaned over her. She was pallid, her lips blue, and a big bruise swelled where I'd bashed her jaw. I worried that I'd taken too much of her blood.

Still she hadn't given up her hold on life. She wasn't just beautiful, she was strong.

"Katrina," I said, stroking her face.

She writhed and murmured.

"Katrina. Are you thirsty?"

Her lips parted just a little, and under her eyelids her

eyes were jerking about in fitful REM sleep. It would take some extreme measures to bring her round.

I reached into my clutch bag and withdrew a single-edge razor blade. Vampires always carried some kind of cutter with them, just in case a bloodletting became necessary. Like now.

I didn't believe in loose ends.

I made a quick incision in my wrist. Blood swelled to the surface.

I squeezed the vein enough to release a small drop, which I let fall between Katrina's sultry lips. Her eyes popped wide open. Vampire blood, my blood, is ten times more potent than smelling salts and twice as stimulating as a shot of adrenaline to the heart. It could also become passionately addictive.

"Lick your lips," I told her and let another blood drop fall.

"Yessss," she moaned, her back arching under her. I'd forgotten about the aphrodisiac properties of vampire blood, as well. Her high was making me high.

"A little more."

She reached up, grabbed my wrist and pulled it to her mouth, those beautiful lips now pressed against my skin, her tongue flicking blood from the wound with the passion of a lover, her body bucking for a moment before settling, and her eyes searching mine for understanding.

How could she, though, understand the woman who had come to kill her, now giving back her life?

Within an hour she was sitting up in the bed, propped on either side by luxurious pillows and sipping occasionally at a glass of water I had drawn from the bathroom sink. No room service for us tonight. Her fingers kept wandering to her neck. While not yet looking entirely human, she no longer resembled a fresh corpse.

"Hello, Katrina. Are you feeling better now?" My voice seemed to startle her, as if she'd just awoken from a

Gem

bad dream, and she curled her legs up underneath her and scooted to the headboard.

"You..." Katrina croaked. "Get away from me!"

"Don't be afraid."

"I'll scream!"

"I'm here to help you."

"You...you hit me... you...you bit my neck. How's that helping?"

"I just saved your life."

"You're crazy!" She scrambled off the bed, but her wobbly legs wouldn't hold her. I caught her fall.

"Let me go. Where's my shoes?"

I set her back down on the bed. "You can't go."

"You can't keep me here."

"Out there..." I pointed to the door, "...you die. In here, you live."

"What are you talking about?"

I sat at the foot of the bed. There was no way I could sugar-coat the truth. "Maloney hired me to kill you."

"Kill me? My Maloney? He wouldn't—"

"You're right, not kill you but...turn you."

"Turn me?"

"Into one of me."

"An assassin?"

"No. A vampire." To press the point home, I opened my mouth, showed her my fangs coming down, and hissed like a mad banshee.

At that, she scrambled back to the headboard. "I'm dead? I'm a vampire?"

"No."

"But I drank your blood."

"I didn't kill you, so I can't turn you. My blood gave your body a kick start. You're very much alive and human, I'm afraid."

"Thank God."

"But that's exactly why you aren't safe."

"Why not?"

"Maloney thinks you overheard him making plans on the phone. His Bosses told him to kill you, or they would, but he opted to have me turn you so he could keep on screwing your brains out."

"That's the only reason?"

"Hello, Katrina. He has a wife. What else is a mistress good for?"

"That lying son of a bitch." Katrina leaned toward me. "He said he left her, moved out, gave her the house. She took him to the cleaners along the way. I felt sorry for the big goof—"

"If that big goof or his Bosses find out you're still alive, they'll all come after you, Katrina. They won't stop until you're dead."

She put her hand on her heart. "What am I going to do?"

"Tell me what you overheard on the phone."

"I knew he was talking to the Columbian. He talked to him differently. That guy scares me."

"Who's the Columbian?"

"I don't know his name, but I know he was arranging for the stuff to get into the country."

"Stuff?"

"Cocaine."

That was enough to make my vampire blood boil. "He told me there were no drugs involved."

"He told me he'd left his wife." The fury of a woman scorned cut deep lines in her forehead.

"The bastard lied to both of us." And he'd cheated me out of my money and threatened to kill Angel, but Katrina didn't need to know that. "Did you hear where the drugs were coming in from?"

"There's a boat down at the docks where they're keeping the cocaine until its ready to be moved onto the streets."

Gem

I had no doubt about what I was going to do now.

"What dock?"

"You're not thinking what I think you're thinking?"

"I am."

Her face wrenched with terror. "They'll kill you."

"They'll try."

She left her sanctuary at the headboard, and knee-walked to me, still sitting at the foot of the bed. "Why didn't you kill me, or turn me?"

"I didn't trust Maloney, besides..." I smiled at her, hoping she'd see the affection on my lips. "You impressed me."

"Impressed? How?"

"Look at you. You're beautiful."

Her eyes turned round in shock. "You're a lesbian vampire?"

"Not that I know of..." I sighed. "Until now."

"I've never been with a woman."

"Ditto."

She swallowed. "I don't know whether to love you or hate you...you... What's your name?"

"Gem."

"Not really."

"Really."

"So what are we going to do, Gem?"

I touched her jaw where I'd bashed her with my elbow. The bruise cleared up immediately. "Sink a boat."

"I'm going with you."

I looked into her determined eyes. "I thought you might want a little revenge."

"Partners?" She held out her hand to me.

"It's going to be dangerous."

"More dangerous than being attacked by a vampire?"

"Point taken." I smiled, took her hand in mine, felt that warm fire still burning. I'm so glad I didn't snuff it out. "They'll be expecting me tonight, and they'll be ready with things that can kill me."

"What do you want me to do?"

"Wear that camel coloured coat of yours and look beautiful as ever."

"I can do that."

Done Dealing

I drove my Porsche towards the docks with Katrina riding shotgun. I couldn't stop my eyes as they flittered from the road ahead to her face and back. She was snuggled in that camel coloured coat, open down the front, and wore the same dress she had on at the Waldorf. I was wearing my active wear, black tennis shoes, black tights, and black jacket. I'd tied my black hair up in a ponytail. Even when hunting, I looked pretty damn sexy.

"Are you sure you are up to this?" I asked as I extinguished the headlights and drove slowly around the cargo containers on the dock front.

She nodded with a determined clench of her jaw.

I brought the car to a stop. We were far enough away from the ship that the mobster drug dealers wouldn't have heard my engine. From here, we'd approach on foot. I took the keys from the ignition and gave them to her, noticing how much colour had returned to her cheeks.

"You're sure about the boat?"

"The Madeira, yes. It made me think of the cake."

"And you know what to do?"

She turned fierce eyes to me. "Don't pin me as a bimbo just because of one mistake. He told me he loved me. I believed him—"

"I meant if things go wrong. You drive away without me, you hear?"

"Don't screw up and I won't have to."

We got out of the car, and I took a moment to remove my tennis shoes and place them under the front seat. I closed the door and moved to her side of the car where she was taking off her high-heel shoes.

"Leave them on. We want them to hear you coming."

She nodded, slipped her heels back on and gently closed the door. She made no attempt to lock the car, just as we'd discussed.

She's definitely not a bimbo.

I grabbed the lapels of her camel coloured coat and pulled them together around her neck. "He's going to shit his pants when he sees you wearing this."

How long can I fight this urge to kiss her?

"The blood stain is awful," Katrina said.

"He was going to give it to his wife."

She bared her teeth, those perfect white teeth. "Go get him, Gem."

"After we're done here. I promise."

"Be careful."

"You too."

We stuck to the shadows as we advanced down the dock. The gentle lapping sounds of the waves on the harbour walls were soothing, in stark contrast to the rage burning inside me. I had to put these guys out of business and save Angel at the same time. It was going to be tricky.

An old and battered trawler was moored fifty yards to our left, the gangplank extended and lights burning in the forward portals. I could just make out the corroded red paint on the bow indicating the name: *Madeira.*

Katrina started strutting toward it.

Car lights suddenly careened around a corner on the opposite side of the ship and sped toward the gangplank.

"Wait, Katrina." I yanked her back into the shadows. "Not yet."

"What is this, Grand Central Station?" she quipped.

Two men wearing suits appeared at the gangplank as the black vehicle came to a halt. The passenger window rolled down. The two men spoke into the open window.

"What are they saying?" Katrina asked.

My vampire hearing picked up: *You got my order ready?* came from the car, then: *You got our money?* came from the dock.

"It's a drug deal going down," I told her.

A third man appeared at the boat rail, holding a small brown parcel. He bounded down the gangplank, and now flanked by his colleagues, he walked to the car, and through the window, they exchanged one parcel for another.

Pleasure doin' business with ya, I heard one of the bastards say. How many kids would be snorting that 'business' up their noses?

The window rolled up, and the car turned around and headed back the way it came. As the engine sound faded, the man with the package spat on the dock and shouted after them, "Idiots," drawing raucous laughter from his friends.

I watched as two of the men went up the gangplank and disappeared below the forward deck with the package. The third stayed on the quayside. A match flared in his face as he lit a cigarette and leaned against a nearby barrel.

"Now," I whispered to Katrina. "He's all yours."

She stepped out of the shadows with all of the confidence I would have shown, and strutted down towards the ship, chin held high and a wiggle in her hips. For a moment I forgot all about revenge, all about why we were here, because her allure could not be ignored. It was only when the man wolf-whistled at her that I pulled myself from my fugue.

"Hey, baby," he called in an unmistakeably South American accent. "You working tonight? Come make a lonely sailor happy."

I had to work fast, now that Katrina was out of earshot. Pulling the cell phone from my jacket pocket, I hit speed dial. Two rings. Three rings.

Come on, answer the damn phone.

Four rings. "Hello?"

"Maria." I had to keep my voice low.

"Gem, it's the middle of the night."

"Get Angel out of there. The safe place. You know the drill."

"What's wrong?"

"Wake her up. I want to talk to her."

"*Si*. I'm going to her room now. You are frightening me, Gem."

"It'll be all right."

Maria's scream shrieked in my ear.

"She is gone, Gem. The window is open. Someone has taken her!"

Maloney, you backstabbing son of a bitch!

"Call the police, Maria." I hung up. Vampire adrenaline seared through my body. Even though Maloney knew I'd made the hit on Katrina, he took Angel anyway. I could only hope she was still alive.

Focus, Gem, focus. One thing at a time. This whole fuckin' mob's going down.

My hands were shaking as I put the phone away. I could see Katrina had the guard's undivided attention.

With his back now facing me, I could make my move.

My bare feet made no sound at all as I sprinted towards the boat. I leapt across the gap between the dock and the ship, graceful as any jungle cat but with ten times the power to span the distance. It felt like flying.

I landed on the rear railing of the boat, toes wrapping around the rust encrusted metal, with hardly a wobble. I stepped down onto the deck and stalked towards the nearest door. All clear. I snuck inside.

There were two sounds within. The first was a loud game of cards being played at the front of the ship. The second was the purr of a generator down the aft stairs to my left.

I slinked down the steps. As I reached the lower aft deck, I sniffed the oily scent of the engine room ahead. The huge storage area, where in a less criminal situation fish would have been stowed, held a much more sinister cargo. I stepped forward to inspect the pallets piled high with brown paper wrapped packages, but a sound reached me and I froze.

Immediately to my right, the tinkling of water made me turn slowly toward a bathroom door hanging wide open. A scruffy haired man dressed in greasy overalls stood peeing into a filthy toilet. The engineer, I assumed. He didn't hear a thing, well, except maybe the snap of his neck. I pulled the door shut, leaving him to sit on the can.

I crossed back to the storage area and dug my nails into one of the packages on a pallet. White powder avalanched to the floor. There were thousands of bags of cocaine, cut and packaged for sale on the streets, to feed the addicted, the downtrodden, and the disenchanted youth. The gear must've been worth a million bucks. My nose itched and my eyes watered. Anger drove me to a murderous rage.

I rushed to the engine room where the generator was running...on gasoline, I ventured, based on the faint smell of petrol in the air. My nose led me to a gas tank, a spare can on the floor, and a steel line leading to a fuel pump on the purring engine. I grabbed the line with both hands and snapped it in half. Gasoline started spewing out all over the floor. It wouldn't take but a couple of minutes for the carburettor to run dry of fuel. The generator would quit, and the lights on this tub would go out.

The puddle growing on the floor soon became a flood that gushed towards the storage area and swirled around the pallets of cocaine. One spark and the whole place would explode.

I picked up the spare gas can, climbed the stairs, and then poured the gas back down the staircase, creating a spill that joined the growing lake below. The generator still purred as if nothing were wrong. Yet.

Gem

As I dug a matchbox from my jacket, I heard Katrina's voice. "So who are your friends?" she asked. Then I heard engines approaching and peeked over the rail.

Three cars appeared out of the gloom, headlights aglow.

"Scram," he told her and then shouted up the gangplank. "Boss, boss, we got company."

I held a match and crouched out of sight, listening to the car doors open, but more importantly, to Katrina's heels clicking away down the dock.

Footsteps clattered down the gangplank. "Who the fuck are you?" demanded a deep-throated South American voice.

"Easy, easy. We're with Maloney."

Maloney's goons. I ground my molars together, wondering if any of them knew where Angel had been taken.

"Where IS Maloney?"

"Who's askin'?"

"I'm the Columbian. I should have you killed for coming here without him."

"Relax. He's back at his suite waiting for us to confirm our business arrangements."

"He sends boys to do his bidding?"

"Look, Pancho. We're ready to move this inventory now. We've brought five hundred grand. Cash."

"You trying to get cheap on us, man?"

"Down payment. The rest on delivery."

From my hiding place, I couldn't see what was going on, but I could hear the clicks of briefcases being opened and the chatter of the Columbians.

"This is good news. You and your boys, you come on board, have a drink with us to celebrate while we get your gear together."

Perfect.

But that generator wasn't going to last much longer. I

could imagine the panic if the lights went out.

But I waited, the match pinched between my fingers.

"We have more gear where this comes from," the Columbian said as he and his new buddies went below.

I looked at the match and felt a warm glow inside. I had the bad ass Columbian's life between my fingertips. He'd just made his final drug deal.

The last of Maloney's goons took their fuckin' time getting up the gangplank.

The generator sputtered.

The lights flickered.

I struck the match.

"Adios mother-fuckers." I tossed the flaming match down the stairs. Now it was my turn to run, and I ran with the speed of a bullet, leaping from the stern as the ship exploded behind me. I flew through the air, my legs pumping, my arms windmilling, the glare from the blast illuminated Katrina hiding in the shadows, her wide open eyes ringed in white. I hoped I looked impressive from her perspective, silhouetted against the orange flare thrown out from the doomed ship.

I landed on the quayside and rolled, jumping straight back up onto my feet. Behind me, I heard footsteps running away. Damn!

"Go to the car," I shouted to Katrina over the roar of the inferno. I turned in the opposite direction. I'd inadvertently left one loose end that needed tying up. One mobster who'd stayed in the car.

As I ran past the burning ship, it warmed me to hear the screams from within, to hear the cracked hull taking on water, knowing the drugs and the lives of the scum on board were being destroyed, and Maloney's *business opportunity* was going up in smoke.

All three Mob cars had been flipped over like toys. Amidst the sounds of the fire, the yells, the gushing water, I could still hear the receding footfalls of the escaping mobster. A smear of blood from a car's broken window assured me he was injured and not going very far very fast.

I tracked him as he limped away from the carnage I'd created, and caught up with him as he finished dialling his cell phone. "The boat, it got hit. It's on fire."

My guess was he'd reached Maloney. Maloney had Angel. But he didn't know I had anything to do with this.

"The drugs are all gone. Fuckin' exploded."

He must've heard me running up behind him. I couldn't get to him fast enough to shut him up. He turned around, his pistol drawn and waving in the air like a television cowboy. "Gem, no. Gem, don't!"

I lunged for his throat, fangs protruded and digging in, hungry for blood and fatal revenge. The cell phone clattered on the ground. Even as he screamed, even as I sucked the life out of him, it was too late. Now Maloney knew that I was behind the attack on his ship.

He'd kill Angel for sure.

Killer Deal

The wind whipped around the corner of the building where Maloney was holed up, flailing Katrina's blond locks and tugging on my black ponytail. We were quite the team, black and blond, ying and yang, human and vampire, our bond forged in fire, a burning ship and a Mob gone crazy for retribution...against us. One would think we only had hours to live. Maloney had less time left than us.

Katrina wore the camel coloured coat buttoned right up to her neck, but she no longer shivered from the cold night air.

"You remember what you have to do?"

"I remember. Tap on the glass until he opens the curtains."

"And don't forget to smile." I stepped to the middle of the sidewalk and looked straight up sixteen stories. We were standing directly under Maloney's balcony.

"What if he's asleep?"

"He won't be. I guarantee it."

"How are you going to get past his goons?"

"One at a time."

"Are you going to kill him?"

"I don't know." I knew I'd have to find out what he did with Angel first. "Depends."

"On what?"

"He has something of mine. I want it back."

"What is it?"

"A long story. You ready."

"Let's do it."

She slipped behind me, slid her arms around my neck, and pulled herself close to my body. Her White Rose perfume inflamed my desire, and I fought to keep a level head. Bending my knees, I said, "Here goes."

She held her breath.

I sprang.

Wind rushed through our hair as balconies whizzed by. We must've looked like something out of a Super Hero movie, though I certainly hoped no one was watching. I was watching balcony sixteen. It rose up in a heartbeat, and I grabbed the banister, lighting on it as easily as I had the rusty ship railing.

"Wow," Katrina said, releasing me and stepping down next to a wrought iron patio chair. "Never a dull moment around you."

The wind was even wilder up here than it was down on the sidewalk. "I'll see you inside."

She hugged the camel coloured coat around her chest. "Be careful."

I stepped over the balcony and let myself fall. When I landed on the sidewalk below, I took a second to address my reflection in the plate glass windows.

I'd do.

I rushed to the entrance and stepped inside the lobby.

Black marble and gold trim flaunted the place. Maloney's floor was only accessible via the lift when a security key card was inserted into the control panel. I had to pickpocket that off the Concierge.

"Excuse me, ma'am," he said. "May I be of service to you?"

I feigned drunkenness and fell into him. "I'm okay, really."

"What room do you wish?"

I stumbled away from him, waving his own key card as if it were mine. "I've got it. I'll be fine."

The lift took me straight up to sixteen. As the doors slid open, I detected the odour of cheap cologne and musk. Two goons, alerted by the lift's arrival, now lay dead at my feet before the doors finished opening.

I'm more than just some vengeful woman.

I'd slashed their throats with my fingernails. Their spilled blood made a mess on the expensive carpet. I'd planned to smash my way into the room, but a glance at the security peep hole in the door gave me a much more interesting idea.

I dropped to my knees and tore the head off one of bodies. Holding the gruesome decapitation up to the peep hole, I knocked on the door.

Footsteps approached.

"Jesus, Mooney, what do you want?"

I conjured up my masculine voice and shoved the head's eye to the peep hole so its mouth wasn't visible. "I gotta go to the bathroom."

The door clicked open. I drove my foot into it, driving the goon backwards across the room until he smashed into a table where two other goons had been playing cards. The first one to his feet got hit square between the eyes with Mooney's head. He dropped immediately, his skull caved in. The final one was trying to wrestle his crucifix out of his jacket when I snapped his neck.

All three mobsters were dead within two seconds of the door opening. I stormed across the room to the bedroom door. Again the garlic was in place around the doorframe.

But now I know what I'm looking for.

All I had to hope for was that Maloney didn't make me kill him before he had a chance to tell me where I'd find Angel.

I stood in front of the door and heard Maloney scream, "Fire!"

Gunshots and splinters exploded in my face. Silver tipped bullets seemed to come at me in slow motion. I turned right, a bullet just missing my chest, twisted around, a bullet just missing my neck, and ducked, dodging a bullet to the head, but dropping my shoulder into the path of yet another silver bullet.

The silver burned my flesh, hot as sulphuric acid. I stifled a scream, gritted my teeth, and lay still on the floor, my breath hitching and my vision blurring. The gunfire stopped, and I heard the sweet sound of Katrina coming to the rescue.

Tap. Tap. Tap.

"What..?" I heard Maloney say.

Tap. Tap. Tap.

"What the..?"

A goon opened the door, looked down at my still body, and then turned back to his boss, all excited. "We got her. She's dead."

Tap. Tap. Tap.

Pushing back the burning pain, I sprang from the floor and into the room.

Oh Katrina, you look absolutely delightful.

All three men were facing the window. Maloney, dressed in a ridiculous striped suit, still held the cord he'd used to open the curtain. His flushed expression looked as if he'd just seen a ghost.

Katrina stood outside on the balcony in her camel

Gem

coloured coat. The smear of blood appeared gravely ominous. "Hello, Maloney. Remember me?"

"She's a vampire!" Maloney shouted. "Kill her!"

His shouting masked the tearing and gurgling sounds as I ended the lives of his men. Only when their bodies crumpled to the floor did he turn to see me.

"You!" he screamed, releasing the cord. "You ripped me off, you... you blew up my ship!"

I stepped towards him. "Where is she?" I demanded in my demonic voice.

"You'll never know!" He jerked a crucifix out of jacket. The blaze of light flattened me. I landed on my back. Between the molten silver coursing through my body and the battering crucifix, I knew I was going to die.

And a deeper dread tortured my mind.

Angel.

I'd failed her. After all I'd promised, after all I'd strived to do for her since her mother died, it was all going to unravel here on the floor of some mobster's drug furnished suite. I hoped that killing me would be enough for him, that he would stop at that, and return Angel back safely to Maria tonight. I hoped he'd leave her alone now that I was gone.

He thrust the crucifix in my face. "Die, bitch, die."

The light tore at my flesh, like the teeth of a thousand bats, burning a hole in my soul, and I could hear the devil screaming my name: *"Olivia! Olivia!"*

And then a shadow fell over me, hauntingly until the pain started to ease, and I looked up and saw Katrina with a gun to Maloney's head, and there's a look of surprise on his face, which disappeared when she squeezed the trigger, and I heard the muffled explosion of the gun, the twack of the bullet shot through his brain, and my voice screaming, "No!" Now I'll never know where he stashed Angel.

And then I sank into darkness.

I had no idea how much time had passed before I sat

up. My head felt like I'd been hit with a brick. The wind that had been severe outside on the balcony seemed worse in here as it funnelled in through the shattered balcony doors. I must've lost my ponytail band, because my hair swirled around as if it had a life of its own. The men on the floor around me had no life left in them at all. Katrina was sitting on the edge of the bed, staring at the floor.

I stood, shakily, and I made it to her in one go.

Very much lacking in elegance, now, but very much glad to be alive...ah...make that glad to be undead.

I sat next to her, my saviour, and looked around the room. It looked like a war zone. "We made this mess?"

"He started it." She indicated Maloney sprawled on the floor, the camel coloured coat draped over his head, soaking up more blood. I resisted the urge to kick his dead husk, but only because my legs felt like the wind could knock me off balance at any second. My body was still fighting the silver poisoning. I moved closer to Katrina and put my hand on her shoulder.

"Are you okay?"

"I loved him," she murmured. "But he was killing you, I could see through the glass, so I grabbed a patio chair and busted in, grabbed a dead goon's gun...I...I never killed anyone before."

"He had it coming." I pulled her face into my shoulder. "You saved my life."

"Does that make us even?"

"That's what partners do for each other."

We smiled, and then a hug.

"Did you get back what you wanted from Maloney?"

"No." I bit my lip and fought back tears. I'd never find Angel now.

"Sorry, but I had to...I mean...I hope it wasn't important."

It was. I glanced around the room, making sure that there was nothing that linked us to any of this mess. As

Gem

exclusive as this apartment block was, a gun shot was likely to have the neighbours reaching for telephones. In fact, someone was already banging on the door.

Thud, thud, thud.

Odd. Last time I saw it, the door was open and shot full of holes.

Thud, thud, thud.

"Where's that coming from?" Katrina asked.

My vampire hearing zeroed in on the coat closet. "In there." Vampire adrenaline launched my body to the door. Could it be? Oh please let it be.

I flung open the door. There on the floor, bound and gagged, lay Angel. My Angel. Now my tears flowed without restraint. With all the vampire speed I could muster, I untied her ropes and the gag.

"Gem," she cried and threw her arms around my neck.

"Oh baby, oh baby, I found you." Still on my knees, I rocked her and rocked her and hugged her and hugged her.

"Who is this?" Katrina was standing behind me.

"It's Angel," I sobbed out. "Maloney kidnapped her, used her as leverage to make me turn you."

"Hi, there, Angel. I'm Katrina."

Angel had on her shy face and buried it in my chest. I stoked her back. "Katrina is one of the good guys."

"Why didn't you tell me?" Katrina asked.

"I didn't want to worry you more."

She knelt next to us in our happy embrace. "No secrets, Gem. Promise me."

"You would've thought it was your fault that Angel was in danger."

"It was my fault. He used a little girl to set you after me. Don't you think I had a right to know that? I wouldn't have killed him until he talked."

"Okay. I'm sorry. I should have told you. No secrets, from now on. I promise."

"Then everything is going to be all right."

My undead heart seized with a sudden jolt of dread. "It's not going to be that easy, I'm afraid. The Mob Bosses are going to be after us for what we did tonight. They'll send hitman after hitman until we are dead."

"Then we better stick together, protect each other."

"It's the only way we're going to survive."

"We better get out of here," she said.

"Yeah." I stood with Angel still clutched in my arms. As I moved through the room, I kept her face pressed to my chest so she wouldn't see all the dead guys, all the blood, all the horrible things that I had done. But one thing I noticed on the way out. Two briefcases full of cash, I was sure.

"Grab those," I told Katrina.

"But it's Mob money."

"They're already going to kill us."

She smiled and picked up the briefcases, one in each hand, and started for the door.

"This way." I tilted my head to the balcony.

We stood in the open air, in the sixteenth story wind, and prepared to go down the easy way. "No loose ends," I told her. "That's our mantra."

"No loose ends."

I embraced her with one arm around her waist and breathed deeply. Everything I loved, I now held in my arms, Katrina and Angel, and my heart felt as warm as the dawning sun on my face. I had to get back to my lair, and safety.

"Ready?"

Katrina looked into my eyes. "So when are you going to tell me about you and Angel?"

"That's a whole other story," I said and leaped from the balcony.

GEM – No Secrets

The Hunter Hunted

They say that if you lie down with dogs, you get up with fleas. What they never tell you is that the goddamn fleas will be armed with state-of-the-art sub-machine guns, spitting out conscience-free silver-laced bullets.

Bullets with explosive slugs!

I ducked as another volley of shots rattled into the stairwell. Shrapnel and dust filled the air. Throwing myself up the final six steps, I rolled and halted in front of the door to my apartment floor hallway with one knee down on the carpet for balance.

The sons of bitches were waiting for me!

I took a second to touch my fingertips to my shoulder where the first shot had grazed me. It had torn my tight black turtleneck and drew a line of blood to the surface of my skin.

That was a five hundred dollar sweater, god damnit!

I'd hardly felt the bullet's brief kiss, but within seconds, my rage turned to self-preservation as the silver toxin seeped into my system and threatened to steal the strength from my legs. Instead of turning on my would-be assassins and ripping their hearts from their pathetic human bodies, I'd fled toward the sanctuary of my lair. I couldn't take chances now. My survival was more than just about me.

This was about Angel...and Katrina too.

I put my fingers on the door handle and listened. My acute vampire hearing picked up on each creaking step taken below me as two hoods edged their way up toward my position. I could smell every bead of sweat running down their overstuffed, out-of-shape bodies. I knew every hand gesture they made, each encouraging the other to be the first to take on the murderous vampire bitch upstairs. I heard the click of metal on metal as one of them changed his ammo clip.

That's my signal!

I popped the door open and sprinted down the wide hallway, the deep carpet masking my footfalls. Somewhere ahead of me, a door slammed, and I could hear a muffled voice calling the cops, complaining of gunfire, asking what the hell was going to be done to protect the residents.

"Because this is a good neighbourhood, we should be safe here," the voice boomed, and then the phone was slammed down.

I had to agree. That was part of the reason I'd chosen this building for my lair. But my mere presence here brought trouble knocking. I reached my door and slipped the key out of my pocket. Wary of another trap, I sniffed around the doorframe seams.

No garlic. The room's empty.

Running footfalls. I glanced back up the corridor. The goons were coming. I felt sick with fear over their silver-laced bullets. My stomach surged with dread. I had to focus and turn the fear into rage.

Unlocking the door, I stepped inside just as the two goons burst out of the stairwell.

"There she is!"

I slammed the door and flicked on the light. My place was a mess. Splinters were strewn across the carpet. A table that cost me over a thousand dollars had been reduced to matchwood. The curtain that divided the suite in two sections hung torn from its railing, and behind it, the gold bier where my coffin had sat for over twenty years now stood empty.

Gem

I'm glad the movers got it out safely! Best two hundred bucks I've spent since the mob started gunning for me.

The footfalls in the corridor reached my door and stopped. The goons' heavy breathing gave away their angst as much as their position. I took a step back and readied myself for their attack, bending my knees to pounce when they broke through the door.

That would put a dent in my damage deposit.

I opened my mouth wide and relished the sexual surge through my body as my fangs extended. Saliva began to drip from my teeth in anticipation of the blood meal to come. I let out a deep and guttural growl, the sound resonating from my throat and through the door in front of me. The fear in my gut left me...not replaced with irrepressible ire but with a passionate sexual desire. I wished it was Katrina out there wanting to come in, wanting to visit me...wanting me. We'd make plans to go out on the town, but we would be happier to just stay here and...

Why am I thinking about Katrina right now?

A door opened outside in the corridor. "What's going on?" yelled my neighbour. "I've called the authorities!"

"Shut the fuck up and get back inside," barked one of the goons, one of Clayton's men, the same guys who'd ransacked my suit, my lair, my home, and sent me on the run.

"You're going to jail, buster," the neighbour snapped.

"I warned you."

The smack of a fist connecting with a face affected me like the crack of a starter pistol affects an athlete.

They're busy with my neighbour! Maybe I don't need to disembowel them right now!

I ran for the bathroom and tore the vanity unit from the wall. There it was, safely stashed away in the cavity I'd cut into the plaster.

I knew they'd never find my laptop in here!

I tucked the computer under my arm and stormed back into the living room just as the front door crashed open.

Keeping my head low, I powered towards the window across the room, my legs driving me faster than any Olympic sprinter had ever ran.

Any human had ever run.

I heard voices. I heard shouts. I heard the whistle of bullets as they rocketed towards me. By dodging from side to side, I made the rounds cut a path around me, and as I drove my left leg off the floor with every ounce of my vampire strength, the bullets shattered the window in front of me, microseconds before I leapt through it. The glass breaking sounded like the cymbals smashing at the end of symphony, drowning out the *crack-crack-crack* of the gun fire.

My legs still pumped as I flew through the cold night air. My jet black hair, tied back from my face, flailed behind me like Medusa's serpents. The falling fragments of glass refracted the yellow glow of streetlights as the ground rushed up to meet me.

I hit the tarmac. My knees absorbed the shock. Any mortal would have broken both legs, smashed her hips, spilled her blood, and died, but not me. I had skills that made me different, that made me priceless.

Because I am Gem.

At 5 a.m. on most streets in most cities, a sexy broad plunging from a fourth floor window may have gone unnoticed, but this was midtown Manhattan, and I felt over a hundred eyes watching me in wide-eyed disbelief. And then I sensed two more sets of eyes looking down at me.

The goons!

From the remnants of my broken window, silver bullets spat down at me, ricocheting off the street, drawing screams from the tourists, from the office staffers heading into work, and causing a rush that quickly became a crush. I dodged the hail of bullets and ran as fast as I could, considering the panicked mob had quickly closed off my exit route.

"Shit!"

Holding tight to the laptop, I dropped my shoulder, ran towards Fifth Avenue, and filtered through the throng, hoping the sheer number of people would mask my escape. Bodies bounced off me with gasps and expletives, and then my legs got wrapped up in a dog leash. I fell. This time I couldn't brace myself because I had to protect the computer, so my face slid across the rough surface of the street, smearing my blood red lipstick across my cheek.

A poodle, whose lead I'd tripped over, licked my chin. *Don't! Stop! That tickles.*

I pushed the poodle aside and freed my leg while listening to the honest apologies of the pet owner.

The sound of fresh shots filled the air, and the crowd around me thinned out, fleeing in panic.

Clayton's two goons had made their way back down to the street, joined with some backup, and now four of them stomped along Grand Army Plaza towards me, weapons drawn and not giving a damn about the approaching police sirens.

From behind them, a car gunned its engine, once, twice, and then accelerated forward, its headlights flashing on an instant before its front right fender clipped one of the goons, which sent him spiralling into his cronies, knocking them to the ground like skittles in a bowling alley. The car skidded to a halt next to me. Burnt rubber stink filled the air. The driver's window slid down.

"Need a ride?" Katrina asked.

I gasped with delighted surprise and then the sickness in my stomach returned, amplified with deep dread. What was she doing here? She was going to get herself killed.

Hunted Down

The crowd around us dissipated, allowing Katrina to ease the Porsche away from the kerb. I stowed the laptop safely under my seat.

Looking over my shoulder, I saw three of the four goons scramble back to their feet, their guns aimed at the car. A fist of panic for Katrina's safety grabbed hold of my lower intestines and squeezed.

"Put your foot on the gas, girl," I shouted.

The warble of police sirens filled the air.

"Just a second," she said. "Let's wait for some interference." The smile she gave me elicited a totally different feeling inside, one of butterflies in a meadow on a spring morning.

She braked, and I rocked forward in my seat, suddenly unbalanced by her beauty and physics. A second later, her flowing golden hair was swathed in blue and red lights as two cop cars rounded the corner from Fifth Avenue. Before they came to a complete stop, officers jumped out, weapons drawn.

They shouted orders at our pursuers. "Hit the deck, bozos."

Gunshots rang out.

"Hold on!" Katrina yelled and plunged her foot down on the gas pedal. Her tight skirt rose up her leg. I couldn't help myself; I had to steal a glimpse of her alabaster thighs.

The engine roared, and she blasted across junction after junction then swung the car right onto Park Avenue.

I had to ask, "What the hell are you doing out here?" I hated the fact that she'd put her life at risk.

"You're welcome," she purred sassily.

"Welcome?"

"I saved your butt back there."

"My butt was just fine."

That earned an approving glance from Katrina.

Gem

She thinks my butt is fine!

I felt giddy.

She swung the car into the outside lane, and I bounced from side to side, almost tumbling into her lap.

I could just let my lips brush her neck.

Lust pheromones shrieked through my body, spooking the butterflies. "Thanks for saving my life."

And for the hot rush!

I steadied myself with a hand on the dash. "Did you check on Angel?"

"She's with Maria. She's fine."

The mobsters had snatched Angel from Maria once, so I didn't feel entirely comfortable.

Biting my bottom lip I tried to work out how to tell Katrina she'd done wrong for doing right without hurting her feelings.

"Katrina—"

"You're hurt!"

I looked down at my injured shoulder and flexed my deltoid. The skin where the silver-laced bullet had grazed me looked like a bubbling Bolognese sauce. The recovery process was ugly sometimes.

"It's healing."

Shame that my vampire powers didn't work on my turtlenecks. This one is ruined!

"But your face? It's all bloody."

I touched my finger to my cheek and simply wiped away the lipstick smear. The damage could have been a lot worse, considering I'd slid my face on the street. Still, that was expensive makeup, and I didn't have my compact with me.

"So you're okay?" Katrina asked.

"Yeah. You should've seen the other guys."

"I see them now, Gem!" Katrina shouted, her eyes wide, staring into the rear-view mirror. "We've got a tail."

I swivelled in my seat just in time to see a black

Mercedes jump a kerb and run a red light behind us, its headlights blinding behind our Porsche. And beyond the glow, I saw what had freaked out Katrina. The goon in the passenger seat was hanging out his window with a pistol pointed at us.

The sons of bitches!

"Turn left onto Forty Second," I yelled.

Katrina had to stand on the brakes to make the turn. The car rose up on its right wheels for a second, and then slammed back down. She retained control and accelerated towards the United Nations building. Clayton's men had more time to prepare for the sudden turn and cornered their Mercedes like it ran on rails. It raced towards us, closing the gap.

"Where next?" Katrina squeaked out, the fear in her voice evident. "I don't—"

The report of a gunshot cut her off, and the *thwack* of the bullet when it hit the back windscreen made her duck.

"Get down," she screamed and looked fearfully over her shoulder.

"Watch where you're going!"

"They're going to kill us."

"Bullet proof glass," I informed her. "Turn right and head for the expressway."

Taxis and delivery trucks veered out of our path, and more shots filled the air. Katrina jerked the steering wheel with every blast, whether it hit us or not, and I could smell the sickly scent of her terror. At the next corner, she was going too fast. The tires screeched through the turn, leaving a streak of black rubber on the tarmac.

A hobo standing on the sidewalk raised a fist and shook it at us. When the Mercedes zoomed past him, he fell on his butt under a hail of bullets fired at our rear end.

"What now?" Katrina shouted.

I could see tears in her eyes, which gave away her true sense of despair.

Gem

The first rays of dawn reflected off high skyscraper windows.

I'm running out of time!

"Head for home," I said.

"I'm not going to lead them to my apartment."

"Don't worry. I'm going to end this now." I depressed the switch that opened my window.

"What the hell are you doing?" Katrina screamed.

"Be waiting for me," I yelled over the sudden rush of wind that filled the car's interior. I pulled the top half of my body out of the window. My long black hair whipped around me.

Damn! It's going to be a tangled mess. I'll have to make an appointment at the hair salon!

"Gem, no! You can't go out there. The sun is coming up!"

"Trust me." I leapt from the speeding Porsche.

Katrina powered the car away.

Any mortal would have tumbled to the pavement, but I rose up in the air, higher than any pole-vaulter ever could. As I reached the apex of my leap, I made eye contact with the gunman. I smiled at his incredulous gape.

The Mercedes hurtled towards me.

I opened my mouth and forced my teeth to extend out of my gums to their most fearsome length.

As I plummeted toward him, he screamed in terror and dropped his gun. He grabbed for it and damn near fell from the speeding car.

I shrieked so loud my throat hurt. "You can't kill me!" Falling feet-first, I tucked my arms in at my side. "And you *do not* threaten my family!"

The Mercedes was directly underneath me.

I became a vampire torpedo and thrust my feet through the windscreen. The safety glass shattered under forces even bullet-proof glass could not withstand. The explosive crash drowned out the driver's howl.

I drove my right heel into his ribcage. I felt bones snap and crunch and then the mushy goo of his lungs. A rib must have burst his heart because a spray of blood erupted from his chest. I threw my face into the spray, like slurping from a drinking fountain.

This is so much fun!

The dying mobster fell against the steering wheel. The car swerved out of control.

My fingers turned into claws so I could latch myself to my mobster lunchbox. The car hit a kerb, flew up in the air, and began to roll. Everything around me streaked to a blur. The squeal of metal on stone made my ears ring above the screams of the gunman passenger.

I felt each impact and jolt as the Mercedes rolled while I fed. Then it screeched to a halt on its roof, slowly rotating, the scraping noise like fingernails raked down a chalk board. Oil and petrol and blood dripped from the wrecked car. To the goons, the end of their lives had fallen upon them in a flash, but I had been able to savour every moment of the crash, every scream, every drop of blood.

I unwrapped my hug from round the driver, my energy reserves replenished. I didn't have to waste time splitting his throat with my razor sharp teeth, though the thought of such pleasure filled me with a bottomless yearning.

For Katrina!

Her last words before I leapt from the car returned.

"The sun is coming up!"

I looked out the shattered windscreen. Shadows leaned across the street, tall buildings and trees were the only shade.

I'm out of time!

As I dragged myself out of the car, I had to push the gunman's legs out of my way. I had no idea what happened to his torso but assumed it had been ripped away during the rollover.

Gem

Ta, ta, ta. You should've worn your seatbelt.

By the time I got to my feet, head down, in the first warm glow of dawn, I noticed my clothes were sodden with dead men's blood.

I'll never get the stains out of this black outfit!

Footsteps and voices closed in, and although none sounded threatening, I had to get away. I had to get home to the safety of my coffin.

As the sky brightened, my pulse pounded in my ears. Before long, my blood would boil in my veins. I looked up at the buildings around me, hoping they would offer me enough shade to make it to safety.

Low sunlight beamed between two buildings. I ducked behind the overturned car, but my hand on the bumper was inadvertently exposed to the sun's rays, which shot a red hot beam across the back of my hand. The skin blistered in an instant.

I retracted my hand and winced in pain.

I can't let my undead life end like this! There's too much at stake!

Despite the offers of help from people now gathering around the wreck, and the all too familiar wail of approaching sirens, I had no option but to turn and run.

I sprinted off as fast as I could and sought out the safety of shadows where the buildings met the sidewalk. My hand screamed with pain. I raised it in front of my eyes to protect my vision from the sun's brightening glare. Every breath burnt in my chest, but I forced myself onward, my legs driving me forward, still moving with the power of a gold-medal-winning runner even though I was nearly bent over double.

Angel!

I found an extra gear in my willpower and shifted into high speed, while my worst enemy, sunlight, pursued me across the city.

Maloney and Clayton were nothing compared to the

sun.

Washington Square Park opened up on my left. I was almost there.

I leapt the low metal fence of the terrace house and descended the steps to the basement apartment. The front door was open.

"Katrina!"

I crashed into the living room, almost lost my footing as I gasped the cooler, shaded air into my body. Katrina was staring at me, but I ignored her eyes and ran for the bedroom. I launched myself across the bed, tearing the sheets loose and wrapping them around me before I dropped into my open coffin with the soft velvet lining.

"Gem! Are you okay?" Katrina stood over me with her handgun at the ready. "How did you get all bloody?"

I sighed as the coolness of my coffin enveloped me.

"Did you lose them?"

I nodded.

And they lost their lives!

Reaching up with charred fingers that looked made of wax, I felt suddenly desperate to pull the lid of my safe-haven shut, to lock out the world and its life giving sun that would kill me.

"Are we safe?"

"For now," I slurred. "But stay alert, Katrina. They're still out there."

"I will."

"Clayton still wants us dead."

"He's got an army out there looking for us."

"The computer, my laptop, do you have it?"

"It's here," she whispered. "Get some rest. I'll stand guard and keep you safe."

She closed the coffin lid.

In the darkness, my energy deserted me, and sleep stole my thoughts of mobsters and murder.

After The Hunt

Dusk.

I sat on the edge of Katrina's bed, still wearing my blood stained and battered clothes as I massaged the burnt back of my hand. It would eventually heal as smooth and beautiful as it was before. Still, it pissed me off that Clayton and his mob of murderers was running amuck in my life. Even if it was an undead life, it was my life, and they had no right to fuck with me.

I watched Katrina scrub dried blood from my coffin lining, blood that had leaked through the sheet. Mobster blood. The best kind of blood.

"What a mess." Katrina wore light-blue jeans and a brilliant white t-shirt that clung to her curves like a Ferrari. Every now and again she'd pause and give me a withering look of disdain that did more damage to me than any ultra violet rays. She finally gave up and dropped the washcloth into the bucket of steaming, soapy water at her side. The splash reminded me that I needed to shower.

"When the hell is he going to leave us alone?" she asked, her voice as weary as an old woman's.

I lowered my eyes to the floor were a series of damp footsteps trailed in from the living room.

No wonder she's so upset! She's been cleaning up blood all day.

"He's not going to stop. He knows..." Seeing the terror well up behind those gorgeous eyes, I paused. The truth of our situation was dire, but I had to sooth her fears. "He knows that I know about his organisation. He knows what information I have on that laptop."

She pushed herself up from her knees and looked down into the coffin. "I can't get all of the blood stains out."

"That's okay. It gives the place a homely feel." I tried to hold back a smile, but it didn't work.

"And all this," she pointed at the blood stains and my burned hand, "for a goddamn computer."

"You brought it in from the car, right?"

"It's on the dining table. What's on it, anyway? The names of everyone you've killed?"

"No," I said sternly, all humour gone. "What good would that be to them? It's not like Clayton wants to hand me over to the cops." I stood up and walked towards her, placed one hand softly on her shoulder. "It's got a lot about Angel on it and nasty information about Clayton's mob, and all the other mobs...enough to get them all hanged, should I decide to turn it over to the District Attorney."

Katrina brought her hand up to mine, still resting on her shoulder. "Couldn't you just trade with him? Give him the computer in exchange for ending this madness?"

Wow, she is thinking one step ahead all of the time.

"Maloney had put in a lot of effort into tracking down Angel and Maria. He was cleverer than I thought. With the information on the computer, Clayton would know her school, the activities she attends, and all the safe houses I've set up across the city. I couldn't take that chance. Everything on that hard drive is too important to be in the wrong hands."

Katrina brought the back of my hand to her lips and gently kissed the burned skin.

My heart is melting. Again.

"Why is this taking so long to heal?" she asked with a this-is-disgusting tweak on her brow.

"Sunlight screws up my regenerative powers."

Katrina bunched up her face when she looked at the slice the bullet had cut out of my shoulder. "Same with that, too?"

Glancing at my shoulder wound, I could understand her concern. The lesion pulsed and boiled, red and angry. "Yeah," I said. "Or it would've been healed by now."

"Get a shower. Then I'll dress it for you."

"It doesn't need—"

"Stop!" Katrina tilted her head to the side. "It's my job to take care of you. Don't take that away from me."

I smiled in agreement.

Katrina held onto my hand a moment longer, and then picked up the water bucket and left the bedroom. I crossed to the bathroom and twisted the shower dial on full blast. As I peeled my blood encrusted black clothes from my body, the room filled with steam. Beads of moisture ran down the chequered tiled walls. I turned my torn turtleneck over in my hands before I tossed it into the bathroom bin.

That's five hundred bucks I'm ripping out of Clayton's rump!

I pushed the curtain open and stepped into the hot bliss of the shower spray. The water at my feet quickly became a deep, gloopy red whirlpool going down the drain. I savoured the shower as it cascaded over me, cleansing my body of last night's feeding frenzy. Closing my eyes, I met the driving force of the water face-on.

"Gem?" Katrina called softly from the doorway.

In the heat of the shower I froze. A shiver ran from the base of my spine to my neck and back again.

"Gem? Are you hungry?"

Only for you. But that's not what you mean, is it?

"I was going to make a salad?"

Not quite what I was thinking.

"Gem? You okay?"

I rubbed the water from my eyes. Poking my head out the shower curtain, I made sure I showed a little flesh as well. "I'm okay," I told her while enjoying her eyes as they danced over my body. Then her cheeks flushed and she left the room. By the time I finished my shower and dressed in a pair of tight blue shorts, white shirt, and a red vest, she was already stuffing my dirty clothes into a laundry bag. She snatched a black pair of jogging trousers I'd left on the floor.

"Not those," I said, tying back my damp hair.

"Feel free to help," she said.

"I'm a vampire, sweetheart. I don't do laundry." I stood with my hands on my hips and one knee bent.

Does she have any idea how hot I am?

"Well maybe you should learn to clean up after yourself." Katrina lugged the laundry basket out the bedroom doorway.

I realised this was going nowhere. She was irritated with the situation, not me, and only because she cared. If she needed someone to vent on, then that person would be me. She'd earned that right, and so much more.

She took me in when I needed a place to hide out.

Shit had hit the proverbial fan less than an hour after Maloney's death, and I couldn't take the risk of being killed, especially with Angel in the mix. Maria knew the routine. She'd met us in Grand Central Station, our emergency rendezvous point, and took Angel to her sister's place in Brooklyn.

It would have been easy for me to board a train, as well, get the hell out of town, but I had just met this gorgeous, interesting, and tantalising specimen of a woman. Katrina couldn't leave her job, or wouldn't, and I simply could not bear to be away from. We were a team. We couldn't split up, no matter how dangerous things got.

And she needed somebody too.

After what she'd been through, with Maloney, who wouldn't? He may have been a mobster, but she'd fallen for him, she'd trusted him, and in the end, she had to put a bullet through his brain to save my life. So I'd listened to her rant about how shitty men had treated her, gave her a shoulder to cry on, and showed her that I cared. She made it easy because she liked to talk, and she didn't ask me too many questions about my job as a hit woman for the mob.

Some things are best left unsaid.

I thought the heat would die down, especially as I

picked off Clayton's hit men one at a time, exposing them for the incompetent fools they were.

However, the sinking of the Madeira had cost Clayton millions in drugs, cold hard cash, and his macho reputation within the mob. He was not going to let me get away with smearing him like that. And even though he considered my talents as a no-loose-ends kind of woman priceless, the five million dollar contract he'd put out on my head got all the two-bit hoods on the East Coast reaching for their weapons and using any trick they could think of to track me down.

Like trying to find my oh-so-valuable computer!

I sashayed to the front room where Katrina was already sitting at the dining table. She'd set the first aid box next to the laptop and had unwrapped a sterile bandage.

"Take a seat, madam," she teased, playing nursemaid.

I did as I was told. The injury would be gone by morning, with or without any treatment, but it was clear she needed to be nurturing.

This feels weird.

I watched her concentrate on rolling the bandage around me arm, over my shoulder, under my tricep time and time again until she held it firm with a safety pin. I'd never bothered with such things, and certainly no one had ever been allowed to take such care of me. A bizarre feeling washed over me, and I felt a tear threaten to slip from my eye.

"Not exactly Versace, is it?"

Katrina stared into my eyes. We reached for each other and our lips touched briefly before she pulled away. She dragged her eyes from mine to the laptop. Her fingers reached out to open it up.

I grabbed her wrist. "Katrina! No! You can't see what's on there."

"What? Why?"

"Because then you'll know what Clayton doesn't want anyone to know. You'll become a target too."

"I'm a target already."

"Whatever else Maloney was, he was good at his job. Clayton isn't going to let the death of one of his cronies go unpunished. And for once, I don't know if I can beat these guys. They're the most relentless, brutal bastards I've ever come up against."

I saw a distant, honest look in those perfect blue eyes that told me she too wasn't sure we'd survive this fight.

"If I'm going to die over this, I should know what for. No secrets between us, right? Isn't that what we agreed?"

"This doesn't count," I said, hoping she'd let it drop.

We sat, hand in hand, eyes locked on each other, offering each other everything but getting nothing, afraid that we'd only just found each other and our time was already running out.

"Tell me about Angel," Katrina murmured.

"I don't know..." Where would I start?

"You promised to tell me the story."

I could see her curiosity boil up to the surface, but: "Not right now."

Katrina's cell phone beeped from the bedroom, indicating the arrival of a text message. It broke the spell between us. Thankfully. She dashed to retrieve her phone. When she returned to the doorway, she said, "I need to know what's going on." Her curiosity had turned defiant.

But the less she knew about Angel, the safer they both would be. "I'll tell you when this is over. When I'm sure you'll be safe."

"And by over you mean when Clayton calls off his men?"

"Or when he's dead. The Organisation, it's like a snake, coiling around our city, our society, but one thing about a snake, no matter how big it is, not matter how strong, cut off its head and the whole thing dies."

"And what if you knew where he was going to be tonight. Would you kill him tonight?"

I could hear mounting anger in her voice, but I could also feel dread, emanating from her body. "I don't know where he's going to be tonight. Your point is moot."

"But I know," she said, her voice sly as a fox.

She is driving me fucking crazy!

My breath came in ragged bursts. I went nose to nose with her, so close I could feel her hot breath on my lips. "What do you know, Katrina?"

The room was suddenly a hot as a sauna. I saw a trickle of sweat run down Katrina's neck and disappear into the heavenly valley of her cleavage.

"That message I just got," she said. "Clayton's having dinner tonight at the Oyster Bar."

"He told you that?"

"I've got friends, you know. People who work as waitresses, as barmaids. While you were sleeping, I made some calls, asked around."

I couldn't believe what I was hearing.

Katrina is full of surprises.

She took half a step backwards and broke the intense gravitational pull that had been growing between us. As if proud of herself, she put her hands on her hips and bent one knee, mirroring the pose I had struck earlier.

Does she have any idea how hot she is?

"So what do you think?" she asked.

"I think there's a snake that needs its head cut off."

The Hunted Hunting

The waiter, wearing a tight black waistcoat, showed me to my table in amongst the riff-raff at the Oyster Bar. I'd eaten here before. Usually I took one of the Oyster Bar's private booths, but tonight was not about me being flashy.

Tonight is about blending in.

Katrina had helped me get ready. The flat shoes, the long drab skirt, and the horrible green and blue chequered overcoat, my disguise looked gaudy on my slim frame. The cheap, mousey brown, curly haired wig made my scalp itch. My new look had been good enough to get me past the two goons Clayton had posted at the door, deep underneath Grand Central Station.

More importantly, I hadn't drawn a glance from the fat slimy bastard, Clayton, as he stuffed his face. He had no clue how close death loomed near him.

He sat at a table with his cronies, slurping oysters and chugging sparkly and certainly expensive campaign. I had no idea what he could be celebrating, but it warmed my heart to see him enjoying his last moments on this planet.

Confident in my disguise, I shuffled past him to a table set for one. The waiter held my chair as I sat down and handed me a menu. "Would you like to see the wine list?"

"No thanks." I needed to stay sharp. "Just a glass of water, please."

"Certainly." He scurried off.

My appearance didn't even warrant a *madam* or *mademoiselle* from the staff.

I might have to see a shrink after this!

My eyes drifted back to Clayton. He had made suggestions over the years that I'd worked for him, about how I could earn extra money. He always said I was sitting on a million bucks.

Yeah, I had a good-looking ass, and he had an eye for ladies of the night, so in this get up, I would have barely registered as a woman, let alone a target. But Katrina had a treat in store for him, one he wouldn't live to enjoy.

Looking over the top of the menu, I scanned the room. In addition to his two doormen goons, Clayton had another bodyguard stationed at the head of the table where he chowed down with three of his chiefs. Compared to Clayton, each one was an Adonis. Back when he'd taken over the family business, he'd been an athlete, a hard man renowned as a bare knuckle fighter, but wealth and the fear others had for him had made him complacent, if not downright lazy.

The waiter returned with his pad and a pen. He placed the iced water in front of me and stood with the nib poised, indicating he was ready to take my order without a word.

"I'll have the fish and chips," I managed to say, though I'd rather have ordered the sea bass and a bottle of Bollinger. My internal disdain for fish and chips was only overpowered by the disdain behind the waiter's smile.

He snatched the menu from me. "Perhaps you'd like to try the—"

"Fish and chips," I said, quietly but firmly.

He jotted on his pad before turning away without a word.

I looked completely out of place. I hadn't even taken off my coat. The couples' tables on either side of me made no effort to hide their snide looks. I didn't care. I pretended like I simply did not exist.

A raucous burst of laughter erupted from Clayton's table, and along with everyone else, I found myself staring at him as he, like a clumsy manatee, dragged his wide ass out of his chair.

Just looking at him makes me sick to my stomach.

The bodyguard moved to his side, but Clayton signalled him to stay put and made some comment to his entourage about his big dick wanting privacy. The mobsters roared again. With a dismissive wave, he made his way toward the restroom, and the bodyguard stood at ease again.

That's going to make this easier. He goes to the restroom by himself. Foolish man.

By the time Clayton retook his seat, my food had arrived. I picked at the chips and disassembled my fish with my fork. What I wouldn't give for a raw, hot neck right now, pulsing with rich red blood.

My vampire hearing picked up on the clip clop of high heels approaching the Oyster Bar's front door. The hubbub of conversation around me faded to static. The door swung open. Katrina thanked one of the goons at the entrance. Her voice oozed sex appeal.

As she stepped inside, she shrugged her long black coat from her shoulders.

Every man in the joint looked her way.

Four inch heels made her as tall as an Amazon princess. Her black net stockings slipped up under a red skirt so short it was barely wider than a belt. The white blouse she wore looked a size too small, and unbuttoned at the top, it exposed a red lacy bra overflowing with round, succulent breasts. She'd tucked her blond hair under a short, bobbed red wig. Like so many hot blooded men whose awestruck gazes gave away their fantasies about her, my heart beat so hard, the fish fell off the end of my fork.

I have never been so turned on.

Clayton's beady eyes landed on her and froze, an oyster halfway to his mouth, his jowl-laden jaw dropped.

Katrina winked at the mob boss.

Oh baby, you are playing your part so well.

I pushed back from the table, giving me plenty of room to get to my feet quickly. If she nailed the next move, I would spring into action.

She smiled brazenly at Clayton, and then let her coat slip from her hands to the floor. With a look of surprise, she turned her back to him and bent over to pick it up.

Holy fuck, she's not wearing any underwear!

I stood and battled to drag my eyes from her ass so I could walk to the restrooms. My legs felt like jelly underneath me, and not because of what I was about to do.

But because of Katrina...and what I would like to do.

She sauntered to Clayton's table. The animal had no clue what she was about to do to him.

I hurried towards the lady's room, and at the last

Gem

instant, confident that no one would be interested in dowdy old me, stepped into the men's room. As the door swung shut behind me, a sudden uproar came from Clayton's table, meaning Katrina had managed to spill Clayton's oysters into his lap.

After scanning the stalls for feet, I took a second to savour the relief that I was alone. I stepped into a vacant stall and locked the door behind me. Men were such pigs. Piss dripped from the toilet seat, and toilet paper littered the floor. The last man who'd sat here had left a reek that reminded me of Maloney. It was cheap and overpowering. I peeled the ugly coat off, draped it over the toilet and took a seat.

I could wait this ass hole out in comfort now.

Not a minute had passed before the door crashed open and heavy footfalls pounded in. There was a momentary blast of noise from the restaurant, and then sound was muted once more.

"Mother fucker," Clayton cursed. "Mother fucker." I heard him pulling paper towels from the dispenser and start rubbing at his trousers. I gripped the door lock and prepared to burst out.

Three, two—

The main door opened. "Hey boss!" called the bodyguard over the sounds of the restaurant. "You want us to kill that bitch?"

My heart froze. Our plan was about to backfire.

"Just get her the fuck out of here!" Clayton shouted.

I heard the goon exit.

"And make sure no one else comes in 'til I'm done!"

Perfect.

I waited until I heard the unmistakeable sound of a zipper being pulled down and the first splash of Clayton emptying his bladder into the urinal. I silently unlocked the stall door and took a step towards the man who had signed my death warrant.

"You shouldn't have come after me," I said softly.

Clayton stiffened like I'd stabbed him in the back. "G-Gem," he choked out. He made no effort to turn to face me. "You mind if I put this big sucker away? I don't want my body to be found with my pecker hanging out." He pointed down at his crotch.

"Just put your hands up and turn around slowly. You do as I say, I'll make this as painless as possible."

Okay. So I lied.

"As you wish," he said, pissing on the floor as he turned. His fat face looked far too smug, he almost seemed happy, but I couldn't find anything funny—

Shit!

The blast hit me like a shotgun and knocked me to the floor. My eyes burned from the glare from a huge crucifix he wore on a gold chain around his neck. I hadn't seen it before. He'd kept it tucked in his suit coat. The son of a bitch was a walking, talking vampire trap.

"I've been expecting you," he drawled out, standing over me. "Fuck, if I'm honest, I was hoping you'd come looking for a piece of me." He began to stroke himself, a glint in his eye more sickening than anything he could wear around his neck.

The power of the crucifix began to burn my body; the back of my hand where the sun had scalded me became the centre of my agony.

He stood between my convulsing legs. "I've always known how to control you, Gem. I just wished it didn't have to come to this." He laughed. "But I'm glad it did."

It became clear that my suffering was his aphrodisiac. I let out a groan as I realised that this upcoming rape would be worse than my death.

Run, Katrina. Protect Angel.

Hunt Over

Gem

Clayton leaned down so the full force of the crucifix's power radiated on my face. I couldn't move. Every ounce of my vampire strength was being sucked from my body like I'd stolen the blood of so many victims. My legs were numb, and I knew that within minutes, the only movement I'd be capable of would be my eyes flicking from side to side.

"Now I could find that little girl, force you to work for me, but I ain't gonna take the risk. Not with you." He looked me up and down, and kicked my dress so it rose up my thighs.

"What a waste!" He reached inside his jacket. "But I can't have the most dangerous bitch on the planet not playing on my team."

As he pulled out a gold plated handgun, I battled the force that was draining me of all my power.

It's over.

"You're a sorry, *sexy* and dangerous bitch." His erection stood out from his trousers like a flagpole.

I have to say I'm impressed.

"As much as I want to hear your howls of pleasure when I stick this baby in you, I can't risk you biting me. So I'm going kill you first and then fuck you." He grinned and licked his lips.

What a fucking idiot.

He was going to save me my final humiliation. How nice. I should send him a thank you note. I'd never feel his fat, bloated, slug-like physique bouncing on top of me, coating me in his sweat. But the joke would be on him. Kill a vampire, the undead body turned to dust. I'd be nothing but a pile of dirt on the restroom floor.

Try fucking me then, you moron!

I wished I could smile.

He extended his gun arm towards me. The barrel grew and grew, and just as it seemed that I was rushing like a train towards a tunnel that led straight to hell, the gun and his chubby fist came between me and the crucifix, blocking its power.

Energy surged through my body.

Fuck you!

I kicked my right foot out as hard as I could, caught him just below his left knee.

"Urgh," he grunted, stumbled backwards, and slipped in his piss on the polished floor tiles. Pivoting as he fell, his prick pointed the way down, and he smashed, forehead first, into the urinal. His obese gut slapped the tile floor, and he slumped unconscious, his body covering the crucifix. The gun rattled across the floor and into the corner.

Obesity wasn't good for his health.

I scrambled to my feet. Although I was not as steady as normal, I had to work fast.

How long before the goon comes in to check on him?

"Like I said, Clayton, you made a mistake coming after me." I reached around to his throat and enjoyed the sensation of my fingernails growing, elongating, sharpening, and then I dug them into the flab of his throat and ripped backwards, tearing his windpipe open. Blood spewed out all over my hands and spilled on the floor. I thrust my head forward, ready to feed, but as the first splatter of his blood hit my lips, I gagged and pulled back.

He tasted like meat gone bad.

I couldn't even bring myself to lick my fingers. Instead, I wiped them on the back of his pants and dragged him, face down, into a toilet cubicle.

He can't hurt us anymore.

I pulled the stall door shut, rinsed my hands at the sink, and slipped the ugly chequered coat back on.

He'd be found with his dick hanging out, after all.

After a quick look in the mirror, I straightened my wig, and then moved to the restroom door. I could hear Katrina swooning over the bodyguard, asking him what time he finished work.

I slipped out unseen.

Katrina didn't even break stride in her chatter.

No wonder the goon couldn't throw her out; he couldn't get her to shut up long enough. Besides, he was getting an eye full of pure womanhood.

This girl is good. Good looking, good smelling, good acting. Good in every way!

As I walked to my table, I slipped a wad of cash from my coat and fished out two fifties, which I slipped next to my hardly touched meal. Maybe the waiter would call me madam the next time he saw me dressed like this, which would be in my next undead life, for sure. I headed for the front door. No one even glanced my way.

Most importantly, Clayton's cronies are oblivious to their upcoming unemployment.

I walked past the goon guards outside and moseyed up the sidewalk away from the restaurant. The clip clop of high heels soon echoed behind me. I turned just as Katrina shrugged off her shoes and increased her speed to catch up to me.

Oh baby, those legs of yours are just fabulous.

She suddenly stopped and rammed her left hand inside her coat and pulled out her chirping cell phone. She read a text message, typed, then began walking toward me again.

"Odd time to take a message," I said. "Couldn't it wait?"

She matched stride with me. "I had to say thanks to my friend who told me where Clayton would be."

"We usually escape first and text later."

"Hey, I'm new at this."

Screams and shouts exploded from the Oyster Bar behind us.

"Let's get the hell out of here."

Hunter's Retreat

We got in and out of taxi cabs four times until we asked one driver to drop us off an easy walk from Katrina's apartment. It may have seemed over-the-top cautious, but I was not prepared to take our safety for granted. Some of Clayton's men may not yet have gotten the memo.

My insides churned in desperate need of a cigarette.

Maybe trying to quit while on the run was not the best move!

It wasn't until we approached the stone arch at the end of Washington Square Park that Katrina, still carrying her high-heeled shoes, turned to face me.

"With Clayton dead, why are you still nervous?"

The wig slipped forward over my eyes.

"Take that ridiculous thing off..." she snatched it from my head. "...and answer me."

I ran my fingers through my hair, untangling it from the mesh net that had kept it in place under the wig. "The message I've sent is loud and clear. Fuck with me and you die. Once the word gets out, it'll keep the goons away from us."

Under the hazy light of the streetlamp, her cheeks flushed red. Her eyes dropped to the sidewalk. "And by *us*, I take it you're talking about you and Angel."

I couldn't believe what I'd heard her say. "The three of us!" I stepped towards her, offered her my hand, but she left it untouched.

"Are you sure? What about our rule, no secrets? No secrets, you said. But it seems that I'm the one who tells all, and you're the one with all the secrets."

"I haven't kept any secrets from you."

"Oh no? How about the information in the laptop. And Angel. You won't even talk about her."

Tears slid down her face, ruining her perfectly applied make up. She must have been feeling pretty disgusted with me, couldn't even bring herself to look into my eyes.

"Let's go inside. I'll tell you."

She finally took my hand. Electricity shot up my arm like a lightning bolt on steroids. I squeezed her fingers. "Wait here while I check the apartment."

How long will it take me to break this habit of protecting her? Probably longer than it'll take me to get over my nicotine fits!

Once I knew it was safe, I signalled her to join me inside. We sat on the sofa without turning on the lights, and in the darkness I began to tell her about Angel.

"Angel is not my daughter."

Katrina's eyes bore deep into mine. I let my mind slip back to the time where this story started, and as I spoke, my voice caught in my throat.

"Her-her mother was my best friend."

I remembered the phone ringing. It wasn't like I hadn't been waiting for it, but I didn't rush to answer.

A girl doesn't want to look too keen.

I'd been listening to the baby cry across the hall. The sound felt soothing next to the shrill buzz of my cell phone. The child's wails stuttered and subsided, and I knew she was being fed, or changed, or simply being cared for by her mother.

The phone kept on ringing.

I answered it. "Yes," I said.

"Tonight. Seven thirty."

"Where?"

"Ice rink, Rockefeller Plaza. You know who to look out for?"

The mob Bosses keep letting their idiots do the calling!

I paused, let the goon at the other end of the phone think I'd hung up on him.

As dumb as he was, he'd still managed to infiltrate Jefferson's gang.

And tonight's target was Jefferson himself, a big fat fish in a small pond over in New Jersey, a drug dealer with high aspirations. He'd inflicted a few serious dents in Clayton's organization, and with every week that passed, his Manhattan client base was growing while he lined his pockets with more ill-gotten dough.

And before long he'll be rich enough to buy himself a small army.

The Bosses had decided enough was enough.

And that's where I come in.

"Of course I know who to look out for, you idiot." I hung up. For a brief moment my anger threatened to bubble to the surface. I looked at my watch. It was only 5.30 p. m. I was prepared for the hit and had a little time to kill. The crying child came to mind. I slipped out of my apartment and gently rapped on the door across the hall.

"Hey, Gem," Clare said with a motherly warm grin across her face. Baby Angel was tucked safely under one arm. Clare's short blond hair was immaculately preened despite the demands a baby placed on her time. "Come in."

She backed up, and I followed her inside. Her apartment was much smaller than mine, but tidy, and there were only the two of them living here. No daddy to be found anywhere.

"Are you sure you're not too busy?"

"Of course not," Clare replied. "I've not seen you all week."

I let baby Angel grip my little finger. She looked up at me from under those cute blond curls. Her crying frown turned upside down. I grinned back at her.

Nine months old and she's got more control over me than the sun!

Clare had never asked about my job, about the late hours I kept, just as I'd never asked about Angel's father. We chatted for twenty minutes, and then a serious look crossed her brow.

"Gem. I have something to ask you. I haven't gotten around to getting Angel christened, but when I do, I really want you to be her godmother. Will you do that for us?"

Emotions welled up inside me that I'd never felt before. "Of course..." I could hardly speak. "You're like a sister to me, my best friend, and Angel, if I were to ever have a daughter, I'd want her to be just like Angel."

"You'll make a wonderful godmother." Clare hugged me.

I hugged her back, but afraid I'd burst into tears right in front of her, I had to force myself to leave.

"We're going for a walk later," Clare said. "You're welcome to go with us."

"I can't," I gasped. "I have to work."

"Maybe next time."

Back in my apartment, I realised I'd been holding my breath. I exhaled deeply. Little black spots appeared across my field of vision. My heart was aflutter in a chest swelled with pride. Tears filled my eyes.

So is this what if feels like to belong?

I liked the feeling and wanted more. Maybe it was time to step away from my job, time to live something like a real life, a normal life with a normal job, well, as normal as a vampire's life could be. I checked my watch.

Maybe after tonight I'll retire. Slow down.

I strolled into the Plaza. It was filthy with tourists. I was bumped and barged into, but I kept my focus. People must've thought I was a goth chick wearing these black designer jeans and a tight fitting black leather jacket. My black Nikes looked right in place, but in these jeans, no one would look below my hips to notice my shoes. I picked Jefferson out from thirty yards away. He was leaning on the railing, a gym bag over his shoulder.

I can smell the cocaine in the bag, sure as a mouse could smell cheese.

I cut a path through the crowd, moving away from Jefferson, as my plan was to double back on him, but right in the middle of my manoeuvre, my cell phone rang. I checked the called I. D.

Clayton? What the hell did he want?

I answered. "I'm a little busy now."

He said something I couldn't make out. Lowering my head, I put a finger in my free ear to block out the crowd noise.

"What's that?"

"Get out of there! We've found Finch dead!"

"Who's Finch?"

"Our mole! Jefferson's on to you!"

Shit!

I ended the call and looked up. Jefferson was staring straight at me over the heads of dozens of people, a confident smile plastered across his arrogant face. The world around me slowed down as I watched him reach inside his bag and pull out a handgun.

Bang! Bang! Bang!

He fired three times into the air. The crowd parted in panic, screaming and terrified. Into the vacating space ran two men aiming hefty machine guns at me.

With vampire speed, I leapt at them, feeling the wind from their silver bullets whistle past me. In less than a second, they were on the ground and throatless. Blood pooled around their heads, and further screeches of terror rang out. I glared at Jefferson and showed him my fangs. He turned tail and ran, firing into the air again.

"Jefferson," I bellowed as he sprinted into the gap created by the departing throng. Only the gap wasn't completely clear. A single woman with a baby stroller stood frozen with fear in the middle of the Plaza, directly in his escape path. She had blond hair. She looked like:

Clare!

He fired two shots at her. She tumbled over, out of his way, and dragged the stroller down on top of her.

Jefferson disappeared.

My hit had gotten away, but I no longer cared. I ran to

Clare and clasped her head to my chest. Angel had fallen from her stroller. Clare had an arm tucked protectively around her.

"Clare! Clare!" Her blood soaked my clothes. She had two holes in her chest, and I fought every urge in my psychic to feed.

"Take her..." Clare coughed. "Love her..." she choked. "You're her godmother," she whispered, gasped, and then her head lolled to the side. The approaching wail of sirens filled my ears.

"She died in my arms with her blood-splattered baby lying next to her. I picked up Angel and ran for safety."

"How horrible." Katrina's cell phone rang, mirroring my memories of the sirens. Dumbstruck, she took the call. I was deaf to her words, lost in my past, in Angel's past. Hot tears flowed down my cheeks.

"Maria will be here in half an hour," she murmured. "Gem, I'm so sorry."

I sniffled. "See why I don't like to talk about what happened. It rips my heart out..."

"And that's why you go after anyone who sells drugs in this city."

Because a drug dealer killed Clare!

Katrina stroked the back of my neck. "And my biggest worry was getting you to do your own laundry. I'm sorry I was being so trivial."

When I found Jefferson, it took three days for him to die.

Wiping tears from my face, I pulled myself together, into the here and now. "We should do the laundry now. Together."

"You sure?"

"We're a team, aren't we?"

Her smile lit up my heart. "We are."

After tidying the apartment, we went back to the utility room. I took the wet clothes from the washing machine and placed them in the dryer. A black lacy bra caught my attention. Katrina's bra. Maybe doing laundry wasn't so bad, after all.

"I've not seen you wear this before," I said.

"You will." She ran a finger softly down my cheek. Staring into her eyes, I felt something more than lust for her, something bigger than the universe.

I could love you forever!

"No secrets," I told her.

Her eyes sought out the floor, as if shamed.

"Hey? What's the matter?"

The doorbell rang.

In The Hunter's Lair

Angel sprinted into the apartment.

"Gem! Gem!" she squealed when she saw me. Her little legs carried her across the floor, those cute blond curls bouncing as she ran, and she threw herself at me, wrapping her arms around my neck in a big bear hug.

"I've missed you!" she cried.

"And I've missed you, too."

Katrina closed the door behind Maria who, as ever, was loaded down with shopping bags.

"Thanks, Maria," I said.

"*Si, Si*, no problem. Angel is a good girl. We have lots of things to show you. She is doing so well at school."

What would I do without you, Maria?

"Can I play on the computer?" Angel asked me, pointing at the laptop on the table.

Aware of Katrina's disapproving glare, I shook my head. "After a while. I need to chat with Maria for a minute, sweetie."

"Okay!"

As Maria filled me in on Angel's schooling over the last couple of weeks while I'd been in hiding, I couldn't help but focus on the conversation between Katrina and

Angel, whom I now considered to be my girls.

"Wow! " Angel said. "You've got lots of books!"

"I read a lot."

Angel took Katrina by the hand and led her over to the bookshelves that filled the back wall. "What's that one about? What's a... umm... Fair Roar?"

Katrina squinted at the title Angel was asking about. "Oh, a Pharaoh? They were the leaders in Egypt thousands of years ago."

"Why do you have books about them?"

"I need to know about lots of ancient things because I work in a museum."

"Oh, okay. You've got blond hair like me!"

"I sure have."

"Maria," I asked. "Would you like coffee?"

"*Si*. That would be nice!"

Katrina followed me to the coffeemaker. "I love Angel more than ever."

"If I hadn't taken her, she'd be lost in the foster care system or stuck in an orphanage."

"About our promise to each other...you know, no secrets?"

Those butterflies swept back into my tummy.

She was going to say something when her cell phone chirped. Frustration drew a shadow across her face. She glanced over her shoulder at Angel pointing out books to Maria.

"What is it you want to say to me?"

After looking at her phone display, "Give me a minute," she said and walked, head bowed, to the bedroom then closed the door behind her.

I hope she's okay.

"Gem, look," Angel sang, holding up a crayon drawing for my inspection, a little red house with a blue roof and big windows and a chimney. A stick girl swung from a swing under a tree branch. "I brought this to show you."

"You did this all by yourself?"

"I'm in preschool, you know."

Katrina emerged five minutes later and subtly tapped her wrist to indicate it was time for me to sleep. She offered to take Angel and Maria out for an early breakfast, and as soon as they were gone, after hugs and kisses all round, I slinked into my coffin.

The darkness was soothing and the smell of the stale blood stains on the velvet lining acted as a sedative. Within moments, the release of sleep creep over my shoulders and drew me down into a black abyss.

After what felt like only seconds, I opened my eyes. My body felt rested, healed even, but that wasn't what had awakened me.

Voices! Men's voices!

There's someone in the apartment!

I gently eased open the coffin lid and slid my body out. Silent as a drifting cottonwood seed, I pulled on a tight pair of jogging trousers and a black t-shirt then slinked to the bedroom door where I peeked through the keyhole.

I could see Katrina clearly. She stood in the kitchen talking to a tall, well dressed man. He had his back to me. Katrina passed him a coffee mug. Another voice, another man, off to my right. I craned my eyes to the sofa. There sat the same three cronies who had been with Clayton during his last supper at the Oyster Bar. Now they were here, in Katrina's apartment, as if it was tea time, or something.

That two-faced bitch!

I had to ram my knuckles into my mouth to stop from shouting out. My undead heart stopped beating.

Where is Angel?

My gaze sliced back to the kitchen. Angel sat at the table, opening and closing the laptop, her feet swaying to and fro. Relief surged through my muscles, but I gritted my teeth.

Gem

Katrina has set me up! She's in cahoots with the men who would kill me with silver bullets and wooden stakes!

My heart lugged back into motion as if suddenly jumpstarted by the ire that coursed through my body. My passion for bloodletting overtook me, and my gums tingled with more sexual pleasure as my fangs stretched out to their supernatural length. I balled my hands into fists, and my fingernails thickened into claws.

That bitch had sold me out!

It suddenly all made sense. The text messages she wouldn't explain. Her so-called friend who knew where Clayton was dining. My knees began to shake. I felt like someone had rammed a stake into my chest.

I'll kill them all! But I'll kill her first!

As I pulled away from the keyhole, I caught sight once again of Angel at the table and stopped. I couldn't just bust in there and start killing everyone, not in front of Angel. I wouldn't want her to see me at my finest... at my worst... doing what vampires do best...killing.

My teeth retracted and my nails shortened.

I suddenly wondered something else. Where was Maria? I couldn't see her, couldn't hear her. Perhaps she was in the closet, gagged and tied.

I couldn't do anything violent. My instincts demanded fast and brutal retribution, but I'd have to play it cool until Angel and Maria were safe. Then the killing could begin. I pulled open the bedroom door and stepped into the living room, immediately positioning myself between Angel and my enemies.

"Where is Maria?" I all but snarled. "What have you done with her?"

Katrina stared at me with those beautiful blue eyes filled with puzzlement.

How could I have been so wrong about her?

"Maria's gone to the store, I—"

"Save it!"

The three Mobsters on the sofa jumped, all three of them spilling coffee onto their laps, just like Clayton had dumped his oysters.

The colour drained from Katrina's face.

Only the expensive suited newcomer kept his cool. He leaned back against the oven and sipped at his coffee.

I stared at Katrina. "What did it take? Money to turn me in?" I looked at the man. "Sex?"

I'll keep that handsome bastard's skull as a souvenir!

Katrina walked towards me, her hands out, her eyes moist. "No! I'd never let anything come between us."

"Don't lie to me! The only reason I'm holding my temper is because she is here." I stroked Angel's soft curls, and she smiled up at me, looking confused.

No damn it, she looks afraid! Afraid of me!

"Gem, can I play with the computer now?" she said, now sounding more bored than worried.

What a kid!

"Of course you can, sweetie."

Angel booted up the computer, and every set of eyes in the room craned to see the screen as it came to life. It revealed a single folder labelled *Angel*. She clicked on it and moved the cursor over one of the icons. She pressed the mouse again, and the screen filled with the opening credits of a Bugs Bunny cartoon.

Angel giggled.

Katrina frowned. "I thought the laptop had information on Clayton and the mob."

"That's what I wanted him to think. He got worried. Made mistakes. Mistakes that cost him."

"Brilliant," the handsome man said.

"And who the hell are you?" I barked.

The three goons leapt to their feet, and Katrina took a step backwards. The newcomer, however, placed his cup down and took a stride forwards.

"Allow me to introduce myself." His accent sounded

as classy as his suit looked. "My name is John Bradley. Dan Clayton was my cousin."

"So you're here for revenge," I muttered, not wanting to alarm Angel.

"No, not revenge."

Desperate to tear him limb from limb, I had to admit he was damned good looking with his thick, luscious brown hair combed in a wave.

"I hated everything Clayton stood for. As soon as he started running drugs, I wanted him out of the organization." He gestured at the three goons. "We all wanted him out, but we couldn't take down a family member. It just isn't done. But because of Katrina's affair with Maloney and the explosion of the Madeira, I figured you two were in cahoots, so I called her and offered a deal. You take down Clayton and we make peace. I'm in charge of the organization now, and I want you back on my team."

"You're the type of man who wanted your own cousin dead. Why would I work for you?"

"I had an older brother. He died of an overdose when I was twelve. I don't want that stuff messing up more lives. We have the same goals, you and I, Gem. We love New York City. We don't want more drugs moving in."

I gave him a look that I hoped told him I understood, and it began to work like an anti-biotic against the rage in my system, which was slowly breaking down.

"I admire your work," he said. "I especially like the way you used that laptop as bait. Clayton had every hood in New York searching for that thing, and all it holds is a bunch of cartoons."

I ruffled Angel's hair again. "Now you see its true importance."

Bradley's eyes showed me he did.

I glanced at Katrina. She was wringing her hands, and her jaw worked nervously up and down. The hurt in her expression pained me.

Oh baby, I am so sorry!

Bradley followed my line of vision to her distress. He put his arm around her shoulders.

"You did well," he told her.

Seeing the two of them together filled me with two extreme feelings. The first was a growing sexual appetite. The second was far more surprising. I felt, possibly for the first time in my undead life, ice cold jealousy.

"I'm sorry I lied about the laptop," I told her.

"I'm not upset," she said, close to tears. "I'm mad as hell. You put yourself, me, and everything we have together at risk for a computer full of cartoons. Are you crazy?"

"I said I was sorry!"

"And you couldn't even tell me why! That's the worst thing! No secrets, Gem! No secrets!"

"No secrets from now on, I swear."

"I want you to know that Angel was never in danger," Bradley nodded. "I've had four men watching over her and Maria in case anyone loyal to Clayton went after her."

"So this is over?" I asked.

"It is over, yes," he replied. "I just need to know if you want a job?"

"A girl's got to work."

"Good." He turned to his men in the front room. "Boys, we're done here. Wait for me in the car." The three goons shuffled out of the door, wiping at coffee stains as they exited. There was a sudden uproar as Maria ambled her way back into the apartment, her groceries now carried by two of Bradley's men.

"Put those things in the kitchen, boys," Bradley ordered, and his men fell into line. "And don't break anything."

I liked Bradley's people management skills. He had an aura of power.

Angel stopped the cartoon and ran to Maria. "Can we

go to the park now?"

"That is a bad idea, I think," Maria said, looking wearily at the mobsters gathered in front of her. "It is getting dark."

Bradley plucked two of his men out of line. "Go with them."

"Yea!" Angel jumped up and down. "You guys can push me on the swing."

In seconds, I was left alone with Katrina and Bradley.

He extended his right hand out to me. "Welcome back, Gem."

I frowned at Katrina. "You should have told me about these guys."

"I was just trying to help."

"But you had a secret all the while you were pissed off at me for having one."

"Two."

The laptop and Angel's story. I felt like a heel.

I will make it all up to you, Katrina but: "Why didn't you tell me about Bradley?"

"If I'd told you that my information came from inside the organisation, you'd have suspected a trap, so I said it came from a waitress friend." Katrina gazed up at Bradley. "I trusted him."

"I can see why his charm worked on you."

The handsome devil's eyebrows arched in approval.

Katrina got all teary eyed. "I swear, Gem, from this moment on, no secrets."

"No secrets." I agreed.

We hugged.

Why do we have clothes on every time we do this?

I accepted Bradley's handshake. "It's good to be back."

And not being shot at!

He held onto my hand for just long enough to make it something more than a handshake. Maybe something akin to affection...

"Maybe we could celebrate. Let me take you both out to dinner?" His eyes glowed.

I think he likes what he sees.

"Umm, excuse me." Katrina interrupted our optical connection. "So this is all over? We're safe? Angel's safe?"

Bradley let go of my hand. "Yes of course."

"Well in that case..." She brushed past him and slipped her left hand through my hair, leaving it settle on the back of my neck. "We're the ones who have the celebrating to do."

And she brought her lips to mine. She kissed me slowly, softly at first, but with each heartbeat, her passion grew to a high I'd not experienced since I became a vampire.

Since before a time I could even remember, another story too painful to tell.

Sensing Bradley's eyes on our gorgeous forms, I could smell his interest in us rise. I placed a finger on Katrina's chin and gently eased her lips from mine.

"Maybe we'll have dinner some other time, Bradley," I said, giving him a wink. "Please, see yourself out."

And this time I kissed Katrina.

GEM – No Choices

Morning

Katrina stirred in her sleep as the nightmare of living with Gem played out in all its grizzly detail. The worry was as real as if she were awake, the terror just as palpable.

In the dream, she paced the hallway of their new apartment, checking her wristwatch every five seconds. It was nearly 6:30 am. The growing warmth from the day's first rays of sunlight had her senses on full alert. In Gem's room, her coffin was still vacant, the lid still open. She hadn't yet arrived home from last night's assignment.

"Gem, where in the hell are you?" Katrina muttered. She immediately conjured up the image of the night Gem had nearly been killed with a silver bullet. She lay prone on the floor of Maloney's penthouse, clinging to her undead life as Maloney pushed the muzzle of his gun against her skull. And then came the ear-drum-shattering blast of a gunshot. But it wasn't Maloney who had fired a fatal shot. It came from Katrina's gun as she fired a bullet into Maloney's head, a shot that echoed through her nightmare and morphed into the *thump, thump, thump* of something striking the front door.

Katrina jumped, almost losing her balance as she burst into action, sprinting towards the front door of their new two-storey apartment. Something hit the door again, but this time the thump was weaker, hardly a slap. She checked that Gem's shotgun was handily placed nearby, and then pressed her eye to the peephole of the steel reinforced door.

Smoke!

The hallway was filling with smoke.

"Katrina, help me," came Gem's weak voice from behind the door.

Heart thrumming, she unlocked the five security locks and pulled the heavy steel door towards her. Smoke swirled in revealing Gem sprawled on the floor, clawing at the air with hands ablaze. "H-help me."

"Gem! What happened? Gem, answer me."

"Sunlight," was all she could manage while rasping in pain. Her once beautiful face was charred black. The pullover she wore looked welded to her skin. Her toasted shoulders bubbled with burn blisters. Pus ran from her eye sockets, and her hair spontaneously combusted into flame.

Gem screamed like no scream she'd ever screamed.

The apartment began to stink of burnt hair, burnt flesh, and burnt vampire. Katrina felt the sick feeling of uselessness roil in her belly. She was incapable of helping Gem. What could a mere human do against the curse of the undead, the reanimated, beautiful body now threatening to burn the apartment building to the ground?

Wake up, Katrina, wake up. It's only a dream.

But this was the hell of living with Gem, sexy, charming, loving, and deadly, so close yet a million miles away from the normal life Katrina wanted to live with her. She'd hoped this day would never come, when Gem pushed the limits too far, danced with death too closely or once too often. Sunlight, a vampire's worst enemy, had knocked on their door and destroyed everything they could have ever had together.

The heat became so intense Katrina was forced to back away from the flames. She had to put them out before the apartment was destroyed. Maria and Angel were still sleeping the back bedrooms. In seconds, their lives would be in mortal danger. Rushing to the kitchen, Katrina retrieved the fire extinguisher that Maria kept in the cupboard under the sink. As Katrina ran back to the front door where Gem lay incinerating, she worked the pin free and fired a frothy mist into the smoky inferno. The flames disappeared, leaving a charred and smouldering husk of a woman on the singed carpet.

"Gem!" Katrina knelt next to her and winced against the eye-stinging smoke and nose-reeling stench. Gem's mouth hung agape, white teeth framing a black hole, and her molars shone through the sinew and tendons of her once beautiful cheeks. And then, right before her eyes, flesh turned to bone...and bone turned to a pile of dust.

Katrina's scream mercifully ripped her from the nightmare. She sat up in bed, panting like a cheetah. One hand went to her chest and her fiercely beating heart. The other groped the sheet beside her, hoping beyond hope that Gem would be there, sleeping next to her like normal people sleep with each other. But the cold empty space further cemented the fact that they were far from normal people in a normal relationship. Even as the morning sunlight sifted in through chinks in the window blinds, so had Gem moved to the safety of her coffin, now locked in her room, a solitary confinement that would extend into eternity, or until the nightmare became a reality.

The alarm jangled. 6:30 am. For real this time. Katrina had to put the nightmare behind her, get up, and face another day that could end in disaster by silver bullets or sunshine's lethal fire. At least Gem's alliance with John Bradley practically ensured the town thugs wouldn't be out to kill her today. On that lighter note, she pushed the Egyptian cotton sheets from her lithe body and slid from the bed.

She pulled on her robe and opened her walk-in closet. As she sifted through the outfits she considered suitable for work at the Guggenheim Museum, she marvelled at how quickly things had changed in her life. After Clayton's grisly execution, Gem found this new apartment. Not just for herself, but for Katrina and Angel and Maria, as well. Once Katrina saw the tenth and eleventh storey condo in a high rise apartment block on Riverside Drive, west of Central Park, she was thrilled. The custom-built steel reinforced front door opened into a large living room from which the kitchen and dining room could be accessed. Down the hallway was Angel's room and quarters for Maria. Upstairs held four bedrooms, three of which were complete with bathrooms as well as a massive main bathroom and a study off the hallway.

Katrina selected a beige trouser suit and a white blouse, and laid them on the bed. She showered quickly and tied her golden hair back in a pony tail. Dried and dressed in world record speed, she skipped applying makeup and headed directly down the hall to Gem's locked bedroom, her vampire lair. Katrina ran the palm of her hand across the polished wood door as if she were stroking Gem's toned and slender back.

"I miss you, Gem," she whispered, knowing the door had to remain shut between them. There'd be no dashing into this room and throwing herself on the bed next to Gem. No sweet nothings. No sweet caresses. Not in this relationship. She had no choice but to stand there, alone and longing.

Gem ruled the night, but sunlight ruled Gem.

Pressing her ear to the door, Katrina wished she could hear Gem sigh and roll over under her satin sheets on a king-sized bed complete with a silk-draped canopy. However, the room beyond the door stood silent and dark while Gem slept the sleep of the undead, tucked into her cushion-lined coffin. It had taken ten of Bradley's most muscle-bound men to carry her *bed* up from the old apartment and place it in her room on a golden dais. There was nothing normal about Gem's bedroom, either.

A sting of selfishness pained Katrina as she wished she could stroll through Central Park on a summer's afternoon, hand-in-hand with Gem while Angel tossed peanuts to the squirrels.

"Katrina." Angel scampered down the hall, night dressing gown flailing around her ankles.

Katrina pushed herself away from Gem's door and reached out to Angel.

The six-year-old bundle of joy launched herself into Katrina's arms. "Good morning."

Savouring the little girl's neck hug, Katrina stepped into her room and sat on the edge of the bed. "Did you sleep okay?"

"I'm not scared of sleeping in a new room." Angel broke free and started jumping on the bed, her gorgeous blond curls bouncing with a joy of their own.

"So you like your new home?"

"*Our* new home," Angel replied, still jumping. "It's great. The TV has cartoons on all the time."

"The Cartoon Channel, of course, only the best for our little girl. Is Maria up yet?"

"Yes, silly. Maria's always up first. She's gone to the corner shop." Angel hopped off the bed. "I'm going to watch cartoons."

"Oh no you don't, young lady. You're going to get ready for school."

"Yea! School. I forgot it was a school day." In a flash of blond locks, Angel swung around and bounded out.

Katrina rose from the bed, energized by Angel's exuberance, and moved to the dresser where she'd laid her museum identity badge. She passed the lanyard over her head. The badge with her photo hung just below her neckline. Very professional. The warmth of pride swelled her chest. Her job as Curator of Antiquities placed her in an enviable position among her piers. She had direct contact with the most interesting and peculiar artefacts to come into New York City. Seemed every day was a new adventure.

A rapping on the door downstairs interrupted her

muse, and Angel's voice announcing, "Maria's home."

"I'm coming." Katrina descended the stairs, snatching up a busy bunch of keys from an ornate, antique table in the foyer. At the front door, she peered through the peep hole and feared she'd see smoke. Maria looked up smiling under her mop of dark curly hair. Four dead bolts and three double locks later, Katrina pulled the heavy bullet-proof door open.

"I'm glad you are still here this morning, Senora Katrina." Maria shuffled inside, laden as usual with shopping bags. She foot-pushed the door shut behind her. "Is our Angel still asleep?"

Our Angel. Maria's words gave Katrina a warm feeling inside, a sensation of belonging that she had struggled to find in Manhattan until Gem, Angel, and Maria had come into her life. She had Maloney to thank for that. If her former lover and now extinct gangster hadn't hired Gem to kill her, she'd never have found this odd but loving family. "Angel is getting ready for school, but I haven't fixed her breakfast yet."

Maria plodded to the kitchen and placed her bags on the table. "Is no worry. You go to work. Gem has left already, no?"

"She's been gone for an hour already." Katrina hated lying to Maria about Gem's activities, but it was for her own good. The truth would make her a target. The bad guys would have someone to torture to gain information on Gem's nocturnal prowling.

"You want I make you some breakfast?"

"I'll get something on the way to work."

"You pick Angel up from school today for me, yes?"

"Yes. And Gem asked if you would be home for dinner? I'm cooking."

Maria pulled a face like she'd licked a lemon. "I should do the cooking every day. You senoritas work hard enough."

"Maybe you're right." Katrina kissed Maria on the cheek. "We'd be lost without you."

"I know, I know." Maria smiled, dragged an eggplant from her shopping bag, and waved her free hand towards the door. "Off to work with you now or I'll be late taking Angel to school."

Katrina donned her beige jacket and grabbed her clutch purse. After a quick peek through the security peephole to ensure the hallway was clear of danger, she opened the door and exited the apartment. She rode the elevator down to the lobby and smiled at the doorman as he opened the gold and glass door for her to pass by.

"Have a good day, Miss," he said as she stepped outside.

On this first true day of spring, the air felt cool and invigorating. It would have taken her just a few minutes to access the Porsche from the downstairs private parking and drive to work, but she decided to walk and enjoy the morning. She set out towards midtown, where she'd cross the park toward the Guggenheim Museum.

As she approached West Drive, she spotted a street vendor. His breakfast cart sparkled in the sunshine. Her stomach responded with a request for a bagel and cream cheese. She joined the back of the queue, directly behind a middle aged couple who were holding hands.

"Cola with breakfast? Better make it a diet," the man teased, wrapping his arm around the lady's waist. "Wouldn't want to ruin those gorgeous curves."

She leaned into him and swooned. "Flattery will get you everywhere, Mister James."

He kissed the top of her head. His salt and pepper hair was thick and luscious, and his smile beamed mature and infectious. Katrina couldn't help but giggle as their good mood vibes filled her heart with romantic notions of Gem...but reality immediately squashed them. She and Gem would never have sweet memories of breakfast in the park together.

"I love you," the lady said. Her summer dress was classy, elegant even, but the cardigan she had tied round her shoulders showed that this woman was no fuddy-duddy.

A flock of pigeons taking noisy flight drew Katrina's attention to a man wearing a suit who'd stormed out of the park. "What the fuck you talkin' about," he shouted into a cell phone pressed to his ear. "Yeah, I'm here. Right on the fuckin' corner."

"Hey," Mister Salt and Pepper called out. "Watch your language, buddy. There are ladies over here."

Lady Summer Dress placed a hand on his chest. "Don, no, leave him be." She positioned herself between her husband and the obnoxious guy in the suit.

"You do what you're fucking told, bitch," the guy spat into the phone, turning his back on Mister Salt and Pepper. "I'm waiting. Where the fuck—"

Rat-a-tat-a-tat.

Katrina felt the concussion of the gunshots just as she heard them. She threw herself to the sidewalk. Her purse flew from her hand and skidded across the pavement. Her knees skinned on the concrete. Bright orange bursts flashed from the back window of a speeding black limousine. The guy in the suit dance around like a marionette, as if its convulsive movements were controlled by some sadistic puppeteer. His spewing blood turned the sidewalk into a macabre Jackson Pollack, a life and death piece of artwork, the remnants of which splattered across her face and her blouse and her beige jacket, until finally the guy slumped to the sidewalk.

Tires squealing, the limo sped off.

A human stampede scattered in panic to get away from the massacred body, its fingers twitching, and the one eye not blasted from his face staring blankly at Katrina.

Mister Salt and Pepper cried out, "No!"

Gem

Katrina blinked, hoping the madness would disappear, but instead of regaining the peace that once belonged to this spring morning, she suddenly became aware of a pain in her elbow. Her heart raced so hard, it felt as if it had been jammed up into her throat.

"No, no, no, sweetheart, no!"

Not wanting to look but knowing she had to, she forced her gaze towards the gut-wrenching, heartbreaking wails of Mister Salt and Pepper as he sat on the ground, cradling Lady Summer Dress to his chest, rocking her body and weeping.

Katrina muttered, "Oh God," in a voice she didn't recognise, a voice that was not her normal smooth tone and texture but cracking at the sight of Lady Summer Dress's head, the back blown off and oozing grey matter, all that was left of her memories.

The beautiful spring day turned black as the darkest night.

***

Katrina stirred, unsure how long she had been unconscious on the sidewalk. The air vibrated to the wail of sirens. Dazed and confused, she was surrounded by people gawking and groaning, some crying in disbelief and despair. Her face felt wet. She brushed her fingers across her cheek and drew them back to reveal blood. Panic started to shackle her, but in a moment of clarity, she remembered the blood belonged to the foul-mouthed guy wearing the suit.

She got a grip on her emotions and took in the scene around her. Someone had placed a gym bag under her head, and her purse lay on her stomach. Her left elbow felt like it was on fire. Venturing a glance, she saw a white bandage. She tried to sit up, but someone told her to be still, a paramedic she assumed by the look of his uniform.

"I'm okay," she slurred, feeling faint and groggy.

"That lady, look after that lady." Katrina indicated Lady Summer Dress and noticed emergency services had already arrived in force. They huddled over her like buzzards on a corpse. Mister Salt and Pepper knelt off to the side, stooped in grief and misery.

She wanted to reach out to him, tell him how sorry she was that their memories would end on this day. They were in the wrong place at the wrong time, caught in a drive-by shooting, a far too often occurrence in the Big Apple.

An ambulance crew lifted Katrina to a gurney and rolled her to the back doors of their vehicle. With a jarring thump, she was loaded inside where other medics fretted over her. They installed a blood pressure cuff and taped wires to her chest. The beep of a heart monitor penetrated the gloom.

"She's stable. Let's roll."

Siren screaming all the way, the journey to the hospital became a disoriented blur. Once she was inside the emergency room, her treatment came quick, efficient, and for the most part painless.

"Flesh wound to the elbow," the doctor said. "A few scrapes and bruises. Not life threatening but painful, just the same. Is there someone you can call?"

Katrina pointed towards her purse that someone had set on the counter. "May I use my cell phone?" While the sun was still high in the sky, the one person she wanted to call most was completely inaccessible. The one she'd have to call would give her the third degree. She could hear him now: *Did you see the shooter? Did you get the license plate number? Did you recognise the victim? What were you doing in the park anyway?*

The doctor handed her the cell phone. "I'll get your release papers shortly."

Katrina began to dial. As she depressed each digit, she felt the dull thud of trepidation rise in her chest, but she had no choice but to call John Bradley.

Gem

What else can I do?

Afternoon

Katrina sat on the edge of the hospital gurney, her torn trousers rolled up, and her knees bandaged like a school kid who had taken a tumble in the playground. Her beige jacket lay across the back of a plastic chair. The hole in its left arm mirrored the wound on her elbow, which was mercifully numb from the local anaesthetic the doctors had administered before they stitched her up.

"That's going to leave one heck of a scar," she mumbled to herself and winced.

A nurse poked her head between the thin plastic curtains. "Did you need something?"

"Sorry, no. I was talking to myself."

"Has your friend arrived yet?"

Katrina grimaced. "Not yet...and he's not my friend." *Bradley is nobody's friend.* "He's just giving me a ride home."

The nurse shrugged. "The doctor should have you released before long."

Katrina tried on a placating smile.

With a rustle of curtain, the nurse was gone.

"He's not my friend," Katrina repeated. She blinked and remembered the back of Lady Summer Dress's head. Or at least, what was left of it. She blinked again and recalled the guy in the suit twitching on his way to the ground.

The doctor swung the curtains back and stepped into her cubicle. "The nurse tells me you've been talking to yourself," he said with a friendly smile. He shined a torch into her eyes. "Is that normal?"

"Normal as what, like getting shot?" She tracked the doctor's finger tip as he moved it from side to side across her field of vision.

"Good, good. If you start to feel faint, or if you start

vomiting, you get back here. Okay?"

"Of course." Katrina began to roll down her trouser legs over her bandaged knees.

"You're a lucky woman."

She lowered her head and focussed on her pants to make sure she didn't look up at the doctor and reveal the angry tears that suddenly welled in her eyes. She'd come very close to getting killed. And that realisation pissed her off.

What had she done to deserve a gunshot to the elbow and skinned knees? What had that couple standing in front of her done wrong? They were there for breakfast, and some bozo with a gun and a fast, fancy car destroyed the future they had together. What right did anyone have to snuff out an innocent life like that? And who was going to do anything about it? The authorities? They couldn't find a burglar in a raccoon den. So who could make the shooter pay? Gem. She was the great equaliser. Katrina wondered how much safer the city would be if Gem didn't have to stay in her coffin all day.

"What time is your ride due?" the doctor asked, breaking her train of thought.

"I'm not sure. I may have to walk to—"

"There's no need for that." John Bradley stepped into the cubicle, a confident smile splashed across his handsome face. "I'll take care of her from here."

What in God's name inspired me to phone this creep?
She had no choice but to go with him.

***

Katrina didn't say a word while she and Bradley walked from the hospital to the parking lot. He opened the passenger door of his top-of-the-range Mercedes and raised his eyebrows at her when she didn't acknowledge his chivalry.

"My pleasure," he said sarcastically and took his place

~110~

in the driver's seat. As the car pulled onto the street, a black SUV with tinted windows tucked in behind them.

"I wasn't the target," Katrina hissed, looking over her shoulder at the tail dogging behind. "And I don't need your goons' protection."

"They've got *my* back," Bradley said. "Not yours. I already know you weren't the target." He accelerated onto the expressway. "You were in the wrong place at the wrong time, is all."

"Did you have something to do with that hit?"

"Whoa, take it easy. It's my job to know what goes on in this city."

Her aches and pains faded. She suddenly realised that getting a ride from mob kingpin John Bradley could garner her some information. "So who was the guy in the suit?"

"They called him *The Banker*. Peter Webb. Crooked as a broken nose. He must've been skimming a little too much cash off the top of somebody's till."

"Money laundering?"

"Don't make it sound so clean!"

Katrina stared at Bradley, incredulous, in spite of the butterflies he'd roused in her stomach. "Do you know the carnage that hit-man left behind? A woman had her head blown off, and her husband is left to deal with her death and a future without her."

"I'm sorry about Don and Betty James, but collateral damage happens."

"Happens?" Katrina's mind became a blur of anger and sorrow. On top of the needless slaughter, she'd witnessed the sloppiest hit in history. Her rage obscured so much of her normal rationale that she envisioned the hit-man suffering and dieing for what he'd done. The image appealed to her. Now she wanted something much darker than simple information. Now she wanted revenge.

"Am I taking you home?"

"To work, The Guggenheim."

"I know." Bradley accelerated into an open lane. "But maybe you should go home and pick up Angel after school like you planned."

"You know too much for my liking," she said and ignored the smirk on his face. "But you don't know everything. Maria is collecting Angel after school."

"That's not the way I heard it."

"What are you...stalking us?"

"I have an investment to protect."

"Is our apartment bugged?"

"I have my sources."

"I'll call Maria from work. She'll get Angel home all right."

"It's none of my business, but—"

"You're right, it's not." Contempt squirmed in her belly. His intrusion into Gem's personal life, and their lives together, bordered on invasion of privacy. She crossed her arms and pursed her lips, swearing to tell Gem of his treachery.

He swung the car to the *Loading Zone* curb outside the museum. The SUV pulled in behind them. Three dark-suited goons got out and cordoned the Mercedes.

"Tell Gem I'll be there at seven tonight."

"You can't just turn up whenever you like!"

"This is business. Gem's business."

"It's our home! What gives you the right to waltz in and disrupt what little time we have together?"

"I'm her boss. I expect her to be at my beck and call twenty-four-seven."

"It's very clear to me what you expect."

"What are you insinuating?"

"I've seen the way you look at her."

"I'm a man. I look at beautiful women, you included."

She hadn't noticed him looking at her. How could she have missed that? "You think I'm beautiful?"

"You're both lovely, but that's beside the point. I have

an important job for Gem. One that could change things for the better in this city."

Katrina stared straight into his eyes. She wished she hadn't. She was appalled by what he stood for, mobs, and guns, and gangsters, but attracted to him in equal measure. "If you know so much about what goes on in this city, then find out who shot me and killed that woman."

"I have no need to involve myself."

"I'm not asking you to get involved. I just want to know who did the shooting. Gem and I will do the rest."

"Don't get in over your head, young lady."

"I have no choice." She climbed out of the car. "Someone has to get justice for that poor woman." She slammed the door. Dizziness engulfed her. She'd gotten up too fast for her weakened condition. Her legs gave out.

One of the goons caught her by the elbow.

Her injured elbow!

Stifling a scream, "Don't touch me." She slapped at his granite arm, drawing odd looks from nearby pedestrians. The goon backed off, a confused look creasing his already bulldoggish face.

Bradley lowered his passenger window. "And you're welcome for the ride."

Katrina rubbed her bandaged elbow, her lips taut against the pain, her head still swimming. "Give me a name...that's all I want."

Bradley shook his head. "I'll see you at seven."

"Great." Katrina stormed towards the museum's staff entrance. She'd be home just in time to watch the pair of them fawn over each other.

Once inside the museum, her mood softened while she made her way down the main hallway. She wouldn't have had to depend on Bradley if Gem could have been available to help her this morning. She was like having a worthless husband.

Raised voices and laughter up ahead hurried her

progress. She edged around a corner and joined the back of a small crowd who had gathered in front of Dr. Amy Jones, one of the more forward-thinking museum curators. She was sharing a newly arrived artefact from Sweden with other members of the antiquities staff. Everyone was so enthralled in her that they didn't seem to notice Katrina, let alone her bandaged elbow and blood-spotted blouse and jacket.

"Now this is a most interesting piece," Dr. Jones announced, lifting a golden pendant above her head so those at the back could see it. The sturdy neck-chain was draped over her wrist. "This pendant is called the Mjölnir," she said, pronouncing it *Me yul neer*, "although the comic book fans amongst you may know it better as the Hammer of Thor."

A wave of laughter swept across her small audience.

"Now this is obviously quite a bit smaller than what the God of Thunder throws around, but legend tells us that this too holds dramatic powers."

Katrina craned her neck to get a better look at the pendant.

"This version of Thor's Mjölnir has tiny words engraved across its surface. *Dåg-gåstol* which translates to Day-walker. This pendant was worn by Nótt, The Norse Goddess of Darkness. A sensual, elegant lady of the night."

One of the men let out a wolf whistle.

Jones wagged a finger in his direction. "Now this is not a lady you would wish to meet alone in a dark alley. If she were around today, some would call her a vampire."

"Vampires don't exist," he said.

Katrina grimaced at the man's ignorance.

"Don't be so sure," Dr. Jones replied. "Nótt was a prisoner of darkness who had never seen the light of day until she wore this pendant around her neck. Legend says it protected her from the light by wielding the power of the *un-light*."

"And she was no longer a prisoner of the night," Katrina concluded for her, somewhat in a daze over the flood of emotions coursing through her body, the most being newfound hope for her future with Gem.

"Exactly," announced Dr. Jones, and with a flourish, she placed the pendant back into its protective travel box. "And that story makes this such an interesting piece. Next month, we'll display it with pride in our museum. Thirty days, ladies and gentlemen, so mark your calendars."

Katrina couldn't take her eyes off the box. If the legend was true, the contents of that box could solve all of her problems. The trick would be to test the pendant's powers...on Gem. Her heart palpitated at the thought.

Dr. Jones engaged in further discussions with the staff. Katrina shouldered her way through the group to get closer to the box. It had no lock, just a basic latch. If she could just borrow the artefact, at least for a day, she could determine its true value. However, Gem would have to risk her life to do it. Wear the pendant, expose her body to sunlight, and see if her skin bursts into flame. Convincing Gem to partake in such an experiment may require some serious prodding.

Dr. Jones' voice drew Katrina from her ponderings. "Gerald," she called to one of the security guards. "Would you mind taking this to the vault room?"

The hulking man stepped forward, his uniform straining at the seams across his barrel belly and over his hoggish biceps. His hair was cropped short and his eyes looked hard, as if he meant business. "Of course, Doctor Jones," he said in a respectful and sheepish voice that dwarfed his massive size.

Katrina saw her chance to get close to the fabled pendant. Gerald was incredibly shy around her, like he harboured a schoolboy crush. There was no better time than now to use that to her advantage. "Doctor Jones."

She and Gerald turned towards her. Both of their jaws

simultaneously dropped open. "Katrina?" Jones gasped. "What happened to you?"

"It's really nothing," she lied, pointing to her bandaged elbow. "I tripped over a kerb. Such a clumsy idiot."

Jones winced. "But your blouse...is that blood spatter?"

"I'll need to clean up."

"Are you sure you're okay to work?"

Katrina watched Gerald's expression in her peripheral vision. By the look on his wrenched face, he seemed genuinely concerned for her well being. "I'm headed downstairs to the washroom," she said. "I'll take that box to the vault."

"Oh...well...that's all right, Katrina. Gerald can do it."

"It's too heavy for you to carry, anyway," Gerald said. "With that broken wing and all...ma'am."

"It's only a scratch." Katrina took the box from Jones. "I'm not an invalid." She tucked the box under her arm and smiled at Gerald. "Lead the way, handsome."

He wilted before her eyes. "Yes, ma'am."

She followed him down a well-lit corridor to the stairs. Descending, he held the handrail as if it were the edge of a cliff. Seemed his size fourteen shoes, which must've been out of sight under the sag of his belly, presented a challenge, as each step had to be taken with extreme care. She doubted he could have carried the box and negotiated the staircase at the same time. While his back was to her and his attention on staying vertical, she opened the box and removed the pendant.

He reached the basement landing and turned around. "I can take that box now."

She barely had time to stuff the pendant in her pocket. "That's kind of you, Gerald, but I've got it just fine."

"You should go home and nurse that so-called scratch." He reached out his shovel sized hand. "I'll sign this into the vault for you."

That was all she needed, him taking a last look inside. "Dr. Jones entrusted it to me. I'll sign it in. Just keep me company and watch out for muggers." She smiled.

He bellowed out a laugh. "Muggers? Down here? You're funny."

She offered up a chuckle. "They wouldn't stand a chance against you, Gerald."

Blushing, he gestured for her to take the lead.

At the vault room, she reached the counter. The back wall resembled the locker bank in a bus station, each thick steel compartment numbered, and a tagged key protruding from the door of each empty vault. There was no one around. "Anybody here?"

A stick-thin sign-in clerk rushed out of the back room. "What do you have there?" he asked with pitched brows.

"Some old pendant," Katrina said and set the box down. "Check it in for Doctor. Jones, please."

"Is this part of the Swedish consignment?" He thumbed the latch, eager as a kid with a Christmas present to open.

Katrina's stomach lurched. "Is it really necessary to look inside?"

"Just making sure there's something in here."

Her throat sized. She was about to go to jail. "But..."

Gerald stepped up. His chest ballooned to button-busting proportions. "Keep your paws off, Fido. I'll vouch for it. Seen Dr. Jones put it in there with my own eyes." He pointed meaty V-ed fingers at his eyes.

"Yes, Sir. Of course." He scooped up the box and with practiced ease, slipped it into a vault, closed the door, and twisted the key. "Just sign it in." He turned back to the counter and indicated a log book.

Gerald did the honours.

The clerk handed him the key. "Don't lose it."

Relief swept over Katrina.

Gerald fisted the key and smiled at her. "I'll take this to Doctor Jones. You go home and get some rest. We got a deal...ma'am?"

She would've jumped his bones for that rescue... Well...not really, but she would've hugged him...well...if she could've gotten her arms around him. "It's a deal," she said, though it would be several hours before she could actually go home.

"Maybe we'll get a cup of coffee some time," he said in that sheepish voice.

"Maybe."

Gerald headed off down the corridor.

Katrina watched him go. A shudder of guilt ran down her spine. If anyone found out the pendant was missing, that teddy bear of a man would go down for stealing it. However, technically she hadn't stolen it, just borrowed it in the hope it would free Gem from the bonds of darkness. If not, she'd find a way to return the pendant to the vault. If so, she and Gem could finally live a normal life together, and the world would be a safer place for everyone.

The trick would be keeping the pendant permanently. But first, she had to try it out on Gem. They had no choice. But she had thirty days to find out if the legend was true or false.

Evening

The instant she arrived home from work, Katrina stashed the pendant in her underwear draw. She desperately wanted to talk to Gem about the implications of finding the artefact, but that conversation would have to wait. John Bradley was due to show up any time now.

She changed into a grey jogging suit. Her bloody blouse and torn-at-the-knees trousers were fodder for the trash can. The skin on her bandaged elbow began to itch. She hurried to Gem's locked door. The sun had set. Katrina no longer considered dusk to be the end of the day but the

Gem

beginning of *vampire dawn*.

The doorknob turned, and the dark haired beauty emerged, smiling. She wore a sleek black dress, low cut, her cleavage exposed to next Friday. Her alabaster skin glowed within the frame of her black combed-down-straight hair, and red-painted lips begged to be kissed.

That little place inside Katrina's stomach tightened like a stretched rubber band then snapped with a pulse of hot desire. She forced the sensation back down into the depths from which it came. "We have to talk."

Gem's eyes darted directly to Katrina's bandaged elbow. "What happened?" Her smile died faster than one of her victims.

"A hit gone bad," Katrina said. "Drive-by shooting in Central Park. I got in the way."

Concern melted Gem's puzzled expression. "How bad is it?"

"It's nothing, really. The bullet just clipped me, is all."

Gem's eyes tightened to mere slits. "Who did it?"

"I asked Bradley to find out."

"Why did you get him involved in this?"

"I couldn't call you."

Gem embraced Katrina. "I swear, if anything happens to you."

"Something already happened to me, Gem. You weren't there for me. You can't be there for me because you spend the day in a coffin. I had to deal with this problem on my own. But when Bradley names the shooter, I expect you to kill him for me."

Gem stepped back, shock and surprise hardening the once-soft lines on her beautiful face. "You want me to carry out a hit for you?"

"The bastard deserves to die."

"For clipping your elbow? Remind me not to piss you off."

"An innocent woman was killed, Gem. The cops got nothing. He's going to get away with murder unless we do something."

Gem wilted. "It's my fault. I've drawn you into a dangerous world—"

"Being with Maloney was more dangerous than this. Hell, the world is a dangerous place. Still, that woman didn't deserve to have the back of her head blown off. I have to do something. You have to help me."

Gem reached for Katrina's hand, but the stern look on her face made Katrina realise she was not going to like the next words Gem had to say. "We can't save the world. Some bad guys get away with murder."

"Bradley got you on that short a leash?" Katrina snapped and immediately regretted saying it.

Gem fired back, "When we do a job for him, he's got our back. We go out on our own, say we waste this shooter you're so hot to make pay, we run the risk of getting busted. You want that?"

"Of course not."

"You think my coffin keeps us apart? Think what a stint on Rikers Island will do for our love life."

"It's not fair."

"Hey, I want to feed that guy his own spleen for what he did to you. But it's not that simple."

Before Katrina could answer, the front door opened, and Angel's voice echoed up the stairs. "Gem. Katrina. I'm home."

"We'll talk about this later," Gem said.

Trying to keep her cool, Katrina followed Gem downstairs, where Angel and Maria had just stepped into the living room. They both noticed Katrina's bandaged elbow. Their eyes grew wide.

Maria spoke first. "You have been hurt. What happened?"

"It's nothing, really," Katrina said, not wanting to

alarm them with another story of gunfire and death. "I was running through the crowd to catch a cab when I tripped over a dog on a leash. I'm such a klutz."

"You must be more careful."

Angel pulled a serious face. "I fell in school once. All the boys laughed at me."

"Well, that's just mean," Gem said.

"I know, but I don't fall anymore. I'm six now."

Katrina patted the top of Angel's head. "Gravity can be such a nuisance."

At dinner, Angel didn't give anyone a moment to ponder the events of their day. Between hungry mouthfuls of Maria's best chicken casserole, she entertained her captive audience with stories about her friends, her teacher, and her activities at school. Katrina couldn't help but smile at the blond girl's enthusiasm and storytelling skills.

"And then..." Angel said, taking a brief pause to sip from her water glass, "... Maria and I went and played on the swings. I can swing much higher than you, can't I, Maria?"

"Yes, yes you can." Maria glanced up at the wall clock. "Now eat your food. We don't want to be late for the cinema."

After dinner, Maria did the dishes and escorted Angel out the door. Katrina locked the locks and tilted her head to Gem. "By the way, Bradley is coming over at seven."

"What for?" As Gem settled on the couch, her dress hiked high up her thighs.

Katrina had to use every ounce of self control she had to keep from jumping on her, so she forced her eyes up to Gem's face. "A job, I guess."

Gem flicked on the television. The news program highlighted the top story of the day, the drive by shooting in Central Park. A photo of Betty James was prominently displayed in the corner of the screen. The reporter said, *"Police are baffled tonight. Dozens of witnesses, but no solid leads to the shooter have surfaced."*

"You see? He's going to get away with it." Katrina slumped on the couch next to Gem, close enough to smell the fragrance of her skin but far enough apart to create an I'm-serious-about-this rift. "Are you going to help me, or not?"

"I didn't say I wouldn't help, but until I get Bradley's backing, I can't do anything."

"What if Bradley was behind the hit and he's just not talking?"

"I'll ask him. If he's lying, I'll see it in his eyes."

"The same eyes he undresses you with?" All right. She'd said it, spread her cards out on the table. Bradley was a wolf in sheep's clothing. Pack leader. Dominant male. Someone Katrina didn't need mucking up their already strained relationship.

"Come on," Gem said. "He's only interested in our well being."

"He's *interested* alright, in the curve of your ass."

Gem smiled. "What's wrong with my ass?"

"Nothing, believe me, but you love the attention he showers on you."

"I do...I mean, I do?"

"And I've seen the way you look at him...all schoolgirl-with-a-crush-on-the-teacher blushing."

"I love you, Katrina. Bradley is business, not pleasure."

"That's what he said. Business." Katrina's fury bubbled in her gut. "But I don't trust him."

"Then trust me," Gem said, almost a whisper.

Katrina squinted, the skin around her eyes bunching up into creases, holding back tears, and as she looked at Gem, so beautiful and sincere, something new struck Katrina, a realisation that no trinket, amulet, or pendant could fix.

I'm going to get wrinkles. I'm going to get old. And

she's never going to change. Immortal beauty, forever. And I'll be dust.

Katrina's pulse throbbed in her neck.

Gem's lips twitched.

She must have sensed Katrina's increased blood pressure. It was anyone's guess the impact that would have on her vampire blood lust. "I trust you, Gem, with my life."

"You did the right thing calling Bradley."

"He'll be here any minute, fawning over you."

"I'll try not to notice."

The doorbell rang.

Katrina rolled her eyes.

"Are you going to get that?" Gem asked her, "or just sit there looking fine?"

She always had a way of taking the edge off Katrina's fears. After padding to the front door, she unlocked the locks and pulled open the door.

Bradley strolled in like he owned the place. He wore an impeccable three piece suit and carried a long canvas bag under one arm, the strap over his shoulder. His scrutinizing eyes darted back and forth between Gem and Katrina. "Have I come at a bad time?" he asked, his lecherous gaze creeping across Gem's exposed thighs.

"Not at all." She stood and pulled down her dress, but not too far. "What do you have for me there?" Gem indicated the canvas bag with a sultry tip of a polished fingernail.

Katrina looked away so she didn't have to deal with the jealousy welling up in her chest, the green-eyed monster roaring. She had to get control of him. It was one thing to be jealous of the coffin that kept them apart, but entirely another thing to loathe Bradley for lusting after Gem, or visa-versa. Katrina was just as much to blame, lusting for both of them the way she did.

Bradley got down to business. "I've got a job for you tonight."

"I'll leave you to it then," Katrina grumped and started for the stairs.

"Katrina, wait," Bradley said.

She stopped and turned to face him, feeling a bit underdressed in her grey jogging suit. He reached inside his suit jacket and pulled out a folded paper. "I was off the mark about Peter Webb. It wasn't a rival mob hit, after all."

"Not about money laundering?"

"Seems he'd given his brother some bad investment advice. Andrew Webb lost a lot of money and killed him for it. You and Betty James got in the way." He held the note out to her. "Andrew Webb has no link to us. I'll put up the smoke screen. You're cleared to take him out."

Gem snatched the note from Bradley. "I think we should turn this over to the police, let them handle it."

Katrina couldn't believe her ears. Gem was going to pass on the hit. "What are you doing?"

"Once I start knocking off everyone you don't like, Katrina, when's it going to stop? I don't want you mixed up in that manure."

"You won't do it for me?"

"The guy will get a needle in his arm. Dead is dead, and you won't be involved."

"I want to be involved."

"Well, I don't," Gem hissed, her vampire fangs flashing.

A chime tone came from the TV. Everyone turned to look.

Breaking News.

Katrina recognised the picture on the screen. Don James. "What is *this*?"

"A man whose wife was shot and killed this morning has been the victim of a hit and run this evening. Don James died as a result of his injuries. Witnesses reported a black limo speeding from the scene. The left front fender was damaged. Police tell us they suspect James was

targeted because he witnessed this morning's gangland-style shooting."

Katrina couldn't breathe. She felt as if someone had hit her head with a board. "What does that mean, Gem? Don James was a witness. Now he's dead. Does that mean I'm next?"

Gem and Bradley stared at the TV.

"I'm as much a witness as he was, Gem. Andrew Webb has got to die...before he kills me. You've got no choice."

Katrina didn't wait for a response. She ran up the stairs to her room and slammed the door. Surely Gem wouldn't let this killer hunt her down. Shoot her like a dog. Run her over with his damn black limo. She sat on the edge of the bed, her knees sore, her elbow ablaze with pain, and wept for the terror this day had brought her: the dream, the drive-by shooting, and now this, being marked for death.

An eye for an eye, is that how it is now?

When she'd made her decision to be with Gem, she knew she'd have to get used to violence and death, but up until this moment she had always been one step removed.

Now I'm the target of a hit.

Katrina closed her eyes and wished for sleep. Even the nightmare would be better than this living hell, the vision of Don James slumped on the sidewalk, holding his wife's bloody corpse to his chest, that heart-wrenching wail coming from his mouth. She saw the flashes of gunfire from the back window of the limo, and she saw the concrete rushing up towards her face. Hot adrenaline spilled into her bloodstream. She snapped open her eyes to stop the flow of memories from her tortured mind.

Gem, sleek as a black cat, was standing in front of her, causing a jolt of surprise. "Gem." Katrina reached out and touched Gem's hand. "I'm sorry. I'm losing it."

Taking Katrina's hand, Gem sat next to her. "I'm going to protect you. You can count on me."

"No police?"

"We'll pay Andrew Webb a visit tonight."

"We're going to kill him?"

"How about we make him beg for his life first," Gem replied, getting to her feet. "Will that be revenge enough?"

"I want him to know it's for Betty and Don James...not me."

"You got it."

Katrina stood and drew Gem into a warm embrace. "Thank you."

"But you have to help me with something first."

"With what?"

"Follow me."

Downstairs, Bradley stood at the kitchen table. In front of him lay the canvas bag, and beside it, a completely assembled futuristic rifle, matt black with a long barrel and a huge sighting scope. Gem picked it up and cradled it in her arms. Her red, sensuous lips tightened into a wicked smile. "You like my new toy?"

Katrina gasped. "What are you going to do with that?"

"We've got a job to do for Bradley. I'll tell you about it on the way. And bring that sexy red wig of yours!"

***

Within minutes, the Porsche was racing through midtown towards the Queensboro Bridge. Katrina sat back-stiff in the passenger seat, watching Gem gun the gas and flick through the gears like an Indianapolis race car driver. Her black jacket was zippered up to her neck, and she'd pulled a black woollen hat down close to her perfectly shaped eyebrows. Gem was so damn hot, even in her prowler getup. Katrina felt a surge of warm desire rush from her stomach and spill into her chest. "Where are we going in such a hurry?"

"You like baseball?"

"What's that got to do with Bradley?"

Gem

"We're off to Citi Field to see the Mets play the Red Sox."

"The Red Sox suck."

"How would you know that?"

"I may be a beautiful woman with an eye for fashion and hot spot for you," she examined her fingernails, "but I keep up with sports."

Gem smiled and signalled to take the road up onto the bridge. "Bradley is doing a solid for an old buddy in Boston. Seems like the Red Sox pitcher has had a bad run on the horses. He owed some bad men some big money, so he started throwing games for cash. The Boston Mob is losing millions, and the Red Sox are playing like they're little league."

"A black eye for Boston fans, I bet."

Gem accelerated to ninety. "The Boston boys have had enough." She weaved through traffic, just missing a bus.

"So they put a hit on him," Katrina shouted over the buzz of the engine. "Can't say as I blame them. What's my part in this?"

"I need you to be my decoy. After all that's happened today, are you up to it?"

"Depends. What's in it for us?"

"This hit is worth a cool million, but nobody can put a value on what you mean to me, Katrina."

"I'm sorry I doubted you."

"This ends tonight." Gem jammed the brakes and careered the Porsche onto Northern Boulevard. "I'm doing the hit for you for free."

Free? I'm worth free! Gem doesn't do anything for Bradley for free, but a million bucks seems rather steep.

"That's a lot of money out of Bradley's pocket. The Boston mob boss must be one hell of a good friend."

"There's more to it than that. The mob boss is fed up with the drug traffickers horning in on his protection business, just like Bradley. We get this job done, Boston and Bradley are going to work together to put dealers out of business up and down the East Coast."

Katrina could see how that plan fit well with Gem's code of practice. Since Angel's mother was killed by a drug dealer... "Count me in."

After fighting traffic down Roosevelt Boulevard, Gem pointed. "There it is."

The stadium opened out before them. Its ultra powerful floodlights made the surrounding area look like a blackout zone.

Gem parked in the side lot, courtesy of Bradley's parking pass, and shouldered the canvas bag strap. "Follow me." She led Katrina to the base of the stands beneath the light tower. "We're going up there." She slipped her arm around Katrina's waist and pulled her close. "Ready?"

Katrina reached into her jacket pocket and pulled out the red wig. "One second." She tugged her disguise into place. No matter how many times Gem carried her up multiple stories in a single bound, she would always feel like Lois Lane. "Ready."

"I've got you," Gem said, as if Christopher Reeve's line would calm Katrina's excited heartbeat.

"You've got me? Who's got you?"

Gem chuckled and leapt into the air.

Blood rushed from Katrina's head so fast she felt faint. The lighted white and red *CitiField* sign went by in a blur. A split second later, Gem set her on the top girder of the floodlight tower, shielded from view behind the bright lights.

"Give me thirty seconds to get into position." And then Gem was gone.

"This is crazy," Katrina muttered as she realised how windy it was up so high. She began to count to thirty in her head. On the field below, the batter stepped up to the plate. The pitch came fast and hard. Strike! Organ music blared

Gem

out in triumph. The crowd erupted in a cacophony of noise. The stands shook. Katrina tensed and wished she had a stabilising handhold to grab onto.

The pitcher readied another pitch. The crowed quieted. Katrina's mental clock hit thirty. Heart pounding, she touched her wig, a salute to the here-goes-nothing god, and stepped to the edge of the steel girder.

She screamed to get everyone's attention then: "I'm going to jump!" she shouted. "I'm going to jump!"

Row upon row of baseball fans turned shocked faces up at her. The fervour of the stadium died to an intrigued whisper. Katrina blinked as flashes from cameras and cell phones captured her red-wigged image. Despite being half-blinded, Katrina's eyes sought out the pitcher. He finally turned his gaze up to her. His expression was pure annoyance. Removing his hat, he wiped sweat from his brow and spat on the ground.

"I'm going to jump," she yelled.

The bright red dot of a laser site appeared on the pitcher's forehead then a dark hole erupted with a spray of blood just as a distant *phut* sound reached her. The military calibre bullet fired from the futuristic rifle exited the back of his skull, followed by a spew of grey matter. What was left of his head jerked back on his neck, and he slumped to the ground. His baseball cap landed next to the dropped baseball. A red stain grew on the mound beneath him.

Katrina stepped back into the darkness and closed her eyes. The impact of what she'd just witnessed hit her like a brick. "Lady Summer Dress, Betty James," she muttered in a breathless whisper, her legs suddenly weak and wobbly. Twice today she'd seen death come from a bullet to the brain. An innocent victim. A baseball player on the take. Both just as dead. Little black dots danced before her eyes. Katrina fought to keep from fainting, but her knees buckled. This high up meant only one thing.

As she pitched over, she heard screams rise from the

crowd as fans realised the pitcher had been struck out for life.

Her mind in a dizzying swirl, she toppled from the tower. Down, down, down, streaking past the white and red *CitiField* sign, the concrete rushing up—

"I've got you," Gem said, catching Katrina in mid air.

The sensation of floating on clouds replaced the thunderous rush of air from the fall. "You've got me? Who's got you?"

"You do," Gem said.

Lois Lane, eat your heart out.

Night

Two hours later, the Porsche crept up a tree-lined street in South Hampton, surrounded by some of the most expensive properties in the United States. Katrina's eyes flitted open, and through a fog she could see Gem behind the wheel. "Are we here?"

Gem stubbed her cigarette butt out in the ashtray and hit the button that closed the window. She powered up the air conditioning. The smoke cleared quickly, and Katrina could see more clearly. "What are you doing smoking again?"

"It's not like it'll kill me."

Point taken. "Sorry I couldn't stay awake. This day has been too much for me."

"We're just down the road from Andrew Webb's house. In spite of his investment losses, it looks like he's done well for himself. Shame he had to kill his brother."

"Greed is a powerful motivator." Katrina felt cold inside. Webb had killed Lady Summer Dress by mistake, that was one thing, and mowing Mister Salt and Pepper down in cold blood was another. Now Katrina was about to have him killed in cold blood. Greed wasn't her motivator. Justice for the James-es of the world. Vigilante justice, to boot. Yet that didn't make her feel like a better person than the killer Andrew Webb.

Gem, the Ninja-looking sex goddess-slash-vampire vixen, went about loading her guns. Business as usual for her, but for Katrina, after what she'd witnessed today, started to baulk and question her decision to take the law into her own hands.

She closed her eyes and took a deep breath. Don and Betty James played in her memory, the happy couple standing at the breakfast cart. Then the image of Betty's brains splattered on the sidewalk hardened Katrina's resolve. On top of that, the news of Don's murder-by-limo-fender cemented her conviction. They weren't given any choices. Andrew Webb took care of that for them. And he'd given Gem and Katrina no choices either. Since he'd set out to kill all the witnesses, Andrew Webb had to die.

"No choices," she whispered.

"We take him out before he does harm to us. A pre-emptive strike." Gem fished her cigarettes out of her jacket pocket, shook one loose, and popped it between those sexy red lips.

It looked out of place, like a turd in a flower vase.

Katrina grimaced. "You're not going to smoke that thing."

Gem produced a metal lighter. "Today has been stressful," she mumbled around the cigarette butt and flipped the lighter lid open.

Katrina plucked it from her fingers. "Smoking makes your breath stink like an ashtray."

"I'm going to murder the scumbag, not kiss him."

Katrina turned the lighter over in her hands. "Not very elegant. I'd expect a sexpot vampire like you to have one much sleeker, maybe with some rubies and gems on it."

"Maybe I stole it from a zombie or a werewolf," Gem quipped. "Or maybe it's something leftover from my life before...either way, give it back." She sounded serious on those two points.

"I'll keep it for now." Katrina stashed it in the inside left pocket of her jacket. "And I'll take that too!" She snatched the cigarette from Gem's mouth and crumpled it. Tobacco rained down on the leather upholstery.

"You're making a mess in my car."

"Sorry, but I don't want you smoking, whether it kills you or not. It's not sexy like it was in the old black and white movies. It's disgusting."

"I suppose you're right." Gem screwed a silencer to the barrel of her gun. "I don't want to wake up the whole neighbourhood," she explained, her voice suddenly business like. She pointed to a house fifty metres away. Like all of the homes around them, it looked big, luxurious, and expensive. "That's where Andrew Webb lives." Gem turned to face Katrina. "You stay here. I'll get in and out quickly."

"Be careful."

Gem raised those perfectly shaped eyebrows. "When has one man ever been a match for me?" Without waiting for an answer, she kissed Katrina on the forehead and got out of the car. While the vampire hit woman slinked towards Andrew Webb's house, Katrina could only admire how hot she looked dressed in black.

"Be careful, anyway," she muttered and slumped down in the passenger seat. She didn't want to raise any suspicions if a cop should drive past or if a neighbour strolled by walking a dog. Her scalp itched. She peeled the sassy red wig from her head and ruffled her blond locks loose. The aftermath of the hit at the ball game entered her mind, the chaos there must've been...

She wished she hadn't thought that thought because the image of the pitcher's brains flying out the back of his head drew her mind straight back to Betty James and how one stray bullet from the back window of a speeding car...

Back window? The shooter was in the back seat. Someone else was driving.

~132~

"Oh shit. Andrew Webb wasn't alone."

Gem could be walking into a trap.

Heart racing with dread, Katrina popped open the door and clambered out of the Porsche. Her knees felt weak, her legs like molasses. She stumbled across the sidewalk, and for a terrifying moment, she tripped but regained her balance.

Get a grip, girl.

The night was humid, still holding the heat from the day, a day that had started so long ago. She ran a hand down her face, mopping away sweat. She'd be no use to Gem if she collapsed in a heap. Focused on putting one foot in front of the other as quickly as she could, she reached Webb's driveway. The black limo was parked there, a chauffeur's hat on the dashboard. She spotted a dent in the fender.

Don James made that dent.

They had the right house. Katrina put her hand on the hood to stabilise herself and take a moment to assess the house. The lights were off, and the front door was closed.

Gem must have gone around to the back.

Katrina followed an unlit path down the side of the house. She crept quietly around the corner and froze in the light spilling out a set of French windows. Unwilling to call out to Gem and attract attention, she edged forward and peered into the room.

Gem stood with her back to Katrina, head down, unscrewing the silencer from the gun. The room was clearly a study or an office. Bookshelves lined two walls, and a desk looked out through double doors and into a deep garden. In front of Gem, slumped in a comfortable-looking chair, sat a bloated fat man with receding hair. He wore boxer shorts and a filthy wife-beater shirt. A bowl of soup was tipped in his lap, and the steaming liquid had spilled across his crotch. A live person would have been screaming in pain. Gem had made sure he wouldn't be a problem for them anymore. A single gunshot wound in the middle of his forehead had left him with a surprised expression he'd take with him into eternity. A gush of blood had run from the entry point and down Webb's face to his hairy chest.

"Gem," Katrina whispered and stepped into the house. "He wasn't alone!"

Gem's face registered surprise. She stopped fiddling with the silencer. "I told you to stay in the car."

"He was in the back seat of the limo. Someone else was driving."

The study door burst open. An obese woman filled the doorway. She wore a long nightgown, furry slippers, and her ratty hair was wrapped up in curlers. In her beefy, hairy-knuckled hands she held a big revolver. "Freeze, you pair of bitches." She snarled and pointed the gun at Gem.

Katrina froze, her heart beating hard. Her eyes tracked to Gem. She looked poised to pounce. Katrina managed a tiny shake of her head, imploring Gem not to do anything rash. She had a gun, sure, but she held it in both hands, one on the grip, the other on the silencer. Katrina didn't know much about guns, but she knew enough to see that Gem's hold on the handgun would make firing it quickly awkward, if not impossible.

Fat Lady took a step forward and glanced at Andrew Webb. Her face scrunched up. "Is he dead?" She looked like Shrek in a nightdress.

"Guess that makes you his widow," Gem said flatly.

"He was a loser." The gun didn't waver from Gem's chest.

Katrina couldn't take her eyes off the weapon. Her stomach churned, and stinging sweat seeped into her eyes. She didn't dare blink. Any movement could trigger bullets into flight.

"Thought you'd burglarise our house, did ya?" Fat Lady sneered at Gem. "Put the gun on the floor, bitch."

"Just take it easy." Gem set the gun down next to her

Gem

right foot. "We've got no beef with you."

"I should thank you. Ya done me a favour." She cocked her fat head at Andrew, jiggling her jowls. "His life insurance will pay out big time. And I'm gonna be a celebrity when I shoot the two bitches what broke into our house and murdered him."

Gem opened her mouth to speak, but Katrina beat her to it. "We're not here to rob you. When he shot his brother, he also killed an innocent woman."

Fat Lady grinned. "Guess it just wasn't her day."

"He shot me too," Katrina added, hoping this woman would realize how reckless her husband had been.

"But now that he's dead," Gem said, "we're done here. We can go. This will be over."

"Is that right?" Fat Lady laughed. "I hate to disappoint you, but that spineless piece of shit couldn't even demand the money back from his brother, must less shoot him."

"He wasn't the shooter?" Gem asked.

"You!" Katrina could hardly speak over the lump of guilt swelling in her throat. They'd hit the wrong man...err...woman.

"He was the driver." Fat Lady groaned. "Except when it came to eliminating a witness. Chickenshit bastard. I had to send Don James to meet up with his wife in heaven."

Gem hissed. "Then you're the one I should have killed."

"Too late, now, but I've got to thank you for bringing the other witness right to my door." She swung the gun to Katrina. The muzzle flared, and the gun bucked in her hands. The room filled with the sound and smoke.

Katrina flinched.

Time deteriorated to slow motion.

Gem leapt into the path of the bullet, a micro second too late, but as the bullet zinged by her, she flicked out her hand. The bullet ripped through a finger, slowing the slug's speed and bumping it off course.

Still, the bullet hit Katrina in the chest, punching a hole through her jacket. She let out a yelp and threw herself to the floor, expecting darkness to envelop her.

"No!" Gem hissed.

The pain was indescribable. Katrina curled into the foetal position, her hands instinctively covering her wound, hoping unconsciousness would take her quickly.

***

"You bitch!" Gem advanced on Fat Lady.

She continued to rip off shots, filling the room with thunder and lightning.

Gem's body flinched from side to side, each bullet a hot poker through her chest. Her gums swelled and split, and her fangs extended, razor sharp and itching for blood. The feeling was orgasmic. The hunger was primal.

With every step she took towards Katrina's killer, Gem's rage grew.

Fat Lady's eyes grew, as well, larger and rounder while she blasted away at an adversary she could never comprehend.

Gem ripped the still firing gun from Fat Lady's hands and threw it to the floor.

Fat Lady screamed, tried to back out the doorway, but with a blast from her nostrils, Gem slammed the door shut. "Not so tough anymore, are you, Mrs. Webb?"

"What the hell kind a demon are you?"

"The best kind." Gem drove her talon-like fingernails into Fat Lady's throat. The ripping of flesh and tendons made a sound like slicing roast beef with a serrated knife. Blood spurted from the wound. Gem would have sucked the blood heartily if she wasn't on a low-fat diet.

The porky body flopped on the floor, spazzing like a blubber-fish out of water.

As blood pooled and splattered, Gem whirled around and rushed to Katrina's side. Her eyes were wide open, and

Gem

her curled-up body shook violently. "Katrina."

She gasped.

Gem rolled her over, spotted the hole in her jacket, but oddly no blood. She ripped open Katrina's jacket, tore her blouse, and pulled down her bra, exposing flesh so white and pure, except her left breast. It was turning black and blue right before Gem's eyes, but still no blood. A quick check of the inner jacket liner revealed no bullet hole. She plunged her hand into the inside pocket and removed her cigarette lighter. The steel case was dented. Another dip into the pocket came up with a mushroomed slug of lead.

Katrina groaned.

Gem's fangs receded back into their gums. Katrina would live, but she would be sore as hell for a couple weeks.

"Katrina. You're okay."

Her eyelashes fluttered, sexy as a princess awakened by a kiss. "Gem?"

"My lighter stopped the bullet."

"You mean..." Katrina coughed, "not smoking saved my life?"

"We have to get out of here."

"Is she dead?"

"Not before she made enough noise to rouse the National Guard." Gem retrieved her gun and hefted Katrina over her shoulder. Back at the Porsche, she laid her in the passenger seat. Distant sirens pierced the night's silence.

***

By the time they arrived back at the apartment, sunrise was only two hours away. Angel and Maria were fast asleep. Katrina walked in under her own power. She sat with Gem at the kitchen table. She removed Katrina's ripped jacket and torn blouse then got some ice from the freezer and poured it into a plastic sandwich bag.

"I'm the one who's supposed to take care of you,"

Katrina whispered, still winded from the collision of the bullet and cigarette lighter.

"We take care of each other," Gem said, "even when you don't do as you're told."

"I couldn't just sit in that car. I had to warn you."

"I can take care of myself, Katrina, but you could have been killed." She knelt between Katrina's spread legs and pressed the icepack to her bruised breast. "From now on you're wearing a bullet-proof vest, you hear?"

Katrina gasped at the cold contact on her hot skin. "You're such a romantic." She took Gem's free hand. Her finger had already healed over. Bullet holes in Gem's prowler outfit revealed perfect, unblemished skin. She'd taken a blaze of bullets, but her body didn't show a speck of damage. Katrina felt like she'd been through World War Three. "I know what we did won't bring Don and Betty James back, but the Webbs deserved what they got."

"You know what they say, *behind every bad man there's a bad woman*. In the end, we came out okay."

"Sorry I'm so much trouble."

"I can't be around all day to look after you."

Excitement shot through Katrina like a howitzer and made her left breast throb, and not in a good way. "I can't believe I'd forgotten." She struggled to her feet. "Wait here."

"What about the ice pack?"

"I'll be right back." It took Katrina longer than expected to get up the stairs. Flinging underwear out of the draw like a gofer digging dirt, she found the pendant and plucked it out. "*Dåg-gåstol*" she read the inscription. "Day-walker." She hustled back downstairs and set the pendant on the table in front of Gem. "This is the Mjölnir, said to have been worn by—"

"Nótt!" Gem jumped in, her red lips rounded in shock and awe. "Or so the legend goes."

"You've heard of it?"

Gem

"The pendant wields the power of the *un-light*, which in the hands of a vampire makes the undead a day-walker. I never thought I'd actually see it."

Katrina picked up the Mjölnir by its chain and stood behind Gem then placed it over her head and down around her lovely neck. The pendant settled into the deep V of her cleavage. Gem touched it with her fingertips. "It's only a legend, Katrina."

"Sleep with me tonight. Awake with me in the morning, like normal people do."

"If it doesn't work, come dawn I'll die."

The nightmare came crashing back, Gem's beautiful face on fire, her flesh melting off her bones, and her bones turning to dust. "It's a huge risk, I know."

"Do I look crazy enough to try it?"

"Just think of it, Gem, you and me living a normal life."

"What's normal?"

Katrina's heart faltered. She was losing this argument. However, something more personal, more dear to her might sway the tide. "If not for me, then do it for Angel?"

Gem stiffened.

"Take her to school. Push her on the swing. Stop lying to Maria about where you are all day."

Gem's gaze roamed over Katrina's face, piercing eyes that for the first time showed a hint of fear. "And if I die in the process, you'll take care of them for me?"

"I promise."

"Then I'll do it for you, Katrina."

"For us," she said and led Gem by the hand up the stairs to the bedroom.

Gem glided to the bed. In the darkness she shed her ruined prowler outfit and tossed it into the trashcan with this morning's bloodied clothes. Her body shone brilliant and smooth in the moonlight seeping in through the blinds, the same blinds that would let in the sunlight come morning. In two hours their lives would be changed forever, one way or another.

Katrina put thoughts of failure aside, stripped, and stood in front of Gem, beaten, battered, and bruised, elbow bandaged, knees skinned but feeling more alive and well than ever. "It's going to work," she whispered into Gem's ear.

They settled into bed together. Gem wrapped her arms around Katrina and spooned her in close. "I love you, Katrina."

Sleep overtook her, and she dreamed again, not about burning vampires, Lady Summer Dress, or Andrew Webb, but of a sunny day walking hand-in-hand with Gem through Central Park as Angel tossed peanuts to the squirrels.

GEM – No Fear

Facing Fear

Lying on my back, I watched a thin beam of sunlight reach across the room to my bed. I glanced at Katrina, still fast asleep next to me, her cheek buried in the pillow, and her gorgeous mane of blonde hair fanned out over her neck and shoulders. The Egyptian cotton sheets, cool on my back, failed to cool the hot anxiety that burned in my chest. My heart pounded harder than a piston pumping in my Porsche as the prospect of excruciating pain and certain death edged toward my left hand outstretched on the sheets.

My breath stuck in my throat like a glob of molten rubber. A tiny chink in the curtains had conspired against me and allowed my most mortal enemy, the sun, into my room. I traced the path the golden beam would take as it slid yet closer, now less than six inches from my perfectly manicured fingernails.

A hundred bucks worth at Madam Lucy's Spa and Tan.

Still, I was surprised to find my memory drawn to a movie I'd seen. A man lay tied to a steel table as a laser sliced a fiery line towards his groin. "You expect me to talk?" he asked. "No, Mister Bond," came the reply. "I expect you to die."

Am I about to die?

My right hand moved to my neck, and trembling fingers snagged the delicate but resilient chain, which I traced to the pendant resting between my breasts. I grasped it the way a little girl would grasp her father's finger and take her first steps into a new world of mobility. If myth and legend were to be trusted and believed, The Mjölnir pendant had protected Nótt, the Norse Goddess of Darkness, from the power of the sun.

But will it protect me?

I had no doubt that Katrina believed it would free me from the darkness and make me a Daywalker. And if what I'd read over the years was true then she was right. I had nothing to fear but fear itself.

And I should fear nothing!

The morning sun's emissary of vampire death edged nearer to my sacrificial left hand.

For I am Gem!

I closed my eyes and flexed the offered fingers. I'd been tensing them so tightly they'd begun to cramp. The waiting was killing me. I should tear open the curtains right now and face the sun with all my might.

But I didn't have to be so dramatic. In mere seconds, the beam would reach my flesh and either pass over my hand harmlessly or sear it to charred meat, drowning me in waves of revulsion, nausea, and ungodly pain.

But I will not scream!

I didn't want to terrify little Angel and Maria asleep downstairs.

I'm risking my undead life here...for Katrina.

If the legend was true and the Mjölnir protected me, then I'd always be available for her, night and day. And for Angel and for Maria too. They'd never have to fear facing danger alone again.

Because of my job, I've put their lives at risk too many times.

If I only had to consider my own safety, then my profession as a vampire hit-woman for the New York underworld was all well and good. But if I accidentally left any loose ends, my family would be the ones unprotected from revenge-seeking thugs, while I slept through the day in my coffin, a prisoner of the night. I couldn't ask my boss, John Bradley, to protect them. He had his own problems.

Besides, if this pendant works, I'm not telling Bradley I'm available during daylight hours. He'll want me to work 24/7.

The spear of sunlight had glided silently, surreptitiously to within an inch of my hand. Time seemed frozen. Impatience overwhelmed my fear. The light wasn't moving fast enough. I was desperate to know if the pendant would protect me. My fangs pricked the inside of my gums, and I felt the rapid, anxious pulse in my left wrist.

Face your fear, Gem.

Unable to wait a second longer, I extended my fingers, squashing the instinct to drag my hand back under the covers, safe from the blazing light.

Face your fear.

Gritting my teeth, I thrust my open hand into the light. The sun struck my skin, and I held my breath, expecting a gush of pain to erupt inside me with the force of a volcano.

But the pendant vibrated in my right hand. My blood didn't boil. Smoke didn't seep from my pores. My flesh didn't turn to flame and burn off my bones. I had been granted a new life, thanks to the pendant's supernatural power over the *un-light*.

Finally I exhaled. The next breath I took tasted like the finest Champagne. A smile grew on my lips, and a delightful tingle ran up the inside of my thighs. Pleasure permeated my entire body in an instant, and as my fangs extended, splitting from my gums, I moaned softly. The blood that leaked into my mouth was an aphrodisiac that simply had to be enjoyed.

"Thank you, Nótt," I whispered. "With you by my side, I can face the daylight and protect my family."

I slid my lithe and naked body out of the bed with the stealth of a vampire...

Still a vampire, baby. Nothing more stealthy than a vampire.

... and stood in front of the window. I took a curtain edge in each hand and readied myself to witness a New York sunrise for the first time in my undead life.

The mattress rocked behind me, and Katrina's voice filled the room. "Gem?"

"It's okay, my love," I said softly. I paused for a second that must have seemed to Katrina like an eternity, and then I ripped back the curtains, filling the room with tame and beautiful sunlight.

I took a step backwards as the power of the sun bathed my body in its heat. My eyes closed, unaccustomed to the brightness, and my mouth opened, and my tongue, moist and hot, flicked across my lips like I'd been fed the most sensuous of nectar. I was gluttonous for every drop. The blood in my body surged towards the warmth, my nipples throbbed, and my knees grew unsteady with orgasmic pleasure. I cupped my breasts. An animalistic sound whispered out from behind my teeth. I sent my fingertips to wander down the inside of my thighs...

I must look fantastic to Katrina in silhouette!

I turned to her and smiled, the cityscape behind me a magnificent backdrop for my supple curves. Katrina lowered the hand she'd raised to protect her eyes from the brightness. Her mouth was a perfect 'O' of wonderment. "It worked."

I purred through puckered lips and sauntered back towards our bed, my body filled with a new fire. "And now I'm going to properly thank you for finding this pendant."

Nothing to Fear

Our kitchen, at 7am, had more life, more hustle-bustle, than Times Square on New Year's Eve. I could only sit at the counter, mouth open, mimicking Katrina's expression when she'd seen me in front of the bedroom window in broad daylight. And my eyes were agog with the pace of real life.

Gem

"Do you have your books packed?" Maria asked Angel and plucked toast out of the toaster. She placed the toast in front of the ravenous blonde noise machine.

"Of course," Angel chimed while smearing chocolate spread across the hot, brown bread, and then she slurped on a glass slopping-full of orange juice. She'd not stopped chatting since she came through the door from her bedroom, school uniform already on and delicate golden curls framing her angelic face.

Angel by name, Angel by nature.

Maria moved through the kitchen like she was gliding on ice skates, skirting us as if *she* were a creature of the night with powers beyond that of mere mortals.

But of course, that's me!

My hand caressed the pendant that had broken my bond with darkness.

"It is so good that you finally take the day off work, Miss Gem," Maria said with a smile and a smugness that told me she thought I worked too hard. She'd always wanted me to take life a little easier.

"My boss can cope without me for one day." I smiled back at her, basking in the love this tiny woman showered on me.

This pendant changes everything.

I'd nearly lost Angel.

I'd nearly lost Katrina.

I'd lost Clare. All because of the path that I'd chosen, the way in which I'd used my powers. I'd stalked the night because that was where the bad guys lurked, the drug dealers and the murderers, the threats to the peace and well being of my family and my business associates. I'd sought out allies who didn't question my lifestyle. I had no social friends, just my adopted family, who now bustled around me on my first morning of real freedom.

Now I could live side by side with my loved ones night and day.

Or maybe I should say day and night.

Katrina lumbered into the kitchen, her body still battered and bruised from yesterday's attack in the park. The clean white bandage around her left elbow looked new. In spite of the bullet wound, she'd managed to dress it, and she'd dressed herself in tight fitting jeans and a pair of knee high leather boots. The white INXS t-shirt she wore was mine, and that made me smile. She looked damn good in it.

I hope I look that good in it, as well.

Without missing a beat, Maria placed a steaming mug of coffee into Katrina's right hand. "You are not working today, too?"

"My boss told me to take off work as long as I needed." Katrina indicated her bandaged elbow. She leaned into me and whispered, "But I'll need to take the pendant back soon."

My eyes were drawn to the Mjölnir hanging around my neck. I was already used to its intense thrum against my sternum as its inner magic protected me from daylight, but I hadn't considered that it may need to go back to the museum where Katrina worked. At least not so soon.

"Where's Norse?" Angel asked, ever the inquisitive one.

"Norway," Katrina said. "It's in Europe. The people once believed in the Norse Gods. One's name was Nótt, Goddess of the Night. She once wore the pendant Gem is wearing now."

"That's so neat. Can I wear it to school?"

"Not today, Angel." Maria swept away plates and cups, leaving a clutter-free trail of cleanliness in her wake. "Maybe we can persuade Miss Gem and Miss Katrina to take another day off and bring it for you to show your friends. But for now, get ready for school."

"Oh, all right." Angel scooted out of her chair and zoomed from the room at high speed.

"And brush your teeth." Maria turned to me with a

wan smile that told me she worried I'd missed out on much of Angel's childhood. Though she'd never say it out loud, she felt that I wasn't seeing enough of our princess. She was right, of course, which made my heart ache within the usually cold cavity of my chest.

Things are going to change for us.

"So what do you want to do today?" Katrina asked me.

Before I had time to respond, Maria answered, "You should start by walking with Angel and me to school. She would like that."

If I had an eternity to ponder Katrina's question, I could never have chosen such a perfect riposte as Maria's suggestion. I'd still have the rest of the day to explore the day-lit city, though I feared it would be like wading through a pool of crocodiles that could turn on me at any second. It was one thing to test the powers of the pendant in the cocoon of the apartment, quite another in the real world.

But now I have no fear.

***

Angel walked between Katrina and I, and Maria led the way along Riverside Drive towards Angel's school.

The sounds were so different during the day than the Big Apple after dark. Children's laughter sang in my ears as kids met up with friends on the route to school. Dogs barked and ran with their owners in the park. Vendors whistled while they set up for the day's business.

I inhaled the aroma of hot food that wafted through the air like a living, breathing entity with a vivacity of its own. The leaves on the trees were green and brown and yellow, not the monochrome I was used to seeing at night. All my senses mixed into one euphoric experience, as if I'd never existed before this day.

This is how it feels to be alive!

I fell in love with New York City all over again.

Angel began singing a song I'd never heard her sing before. Both Katrina and Maria joined in. I couldn't help but sing along too. *The Alphabet Song.* Somehow I knew the tune though I couldn't remember ever singing it. I probably knew it back when I had a different life that I couldn't remember either.

My human life.

Minutes later, we kissed Angel goodbye, and in a flash she ran through the open wrought iron gates and across the schoolyard to her friends. As we turned to walk away, she gave us one final wave. Hot tears of pride welled in my eyes. She was so strong and brave in her daylight world. For me, it was like my first day at school in a whole new life.

"Are you okay?" Katrina asked.

"Yeah, yeah, it's just..."

"Okay then, girls," Maria broke in. "I am off to meet my friends at Starbucks, and then I will go shopping. I'll collect Angel after school, and we will see you at home later. It is good you two have the day off together for once. You both work too hard. Enjoy yourselves."

"Thank you, Maria," Katrina said. "Have fun, too."

I was too choked up to say anything as I watched the dear lady hustle off toward the stairs to the subway.

Katrina grinned. "I never pictured Maria in a Starbucks."

"There's a lot we don't know about her," I managed to say. The same could be said for Katrina and Angel's daily lives, so far removed from mine, until the pendant worked its magic on me. My sense of euphoria mingled with a new light-hearted hope for the future.

Katrina took my arm. "So what do you want to see today?"

"Everything!" I replied. "Absolutely everything."

***

Gem

The morning's sightseeing became a sensory overload on my brain. Before long, my temples throbbed with pain. I must've been overdoing my first day in the sun.

Maybe I should rest. Slow down a little.

Katrina offered to buy me a pair of cheap sunglasses from a street vendor, but instead, I took her into a department store and treated us both to a pair from Versace. However, the expensive UV protective lenses brought no relief for my headache.

Walking along 42nd Street towards the U. N. Katrina pointed out the Chrysler Building, taking on the role of my daytime tour guide. "It was the tallest building in the world for almost a year before the Empire State Building was finished."

As I gazed at the building, the Mjölnir began to jump around under my blouse. Must've looked like a hamster was trapped in my bra...

Oh...I don't wear a bra.

I stopped walking to take a firm hold of the pendant before it drew anyone's attention. My head pounded bongo drums.

What is wrong with me?

I couldn't take my eyes off the Chrysler building. I'd been up there before, when I stood atop the spire and surveyed *My City* that first night I became a vampire, the farthest back in time my memory would go. But now, with the sun glinting off the arcs and spires, I was hit with something intangible, something...frightening.

An older memory?

A woman, carefree in heart and spirit, stepped out of the Chrysler Building and waved at some one on the opposite corner. A man wearing a dark suit, black hair slicked back, handsome chin, bright smile.

Pedestrian traffic flowed around me as if I were a boulder in a rushing stream. I scrunched my eyes shut. Emotions surfaced. The woman was in love with this man.

She rushed across the street, a joyous smile on her beaming face.

My head felt like it was going to explode.

The woman is me.

Somebody bumped into me, nearly knocking me over, but I was too shocked to say excuse me.

Katrina caught hold of my arm. "Gem? What is it?" She steered me to a bench.

"I don't..." I began, but my eyes, underneath the dark shades, sling-shotted back to the Chrysler Building. We stood two blocks from it, but its sheer presence under the sun felt like a powerful electromagnet that was pulling metal shards from the centre of my brain. The pain sliced through my skull like grenade shrapnel, so violently that I feared Katrina would be injured in the explosion.

I forced my gaze to the sidewalk and sucked deep gulps of air over my pursed lips.

"You better sit down." Katrina all but shoved me onto the bench. "I'll get you some water." She rushed off toward a street vendor.

The pendant pulsed in panic against my skin. My scalp felt like it was trying to pull itself off my skull, and the skin down my spine itched like I'd been rolling in nettles.

The vision of me and my mysterious lover faded, and so did the intense pain. I wanted the first one to continue so badly, but not the other. The pendant had a horrific side effect, teasing my brain with a past life, and then tearing my cerebral cortex from my head.

Katrina returned to my side and jabbed an open bottle of Aquafina at me. "Drink this."

I forced water down my throat. After taking a moment to calm down, I stood, making sure the Chrysler Building was at my back. "We have to get out of here."

"What the hell is going on?"

People around us were staring but not offering any

Gem

help. This was New York City, after all, where freaks congregated on every corner. I didn't want to be noticed. "Get us a cab."

Katrina rushed to the kerb and hailed a passing taxi. It just drove on by. Two more cabbies ignored her upraised arms and waving hands. She stepped into the street, more determined than ever to get us a ride...or get run over in the process.

I forced my feet forward and pulled her out of traffic. "Nevermind. Let's walk."

Two blocks west and two blocks farther from the Chrysler Building, the headache dwindled, leaving only a residual pulse in my left temple.

"I'll be okay now," I said, but if Katrina had heard me over the drone of the city, her ashen, worried face showed no relief.

"You're going home to lie down and rest," she commanded like a mother hen.

I gently nodded in acquiescence but grimaced at how much that small action actually hurt. And I started to get dizzy. The pendant began vibrating between my breasts like an alarm clock on steroids.

Now what's wrong with me?

A young couple ahead of us, holding hands and giggling, joined the queue for a hotdog vendor, and behind them a woman pushing a stroller stopped.

My eyes were drawn to the child. She was petite, gorgeous. Her lips moved as she silently chatted to a Winnie the Pooh cuddly toy she cradled in her arms. Her smile would have lit up all of 42nd Street at midnight. Her familiar smile...

I panned my eyes up to the woman behind the stroller: young, slim, pretty, now rummaging through her purse. She had short blonde hair... like... Clare.

My mouth dropped open.

Clare?

It couldn't be. She was dead. I looked harder, closer, my heart a caged animal trying to escape my chest. But I wasn't mistaken. It was them.

Clare and Angel!

Miraculously alive...

Behind them, movement jarred my peripheral vision, someone running toward her.

It can't be her killer. Not again. What's happening?

A man wearing dirty jeans and a grease-smeared jacket snatched Clare's purse, and although she tried for a second to fend him off, her hands returned to the stroller to protect her child...

Just like Clare had done moments before she was killed.

...and then he yanked the purse from her grasp and sprinted off, shoving through the crowd toward me, and no one did anything to stop him, and Katrina called to me because she had finally hailed a cab, and before I could stop myself, my left foot arced though the air in a roundhouse kick, and my shoe connected with his jaw, which knocked him unconscious before he hit the sidewalk, and I looped my arm around Katrina's waist, just about to Superman-leap us out of there when she shouted, "Gem, don't jump!"

That stopped me.

"Let's just walk away," she whispered in my ear. "Real calm like. There are too many people around to witness your powers."

She was right. There were no dark shadows in daylight to mask my movements.

I took her hand and started to lead her away from the fallen mugger and the woman who rushed up to claim the purse. Dead Clare.

The pendant shook violently against my heart. My headache came back without mercy.

A cop stepped in front of us, stopped me with an

outstretched hand. "I saw you nail that purse snatcher."

"I... It was nothing," I stammered and pinned the pendant between my right palm and my chest, fearing he'd notice the commotion under my blouse and start asking questions.

"Well you nailed him, sweetheart, and thanks to you that's another creep off these streets. But if he'd had a gun, we'd be sweeping you up off the sidewalk right now, so don't be a hero next time, capiche?"

I nodded, playing the pretty little lady who would take the advice of a big, strong policeman.

The blonde woman with the stroller, a woman who now looked nothing like Clare, pushed the child who held no resemblance to Angel towards me. "Thank you so much for stopping that man and getting my purse back." She spoke in an accent I didn't recognize, something European. "You're so brave."

"You're welcome."

"Officer," Katrina said, "I've got a cab waiting. Is it okay for us to leave?"

"Yeah, but be careful, girls. The streets aren't safe nowadays."

You don't say! Who is this guy, Sherlock Holmes?

Before I could open my mouth to lambaste the guy, Katrina steered me toward the cab. "I think the sun is getting to you."

"No shit!" I got into the cab. The pendant became still again. Perhaps it was more of a curse than a blessing. Magic always carried with it a price. What would it cost me to be free of the night: visions of memories lost to my undead existence, hallucinations of dead people from my past come back to life? What other horrors awaited me?

A cold blade of fear pierced my heart.

Friends In Fear

It took the rest of the afternoon for my latest headache

to completely dissipate. Katrina didn't object when I'd spent the last hour of daylight locked in my room and entombed in my coffin. Somewhere familiar. Somewhere safe. I wasn't sure if it was the nap or the removal of the Mjölnir from around my neck that had improved my health. *Or maybe I had simply spent too long out in the sun.*

I slipped into a tight pair of blue jeans and a pale blue t-shirt that caressed my Ferrari curves. I wanted to show Katrina that my body was still in good shape since my morning exertions.

Leaving the pendant on the lid of my coffin, I walked into her bedroom, disappointed she wasn't there to see me. Everything was in its place, the bed made without a crease, wardrobe closed, not a speck of dust anywhere, not on the nightstand or the dresser or the lock box where she kept her gun.

Never can be too careful in this town.

I jogged down the stairs to find her perched in front of the television. The news played out, the police asking for any information on the death of Mr. and Mrs. Webb to come forward. Our hit on the drive-by shooters the night before seemed a lifetime away.

"Looks like we got away clean," I said soft enough that Katrina wouldn't be startled by my stealthy entrance.

She muted the TV volume and faced me. "Wow," she chirped with a naughty glint in her eye. "It seems an afternoon nap did you well. You look much better."

"You mean I look absolutely stunning, right?"

Before she could confirm and stroke my ballooning ego, the telephone rang.

Pop! Damn phone.

Katrina picked it up on the second ring. "Hello." She tilted her head to the side as she listened to the caller, and then mouthed the words *John Bradley* at me, her eyebrows arched in surprise. She and Bradley had gotten into a tiff. The handsome bastard would show up at our door

Gem

unannounced. She hated when he did that, but now it seemed he'd finally gotten the message: *Call first.*

Personally, I was impressed with his smooth approach to us and his impeccable manners. He may have been a gangster, but he was a classy gangster.

Katrina held the handset away from her mouth. "He's got a job for us," she said in a positive voice, clearly happy that Bradley had adopted the preferred protocol. "He wants to know if you want to earn a quarter of a million dollars for an hour's work."

A quarter mill? Hmmm. I did have an appointment at the hair salon next week. I could use the cash. "Tell him I'll think it over."

***

Bradley pulled up outside our apartment at 10pm. I didn't have to think it over for long. A quarter mill was a no brainer for a girl...er...vampire like me. Besides, the *job* he had in mind would be more pleasure the actual work.

Earlier, as I'd changed into a sleek black cocktail dress, a favourite requested by the mob boss himself, Katrina had bombarded me with questions to ensure I was at my physical and mental best.

"Are you feeling all right?"

Other than starving for fresh blood, I'd never felt better as I slipped into a shoulder harness and holster.

"Is your headache completely gone?"

My answer could have sounded like an aspirin commercial, but I just answered yes instead. I checked the clip in my .40 calibre M&P, decided by the weight that it was full of bullets, and tucked the gun in the holster.

Beautiful and deadly stared back at me from the mirror.

"How many fingers am I holding up?"

I'd said, "All five" and slinked into a mink coat that hid my weapon completely.

She kissed me on the cheek. "Be careful."

Yeah, I don't want any bullet holes in this ten thousand dollar mink. I will be very careful.

I stepped outside the apartment, closed the door, and waited to hear the click of the lock. She knew I left little to chance, but even the best of intensions were no match for a solid deadbolt.

Walking toward Bradley's bright red Bugatti, I thought why I'd left the pendant in my coffin. For one, I didn't need it at night, but mostly, if it was messing with my mind, I could do without the headache tonight.

Bradley held the car door open for me. "You're looking lovely as ever, my dear."

I climbed into the passenger seat and allowed myself to be swallowed up in a luxurious leather and aluminium-trimmed cabin that befit the Bugatti's $1.9 million dollar price tag.

"Nice car." I buckled the seat belt. "But not very subtle."

"I'm not a subtle man." He closed the door.

I watched him walk around to the driver's side and get in behind the wheel of his pricey toy. Even his suit looked expensive, a William Fioravanti black pinstriped job.

This slick mobster has style. I'd snag him in a heartbeat if I didn't have the hots for Katrina.

He fired up the sixteen-cylinder one thousand horsepower engine...

I know my cars.

...and accelerated towards midtown, his million-dollar smile beaming bright as the four Xenon headlamps that lit up the night in front of us.

He got down to the job at hand. "This is a negotiation. Two suits over from Britain." He shifted the seven-speed transmission. "Looking to discuss our mutually beneficial businesses. I'm pretty sure they're not here to sell shoes."

"Drugs?" I asked, my fangs itching inside my gums

for a drug dealer to drain.

"You know I won't back that sort of action. If this meeting is about drugs, I want to send a message to their people across the Atlantic."

He made a hard left on Lexington. The tires didn't even squeak.

"Fire and ice, baby, that's us. I'll be the fire, the passionate one, hot to make a deal. You'll be the ice. Cold and calculating. Ruthless if you have to be."

He wound the engine to redline and slammed another gear.

"What do you want me to do?"

"One word about bringing more drugs into this town, I want them back on that plane with a twitch so far up their asses that they could hit the spot with their cereal spoons at breakfast tomorrow."

"So it's a no-kill operation?" I expected him to hear the disappointment in my voice.

"Not unless it takes a bad turn and somebody gets trigger happy. Then we wipe them off the planet and ship their heads back to their Limey bosses via FedEx to London town."

That put a smile on my beautiful lips. I dropped down the visor to admire them in the lighted mirror. It may not have looked like it to Bradley, but I was focussed, already formulating a plan.

I was packing heat in my shoulder holster under my mink coat. It would come off as soon as we got inside the Brits' suite. My glamour would disarm the *businessmen*, but the sight of the weapon would knock them off balance.

Bradley would then be on the front foot once the negotiations began. If it came down to gunplay, this mink better not catch a bullet. Bradley thought his car was expensive. Wait until I send him the bill for fixing this beauty. I stroked the fine, furry lapel.

Bradley reached inside his jacket and pulled out an

envelope. "This is for Katrina."

Surprise slapped me across the face like an abusive lover. Why would Bradley have a gift for Katrina? "Is this something I should know about?"

"She called and asked for it. My hacker says she'll have to programme the codes, but once that's done the swipe card will do the rest."

I was glad Bradley had his eyes on the road because the incredulous look on my face would have distracted his driving.

What is Katrina up to?

I plied the envelope with the tips of my fingers and felt something like a credit card, obviously the swipe card he'd mentioned, but it had wires attached which joined it to something short and stubby, a computer flash drive, I guessed. Curiosity itched under my bra strap...

Oh...I'm not wearing a bra.

As much as I wanted to open the envelope, I wouldn't. I respected Katrina too much to invade her privacy. "I'll see she gets this," I said. "I'm sure she'll appreciate it."

"It's good she feels she can ask me for what she needs," he said. "Maybe one day I'll find out what she's got planned for that bit of hardware in the envelope."

Maybe she'll tell me too!

I stowed the envelope inside my coat.

Bradley swung the car into the Ritz Carlton, a hotel where I hadn't killed anyone, yet, and parked in front of the main doors. Attendants and valets rushed us like a pack of wild dogs.

"Ready?" Bradley asked me.

I stay ready so I never have to get ready.

We exited the car together. Bradley flicked the keys to a wide-eyed valet. "Be careful with it."

A throng of people gathered around us, staring at the sports car. For once, my good looks were ignored in favour of an automobile. My temples began to throb. Then the headache hit me, migraine strong.

No, not again.

I thought my head was going to split in two.

And it can't be the pendant's fault. I'm not wearing it.

Pain shot up from the back of my neck and drilled in between my eyes. My knees almost buckled. I had to place my hand on the car fender to steady myself.

Bradley had his back to me, issuing strict instructions to the hotel attendants. As quickly as it struck me, the agony departed. I stood upright and took a deep breath. My hand pawed at my throat, double-checking to be sure the Mjölnir wasn't there.

What is making me feel this way?

From across the street, in the shadows of a recessed entrance to a closed boutique, the flare of a cigarette lighter briefly illuminated the strong, square chin of a handsome man.

My breath hitched.

Even after the flame went out, the eyes glowed like a wolf in the headlights.

I blinked. Those eyes were directed at me.

What the hell?

I recognized the man's face from the vision I'd had earlier: my lover from a previous life.

For the briefest of moments, his bewitching spell made the bustle around me slow. Cabs drove by at a snail's pace. The people close to me turned gossamer, as if their presence carried no weight. The constant noise that was inherent to New York City became conspicuously absent. Only the sound of my heartbeat drummed in my ears. The man tipped his head, like an old friend acknowledging me from across the room at a dinner party. His hat brim suddenly hid his eyes.

In that moment, the spell was broken.

"Gem?" Bradley called. "If you're quite ready, may we go inside now?" His voice carried a playful tinge of sarcasm yet gentlemanly and full of respect. To anyone watching us, we were an established couple, comfortable with our banter.

"Of course, darling. Are you sure you can leave your true love?" I pointed a slick fingernail at his car, drawing laughter from the crowd.

"Only you could take its place, babe."

I accepted Bradley's outstretched hand in mine, and as the concierge opened the doors for us, I peered over my shoulder. Whoever had taken an extra long look at me was no longer there, just like the icy pain in my skull.

***

A fat British gangster welcomed us into his suite. As planned, I slipped out of my mink and draped it over the back of a chair. As I stood with my back to the door, I surveyed the spacious room. The suite boasted Victorian furniture, a polished conference table, and modern entertainment electronics. A flat screen took up an entire wall. Huge curtain-framed glass doors opened out to a balcony. The dull hum of the air conditioning reached my acute hearing.

I imagined myself staying here with Katrina. We'd lounge about in our lingerie, wine glasses filled...

A warm flutter flitted through me. I bit back my thoughts so my musings wouldn't develop into anything more sensual and distracting.

This is business.

A hallway with three doors led off from the living area, and I guessed that one was a bathroom and the other two were bedrooms. My vampire hearing detected rustling from the nearest bedroom. The second British gangster was towelling himself dry after a shower. He probably thought it was appropriate to keep a man like Bradley waiting.

The first British gangster, the one who had opened the door to us, wore a cheap suit that didn't fit around his belly

Gem

properly. He shook hands with Bradley and made no effort to conceal his head to toe appraisal of me.

For the moment, I stood with my killer body sideways to him to block his view of my killer weapon holstered from my shoulder.

"You want a drink?" he asked Bradley, reaching into the mini bar and pulling out a can of beer. He popped the ring-pull and drank straight from the can.

Bradley grimaced at the low level of scum he would be dealing with. He glanced into mini bar. "I'll have that Sambuca. No ice."

It's not like Bradley to drink on the job, much less choose a 42% alcohol drink made with star anise oils. Highly intoxicating, not to mention flammable!

The goon poured Bradley his drink and turned to me, I assumed to ask me if I wanted anything, but the sight of my gun turned his face red as a flustered school girl's cheeks.

"Whoa, nice gun, little lady. Let's all put our pieces down so we can have this chat without any tension." He pulled a short barrelled handgun from the back of his pants and laid it on the conference table.

This guy is such an amateur.

I drew my Smith and Wesson M&P. "You sure you want me to put my big weapon next to that little thing?" I ejected the clip so he wouldn't die of a panic attack.

"Yeah, just on the table," he replied, not getting my sarcasm.

I laid my empty gun and fully loaded clip next to his dainty lady's pistol.

Bradley shot me a look that said I'd better know what I was doing.

I shrugged.

What's wrong with keeping him guessing?

"You got a smoke?" he asked the British buffoon.

"Yeah, sure." He tapped a cigarette from a pack he carried in his coat pocket, and then offered him a light.

Bradley sucked in the flame and exhaled smoke from his nostrils.

I've never seen him smoking. He's up to something.

The fat man fell back onto one of the sofas. "Make yourself comfortable, mate." This guy had the lamest British accent since Dick Van Dyke.

"When is your partner going to join us?" Bradley asked, cigarette in one hand, glass of liquor in the other.

"Be any second now, I'm sure."

The nearest bedroom door opened, and the biggest man I'd ever seen emerged from the hallway. Wearing only track pants, he went shirtless for good reason. His pectorals were huge and well defined. His biceps had biceps. His abs were ripped, and I could have played his ribs like a xylophone.

I hope I don't have to kill this exquisite specimen of a man.

"Sorry to keep you waiting, Mr. Bradley." But he made no show of respect by offering a handshake or initiating an introduction.

I thought for sure Bradley would have knocked back a swallow of his drink by now, but he just stood there gawking at the Brit. His late appearance and grand entrance were clearly part of their plan. Soften us up with the douche in the cheap suit, and then send in the Terminator.

"What's this all about?" Bradley asked.

"I won't hold you up for too long," the Brit said, his voice full of culture and education, out of place coming from that steroid-enhanced body. "It's apparent to us that there's a gap in your market."

"I'm intrigued," Bradley said. "Tell me more. I hope you make it worth my while."

The human hulk met Bradley's eyes with a stare of arrogance. "Would you now?"

I need to be on my toes tonight.

"Back home, we're called The Gods." He cockily let

his eyes drift down over his chiselled form.

Bradley raised his eyebrows and tilted his head toward the fat sloth on the sofa. "The Gods? Really?"

"The Gods reward loyalty," the big Brit said, earning a smile of approval from his cumbersome colleague. "And if you get on board with us now, we won't forget it. The rewards will be greater than you can imagine."

"I've got a pretty big imagination, so cut to the chase."

"We've developed a product that gives our clients everything they need. Extreme confidence, sexual pleasure, intellect, you name it, you get it. And the side effects are equal to a full course of anabolic steroids. Body fat drops off, and muscle tone gets firmer. Trust me, I know."

"So this proposal of yours is just about drugs."

"Puritan is more than a drug." He flexed his chest muscles to emphasise his point.

"Puritan?"

"That's what we named it, yeah. It becomes a way of life."

Bradley frowned. "Then it's addictive?"

"Addictive is not the word."

"Then what is the word?"

"Necessity." The bulky Brit moved to the glass doors and looked out. "And expensive. We market to the rich, high-society types, the corporate tycoons, the Wall Street top guns who control the money."

I looked at Bradley. His eyebrows twitched like the gears were grinding in his brain, mulling over some unexpected information. He glanced at his glass of liquor like he might take a belt. "So this product isn't for momma and papa and baby bear, I take it."

The Brit didn't react to Bradley's attempt at humour. "Puritan makes cocaine seem like nothing more potent than saccharine. We'll sell it on the cheap and get the suckers hooked. Then we bang up the price, and they'll be so desperate for their next energy boost that they'll gladly drain their fat bank accounts."

"They go broke," Bradley said, grinning. "We get rich. I like it already."

I have to give him credit, he's one hell of a good liar, but that's my cue to step in, the cold, calculating one.

"So you bankrupt the rich?" I glanced at porky on the couch. "And give the money to the likes of him. That's not a good idea."

"Puritan will purify the system, create massive business failures, loss of jobs, corrupt the health care system..." The Brit turned toward me, drawing my eyes to the bulge in his track pants. "And break the Federal Reserve's back."

One peek, that's all I want. Then I'll kill him.

He paused as if letting his words settle in our minds. I could see by my boss's face that the meeting was going to end badly.

He looked at his cigarette. "And why would you want to do that?"

"Because that's what you American's want, right? We watch the news. Occupy Wall Street. You're anti-bank. Anti-corporation. Anti-government. Anti-rich. Ninety-nine percent of you, anyway. No Sweat. We'll take the money. Just trying to help."

The fat guy spoke up. "Puritan will bust you cry-baby Americans back to the Stone Age."

"And you don't have to go with them," Muscles added. "You can hop on board with us."

"My lucky day." Bradley hoisted his glass in salute.

Do I go for my gun now?

I had no doubt that I'd be quicker getting my clip into my gun before the fat man could wobble to his feet, much less reach his gun, but I'd wait for a signal from Bradley before I made a move. What worried me more was the bulky guy.

Gem

He's closer to Bradley and could snap his neck by the time I get off a shot.

The Brit smiled a disarming smile. I'd give him that. "Luck has nothing to do with it."

Despite the words that slickly slid from his mouth being against everything that Bradley stood for, I could imagine the Brit smooth talking weaker-minded fools.

"We need you, *Mister* Bradley. You know how the dark side of this city runs. Your mob, along with me and my fellow Gods, we'll make a killing."

Bradley sighed. "So I was wrong. This *isn't* just about drugs." He sucked hard on his cigarette. The ash glowed yellow and hot. He removed the butt from his mouth and examined the smouldering stub. "Sorry boys, I expected something more lucrative. You've wasted your time asking me to help you."

"Oh, we're not asking. We're telling you...out of courtesy."

"And I'm telling you you're not coming into my town," Bradley responded, cool as a summer salad.

I noticed him lock the cigarette butt between his thumb and middle finger, preparing to flick it.

A signal?

"Imagine twenty of me," the big oaf went on, oblivious to the storm his words were brewing behind Bradley's eyes. "Backed up by twenty more, backed up by twenty more. You don't want to get in the way of The Gods."

The big guy with the big mouth is mine.

"Fuck you and your *Gods*."

The fat gangster on the couch pulled a hidden gun.

Bradley tossed the contents of his glass into the fat man's face and flicked the cigarette straight afterwards.

Time paused as the cigarette, ash glowing red hot, flipped end over end in slow motion, tumbling through the air to the gangster's Sambuca-sopped shirt. On impact, the ash exploded in a shower of sparks. With a *whoosh*, blue flame engulfed the fat man's face, and the anise-sweet smell of Sambuca morphed into the stench of burning hair and roasting flesh.

Screaming like a girl, he slapped at the fire with his chubby hands.

I crouched to spring for my gun.

Roaring like a grizzly, the big Brit reared back a shovel-sized fist and attacked Bradley.

I leapt.

Bradley ducked as I flew over his head so fast my motion must've only been a blur to the Brit. My knuckles smashed into his larynx, dropping him to the floor. He gasped at my feet. All that muscle was useless under the power of a well-placed choke punch.

But damn it, I broke a nail. There goes another hundred bucks to Madam Lucy.

"You bastard." I kicked him across the jaw, sending the gangster straight to Sleepsville.

I immediately turned to pamper my broken fingernail.

A gunshot went off behind me. I whirled around. A single bullet hole leaked blood from the fat man's scorched forehead. Bradley held a smoking pistol that he'd pulled from his ankle holster.

Nice to see my boss isn't afraid to get his hands dirty.

He grabbed a sofa cushion and suffocated the flames in the fat man's hair before the smoke alarm could go off.

"You want this hulk dead too?" I asked, my fangs begging for something muscular to bite into.

"He's all yours." Bradley re-holstered his pistol. "When you're done with him, his head is going back to Britain in a box."

I raised my eyebrows. "You think that'll be the end of Puritan?"

"There's no room in this town for The Gods. If the Limey bastards send anyone else, they'll get the same reception."

That sounded fine by me. I knelt next to the gorgeous Brit, fully intent on giving him my kind of reception.

He moaned.

Not long ago I'd have fucked him first, and then drained him. But now my true passion was for Katrina.

Still, it's been a long time since I've had fresh blood.

"Sucks to be you," I muttered and turned his head to give me a clear shot at the pulsing vein in his neck.

My fangs sprang from my gums with an orgasmic burst of pleasure.

"You might want to look away," I told Bradley. "This is going to get messy."

Follow Fear

I lay awake in my dark coffin, having slept most of the day. My silk dressing gown felt warm against the chill of my undead skin. I'd convinced Katrina that last night's job had been more taxing than it actually was, so she didn't ask me to stay up with her all day.

Just because I could, didn't mean I would. I still longed for the comfort of my coffin.

I'd put the pendant in my jewellery case, safe with my diamonds and other precious gems. A deep and secret part of me was relieved that I hadn't worn the Mjölnir since we'd returned home from the Chrysler Building.

I am afraid of it.

The visions it threw at me were something to fear. They made me weak. They brought about painful headaches that I had never experienced before.

And ghosts.

The ghosts of a life past. Of Angel with Clare before her murder. Of myself, apparently working, seemingly happy.

And most worrying: *the smoking man.*

I had been in love with him...in a past life I didn't

remember. And he was real, I'd seen him, not some random face stored in my subconscious mind. Whoever, whatever he may have been to me, he had to know what happened to me, to us. What changed our lives. And now he'd found me, but he too must have been afraid. Afraid to approach me, to talk to me, to see what I've become. Why else would he stare at me from across the street?

I pushed the coffin lid open to let in the soft light of my room. A satisfying meal of British blood and a good day's sleep had given me a more rational state of mind. I couldn't expect to go from blood sucking night dweller to a guest star on Friends in one go.

I had to slow down, quit rushing the process.

The Mjölnir and I could learn to get along. I would learn to control its powers and be a Daywalker without fear.

I need to focus on what good this can do for us all in the long term, despite what is happening to me in the short term.

A gentle rapping on my bedroom door drew me from my introspection. I stretched my undead joints, enjoying the sensation of a recharged body, and pounced out of my coffin. After checking to be sure my dressing gown exposed just a hint of cleavage, I sauntered across the room and opened the door.

Katrina looked, as she always did to me, irresistible. Her blonde hair was tied back from her gorgeous face, and her eyes sparkled at the sight of me.

My first instinct was to take her, right then and there, drag her to the floor, tear those jeans and her t-shirt off, and in the throes of our passion...

"Gem? Are you all right?"

I must've been staring at her. The look on her face told me that she had other things on her mind besides frolicking with me.

"What's wrong?" I asked.

Gem

"I need the Mjölnir. I've got to take it back to the museum."

But I'm not ready to give it back!

"Gem? Did you hear me?"

I had heard her, and her words had slapped me with surprise, but I felt a more profound jolt of shock at my own reaction. For all my fear and concern over the pendant, I did not want to let go of its connection to my past.

"Gem? You're freaking me out!"

"I'm sorry." I blinked the confusion from my mind. "You can't have it back."

She closed the door and pressed her back to the doorframe as if to keep me from leaving the room. "Please, Gem. I took it to see if it would work. Now I have to put it back or they'll find out I took it, and they'll throw me in jail."

"Don't worry. I'll visit you during daylight hours."

She scowled. "Gem. I'm serious."

I smirked. "Okay, I'll buy it from the museum. How much do they want for it?"

"It's priceless, Gem, like you. Like us. Like our family. But if I get busted, we may never see each other again."

I didn't want that to happen. She'd risked a lot for me. I'd rather only see her at night than never. "All right. I'll get it." Swimming in mental turmoil, I crossed the room to my dresser and drew the Mjölnir from my jewellery box. The moment it touched my hands, the thrum in my body kicked in, but I no longer resented it. I would miss it.

So this is as close as I'll ever get to normal.

I passed the pendant to Katrina.

"Thank you." She kissed my forehead and slipped the Mjölnir into her front jeans pocket.

Her lack of remorse set me back a step. "I don't understand. You wanted us to be together during the day but you seem happy to give up the pendant."

"It won't be gone long."

This time I saw a glint in her eye. "How will we get it back?"

"You're going to steal it," she said, and the warm look of hope on her face smothered the cold dread I had felt for my existence without Nótt's charm.

"And how do you expect me to do that?" I placed a hand on my hip and let my dressing gown fall open to reveal a slender leg.

I must be crazy. In the middle of this disaster, I can't stop flirting with Katrina.

But she didn't respond: no wink, no twinkle in her eye, no smile, as if she was focussed on something else, and none of my love games were going to distract her.

She reached into her back pocket and brought out Bradley's envelope I had given her the previous night. She opened it and tipped the contents into her open palm.

I had been right. It was a swipe card attached to a flash drive by a couple of thin wires.

"This little thing is genius," she said. "The card is a clone of my access swipe for the museum." She touched the tip of one perfectly manicured fingernail to the flash drive. "The programme Bradley's IT man loaded on here will shut down the entire museum security system for fifteen minutes. Just swipe the card on any door lock."

I found that hard to believe. "The computer will know something's wrong. It'll sound an alarm."

"The system won't know it's been shut down because shadow data on this flash drive will upload and mask your movements. Everything will appear normal while you go down to the vault, retrieve the pendant, and get out safely."

"Come on, Katrina, nothing is that easy."

"You're right." She led me to my coffin and sat me down on the edge. "You'll have to avoid Gerald."

"Gerald?"

She sat next to me. "The security guard. Don't let him

see you."

I saw a fondness in her eyes. "You don't want him to get hurt."

"He's such a Teddy Bear."

"But if he sees me, I'll have to kill him."

She wagged the swipe card at me. "I want us to live as normal a life as possible...but not that badly. Nobody gets hurt, you hear. Or I'm through with you, Gem, your assassin's lifestyle, your loving kisses, none of it's worth the loss of a life."

Katrina, you continue to astound me!

"Promise me you won't hurt him, or I'll bust up this flash drive and cut up the card."

My reaction to giving the Mjölnir back to the museum had put me on my back foot, but this prospect knocked me into next week.

I can't live without Katrina, not after all we've been through.

I wanted to take care of her forever. Money wouldn't be a problem. I didn't have to work for the mob. Over the years I'd accumulated millions of dollars, now stashed away in numerous accounts, safe deposit boxes, and investments. I could take care of her for ten lifetimes over.

But she doesn't have ten lifetimes. Only I have that.

If only I could turn Katrina safely, but I knew the consequences. The second she became a vampire, she would forget her mortal existence, as I had forgotten mine. She would forget me, as I had forgotten my sire. The only way I could keep her was if she wanted to be with me. If stealing the pendant meant killing someone, then losing Katrina wasn't worth the risk.

"Do we have a deal?"

"The museum can keep their pendant." The words were like knives in my throat. "Gerald might get in my way and ruin everything we have. I'll sleep in my coffin all day."

Katrina stood. "I'm only asking you not to hurt him. If he sees you, run."

"I don't run."

"Do it for me, for us, for Angel."

The passion in her eyes was unmistakable. She wanted me to steal the pendant. She wanted us to live a normal life together. And we could. All I had to do was not hurt anyone. That wasn't too much to ask. Not really. I was just being stubborn.

"Well?"

I got to my feet and faced her, so beautiful and determined, and held out my hand, palm up. "We have a deal."

She smiled.

I wanted to draw her into my arms and hug her and kiss her, but I stood firm with my hand out.

She set the swipe card and flash drive on my palm. "Be careful."

Closing my fingers around the card, I felt as if a breath of fresh air had swept me off my feet. "When do I go in?"

"Tonight." She patted her jeans pocket. "I'd better get to the museum and put this little thing back where it belongs."

I kissed her on the lips, and then she was gone. Only as the door closed behind her did I realise how naked my neck felt without the Mjölnir, how suddenly vulnerable I had become.

**

Wearing my tight-fitting black leather jacket knee-high leather boots over black leggings, I could move like a cat burglar and mingle with a fashionable New York crowd in equal measure. I walked casually along 5th Avenue, across the front of the Guggenheim. It was five minutes before 2am, but in New York City, that was prime time. I wasn't going to get a quiet window of opportunity for privacy, so I simply stepped into the shadows next to the staff entrance to the museum. I could have made one of my Superman leaps to the top of the museum. If anyone happened to see me, I'd be only a blur to human eyes. Besides, people only saw what they expected to see.

And I'm far from the expected!

But with the swipe card Bradley had provided for Katrina, for once I didn't have to be so dramatic.

A drama queen? Moi?

And anyway, this was New York City. No one could care less about what I was doing. But I still had to blend in, look like I should be here, that I was simply a member of the staff working late.

If I get caught, there's no way I'm getting the Mjölnir back.

I gently eased the swipe card and flash drive out of my jacket pocket. My only worry was that the swipe wouldn't work. I'd have no problem once I was inside. Well, just the one.

Avoiding Gerald.

Gerald, Katrina's unwitting stooge when she took the pendant the first time, was on night watch and would be surveying the building from his office. He'd be monitoring over forty television screens, and if this plan worked, he wouldn't see my cute ass on a single one of them. The programme Bradley's hacker had installed on the flash drive would ensure the scenes would not change on his monitors, and not record me moving through the Guggenheim.

But I'd better move fast anyway!

Mounted to the right of the staff door was a small console with a numeric keypad and a swipe card reader. The light currently on display glowed red. *Locked.* I silently drew Katrina's card through the reader, and nothing happened while the flash drive downloaded its shadow data.

I hope this doesn't take too long.

The headache slammed me like someone had hit me from behind with a sledgehammer. I brought my hand up to my temple as if it could ward off the pain with a simple swipe, but my eyes blinked spastically as a lightning rod of agony etched itself across my forehead. When I managed to focus my eyes, moonlight revealed the smoking man, hat in place, long black coat, smiling at me from the corner of the building. Despite the pain in my head, I took a determined step towards him. "Who are you?"

He looked at me with those tantalizing eyes that glinted like captured starlight. He knew me. Maybe he was just too shy to come forward, to introduce himself. "Do I know you?"

The red light changed to green, and a *click* indicated that the door had unlocked. In that moment of distraction, he had disappeared. My heart sunk. I pushed the door and slipped inside, quickly closing the door behind me.

I hope he's out there when I come back.

Meeting him would have to wait. I was on a limited timescale. Fifteen minutes. Then all hell would break loose.

The corridor was long and dark. Night lights glowed along the hallway floor and above the doorway at the far end of the corridor. The amount of light made no difference to me. My vampire eyes instantly adjusted to the dark, and I could see as if I stood in full daylight.

I know what that looks like now.

I moved. Quickly. From door to door, listening for a moment before entering, my movements nothing more than a whisper, skirting around the edges of the displays until I reached the main display room. The moon's glow was painted across the floor in a criss-crossed spider web pattern born of shadows cast down from the massive glass skylight many floors above.

So far, so good.

Gem

No alarm had rang out. No security guard had come running. For once it was nice to do a job without a rain of bullets pelting my ass.

I took a millisecond to orientate myself and moved towards a door to my left. It was locked, but with the swipe card I was able to access the storeroom inside with no problem. I ran to the back and down a flight of stairs to the vault door.

Here goes nothing!

I tried to spin the massive wheel that was the vault's door handle.

Nothing!

It wouldn't budge an inch. I tried again, this time injecting a little more of my vampire strength into the process.

Is it stuck?

My undead heart stopped in my chest. I had failed.

I won't be able to rip this thing off its hinges.

So close, yet so far. It must have been on another security system, possibly even one of its own. Or a time lock.

Focus, Gem!

I swept my eyes around the room with vampire speed and spotted another console, just like on the entrance door of the building, built into the wall: red light, numeric keypad, and swipe slot. Either Katrina had forgotten to tell me about it, or it was a new addition to the security system to protect the Mjölnir.

I swiped the card. The red light switched to green. I spun the wheel and opened the thick steel door. Ceiling florescent lights blinked on.

I rushed in.

Now where are you?

Selves lined the walls, stuffed with boxes, scrolls, and priceless artefacts, but only one called out to me. A faint vibrating sound emanated from a blue box, a sound only a vampire could hear. The pendant, like any lover, wanted to be next to my skin again. Even though it made my dead heart ache with memories, I wanted the pendant too.

The Mjölnir!

I opened the box and lifted out the pendant. Holding it up before my eyes, I basked in its powerful aura.

"Welcome to my new world," I whispered, and then I looped the chain over my neck and tucked the hammer-shaped pendant inside my jacket. I felt whole again. Renewed.

I closed the vault. The LED turned red. My passing would be forever erased. I couldn't resist a satisfied smile.

On the move again, I backtracked, closing every door after me, moving with the silence of a ghost, making sure that Gerald had no reason to leave his station to check out any suspicious sounds.

I slinked into the main display room. Clouds must have blotted out the moon over Manhattan, as the spider web pattern on the floor was now obscured. I ran, no longer keeping to the edges of the room, towards the exit door.

Then the world around me exploded.

A massive crash filled the room and reverberated around the sloping curved walkways.

I hit the floor on all fours and looked up. The skylight above me had shattered, the shards of glass raining down like a brutal hailstorm. And in the midst of the falling glass, the smoking man floated down, defying the laws of gravity, his long black coat fluttering in a tornadic wind. He landed, that handsome hat still perfectly in place, five metres away from me and, of course, he smiled like he was some kind of game show host.

Who in the Devil's name are you?

I bared my teeth as the last of the glass tinkled to the floor, and I realised other sounds had joined the party.

Footsteps! Running! Closer! Obviously, Gerald may not have seen anything on his monitors, but he'd definitely heard the breaking skylight, loud as a bomb.

And the alarm counted down, a steady and monotonous beeping. In minutes this place would be swarming with cops. How was I going to get out of this mess without killing anyone?

But I'd promised Katrina no one would get hurt.

Except this gorgeous man...this bozo who has just botched my burglary.

I hissed a warning and extended my fangs to their most vicious peaks. The smile on his face faded, and he returned the gesture with twice the ferocity I could ever muster.

Hey, I'm a lady.

I took a step backwards. He too was a vampire, the first I'd ever come face-to-face with; I didn't know whether to piss in my panties or go blind.

The burglar alarms shrieked.

"Hello, Olivia," he said. "It's been a long time."

What the fuck? He must think I've got all night to have a little chat with him.

"Who are you?" I snapped.

Gerald's running footfalls came closer.

I needed to get moving. He may not be able to stop me, but he'd recognize me as Katrina's friend. And I wasn't allowed to kill him.

The smoking man said, "Give the Mjölnir to me."

Footsteps, closer, closer.

"Give it to me, Olivia."

His voice was powerful, earthshaking.

I moved my hand over the pendant protectively as it hung between my breasts under my black jacket. "It's mine. You can't have it."

Gerald's footsteps were now descending a final flight of stairs. In just seconds he'd be in the main room, and he would see me.

"Olivia, you cannot resist me."

The pressure inside my head intensified, and I found myself on the floor again in Maloney's apartment, reliving the time that a searing light tore at my flesh like the teeth of a thousand bats, burning a hole in my soul, and I could hear the devil screaming my name: *"Olivia! Olivia!"*

I squeezed my head between my hands and wanted to cry out for mercy.

Before I could move, he was at my side, an arm, vice like, around my waist, and just as Gerald burst through the door, I turned my face away from him.

And now it was my turn to be Lois Lane.

The vampire leapt back up through the shattered skylight and deposited me on the highest point of the Guggenheim roof.

Pain hacked at my scalp like a tomahawk. I pushed myself away from him. The Mjölnir trembled inside my jacket as if it too were afraid of the male vampire.

His face, handsome, chiselled, was suddenly shadowed in sadness.

I didn't understand where that was coming from. A memory? A thought that he'd have to kill me to get this pendant, pry it from my dead fingers. I stepped back, the gravel on the roof crunching under my boots. "Leave me alone."

Finally a smile swept across his perfectly formed mouth, and he revealed his long, sharp teeth.

This was it. He'd decided it was time to kill me. I staggered, almost fell.

He grabbed my arm, steadied me, and bore his soulless eyes into mine. "Now give me the Mjölnir."

I couldn't let him have it. My plans with Katrina would be forever ruined. And I'd miss Angel growing up. I'd sooner die. "You'll have to take it off my dead body."

He pushed me back, pressed me against a nearby roof-air unit. "That can be arranged." With one swift swipe, a razor sharp fingernail sliced open my black jacket. He

~178~

reached in a grabbed the pendant.

A sizzling sound and a wisp of smoke sent him reeling backwards. I smelled burned flesh. He gripped his wrist, his upturned hand a claw, scorched and smoking. "Curses!" he hissed at me, fangs bared.

I cowered back, wishing I could shrink down into my sexy boots.

"I cannot take it from you by force," he growled out. "You must give it to me of your own free will."

"Who the hell are you?"

"Sleep with the Mjölnir around your neck. It will tell you everything."

The screech of police car sirens rolled up on the streets below. The noise made me wish my head would just explode and be done with it.

"You have twenty four hours to give me the Mjölnir. I'm staying at the Helmsley Hotel. Bring it to me there."

"Never."

"Oh I think you will...after you learn the truth about who you were."

And with a flip of his long coat, he was gone. The headache's intensity dropped like a stone.

A police helicopter's battering whine joined the cacophony of the night. I leapt across Fifth Avenue and into Central Park. Landing at a run, I stayed off the path and ran across grass and through the trees until the alarm and sirens were far behind me. I emerged from the park less than half a mile from home and slowed to a walk, still shaking from my encounter with the vampire. He knew who I was...before.

My name is Olivia.

The pendant was now calm against my skin.

I reached our apartment and let myself in.

Katrina greeted me with open arms and a nervous smile. "You have it?"

"Yes, but there were...complications."

I would tell her the full story, of course I would, but already I yearned for my coffin and the truth that the Mjölnir would reveal to me.

Final Fear

Lying in my coffin, darkness rushed at me, and for the first time, fear invaded my safe place. My coffin became claustrophobic, the air thick with the charge of the Mjölnir as it vibrated against my breast bone. I resisted the urge to punch an escape hole through the lid because I wasn't going anywhere. The pendant had something to show me.

I closed my eyes, slowed my breathing, and then I heard gasps from a frightened young woman in the dark, and I had never heard a person so in need of solace and...oh, no:

The frightened young woman is me.

My eyes blew open. I was no longer in my coffin. I was sitting in a spacious open-plan office. Around me, men dressed in suits packed papers into their briefcases and donned their hats. Ladies in knee-length dresses fixed their hair and slipped cigarette boxes into their handbags. En masse, employees headed for the doors, for the elevators.

"Goodnight, Olivia." A few of them smiled at me and I felt my face smile back.

There's that name again.

"Don't work too late," the girl at the desk next to mine said, and then leaned close to me and whispered in my ear. "What time are you meeting him?"

"The usual," I said. "Seven on the dot."

"Well, have fun." And then she merged into the exodus.

I went back to work, fingers racing over a typewriter in front of me, the words appearing on a white sheet of paper.

I'm writing an advert.

Finished, I whipped the sheet free from its roller and

Gem

crossed the room to one of the corner offices. The windows around me revealed a vista of New York City alien to me. I looked down on the Empire State building, just a maze of steel girders and cranes.

I'm in the Chrysler Building. This is where I work.

I tapped on an office door, and a man's voice called for me to enter. I stepped inside and held out the typed sheet to him. He was short, rotund, and smiling.

He took the paper with a flourish, and his ruddy cheeks glowed as he read.

"Olivia Martin!" he exclaimed. "To think your first job with us was in the typing pool. Before too long you're going to be my number one copy writer."

I felt my cheeks blush. "Thank you, Mister Draper." I smiled with pride.

I loved my job back then.

"Now get out of here. A lovely young lady like you should be out on the town with a gentleman on your arm."

"Yes, sir." I slipped out of his office. It was ten minutes to seven. I exited the elevator, and as I approached the door that would take me out onto 42nd Street, my heart fluttered in my throat...in anticipation of... Victor.

His name is Victor.

Outside, as dusk turned to night, darkness crept into the canyons of the city, coaxing streetlamps and neon to lustre. I easily picked him out of the crowd. That perfectly fitted suit, long black coat, his rugged, chiselled chin, those piercing eyes, and his trademark fedora. And of course, that ever-present cigarette.

Victor Kyle.

Butterflies flitted in my stomach.

I crossed a street jammed with vintage *Bonnie and Clyde* style cars and rushed to him. He took me in his arms, strong and secure, and I got lost in his eyes, beautiful, seductive.

The Mjölnir hummed.

I glanced down at it...but it wasn't hanging around my neck. Confused, I looked up. I wasn't on the 42nd Street anymore; I was sitting in a speakeasy, cocktails in front of us, and Victor was talking to me.

"I knew you were different the first time I met you."

"Different how?" I purred, fishing for compliments.

"Olivia, Olivia. This is 1930. Most girls your age are flapping in night clubs and swooning over Maurice Chevalier and Guy Lombardo, but you, you know what you want."

My body tingled with desire. "You are what I want." My voice sounded breathless.

He brought his lips to mine.

The Mjölnir sang out with glee.

Next thing I knew, I was in a hotel room, in a bed, my naked body intertwined with his, my heart racing as I cried out, "I love you," over and over again in the throes of passion and orgasmic release.

The Mjölnir thrummed wildly in the valley between my breasts.

Time shifted forward. I was sitting on the bed, sheets scrambled, my hair mussed, my body exhausted. Something was wrong. I could feel the tension in the air, tension between us, between lovers, and my heart felt heavy with worry.

Victor stood in front of the closed drapes. "You've know there is a secret within me." His face was pale, ashen.

I let my eyes implore him to say the words to explain himself.

"I am not of this world. I was once, but I am not now, for I am a vampire."

But I knew, somehow, deep in my heart, at the pit of my soul, I knew there was something otherworldly about him. But a vampire was not on my suspect list. If not for the love and trust I had in him, I would have run from the room, screaming.

Instead, I sat stoic, my heart jamming about in the throes of shock. And I feared what he was going to ask of me next.

"Will you join me for eternity? Will you become a vampire with me and be by my side forever?"

I knew he was sure my answer would be yes, or he would not have asked this of me, and when the word left my mouth, he glided across to me, and although the tremble in my body was apparent, he laid me back onto the bed, and I hardly felt his teeth on my neck and then...the bite...the pain...the ecstasy.

Victor Kyle has come back for me!

My eyes snapped open in the darkness of my coffin. The Mjölnir was writhing against my skin. Suddenly its power was wholly evident to me, it was my link to Olivia. I had no idea how far back in time I could go...and...

And there's no way I'm giving it up.

I may have been in love with Victor Kyle in 1930, but that was eighty some years ago.

Eighty years? I'm an old lady. Old woman. A hag. No!

I shoved the lid off my coffin, ripped the Mjölnir from my neck, and tossed it across the room. My life was now about loving and protecting Katrina and Angel and Maria. I would go to Victor's hotel tonight, but he would not receive the Mjölnir from me. He would get the tips of my fangs in his fucking throat.

***

"Where are you going?" Katrina shouted at me from the couch in front of the television.

I strapped on my shoulder holster. "The Helmsley Hotel. I'm not giving up the Mjölnir, so I'll have to kill Victor."

She sat up. "Who?"

"My sire."

"You found the vampire who turned you?"

"He found me." I ejected the clip on my M&P and inserted one loaded with silver bullets. "And he's one nasty son of a bitch."

She scrambled to her feet. "What if he kills you instead?"

I holstered the gun. "This is our chance to live a normal life. He's not going to ruin it for us."

"But if you kill him, the bloodline ends." The harsh look on her face radiated lines of terror. "Isn't that the legend?"

"It's just a legend."

"Like the Mjölnir. It's just a legend, but it's true. If you kill your sire, you'll become human again. Like me. Like Angel. It might happen."

"You better hope it doesn't because I'll be an old woman."

Her face scrunched up. "How long ago were you turned?"

"Trust me. You don't want to know."

I slipped into my black jacket, the one Victor sliced with his fingernail...

It's going to cost me a fortune to repair this thing.

...then I ran the zip up over the holstered gun.

"But if someone else kills your sire, you're not changed back. Isn't that right?"

She doesn't want me to give up what I am!

"It's just a legend, Katrina, so drop it." I stepped into one of my knee-high boots, pulled it up tight.

"Well, maybe I can't!"

Stabbing my foot into the other boot, I was about to tell her not to worry, when someone hammered on the front door.

We both stopped and looked at each other. My heart was beating bat wings.

"Maybe that's him now," Katrina said.

Gem

"Gem! Gem, are you there?" John Bradley's voice. "Open up."

Katrina jammed her hands on her hips. "I told him not to show up here without calling first."

"His memory is probably as short as his dick." I opened the door.

Bradley cannonballed into the apartment. "Gem, I've underestimated the Brits. The Gods are really pissed off at me!" His clothes were dishevelled, his face unshaven, his hair a mess. He glanced back and forth at us. "What the Hell is going on with you two?"

"Nothing," I snapped, hoping Katrina would keep quiet—

"Everything," she said, completely contradicting me. She stormed out of the room.

"Gem, you have to help me!" Bradley went on like he was the only one with problems. "They've already killed five of my best men. In their own homes. In their beds. Christ, two of them were on my personal protection detail, the best men I had. You've got to help me."

I'd never seen my boss panicked like this before. I wanted to help him, but I had more pressing matters at hand. I had a vampire bastard to kill.

Katrina stormed back into the room, this time donning her coat. "I'm going out."

"Where?"

"To get a drink."

"You don't drink."

"I do now."

I stepped forward to block her path, but Bradley ran interference. "Let her go. You've got to help me, Gem. The Gods skinned my men alive. I shouldn't have sent the Brits' heads back to the Limeys in a box."

It took all of my self control not to knock him out of my way. Meanwhile, Katrina ran out, slamming the door behind her.

"You're not the only one with issues, Bradley. There's another vampire in town, and he's not as cute and cuddly as me."

"Another vampire?" Bradley's eyes lit up. "Whoever he is, get him on the payroll."

How much does a girl have to deal with in one day?

"With two vampires on my side, the Brits won't stand a—"

"Don't utter another syllable!" I shouted. "Go to ground for tonight. Tomorrow I'll solve your problem. Tonight I have enough to deal with."

"But..."

I let my canted eyes show him I meant business.

His deflated expression told me he understood. I left him to let himself out and ran up to my room to get the Mjölnir and my lipstick.

I have to look my best when I kill Victor.

Katrina's bedroom door stood open, and I could see she'd left her wardrobe agape and clothes scattered on the floor. She'd dressed in a hurry. I was about to turn back to the stairs when I spotted the box on the bed, lid off and laid to the side.

The lock box where she kept her handgun!

Empty.

Panic filled my body, and my knees almost gave out underneath me. Katrina had taken things into her own hands. She'd gone after Victor by herself.

I have to stop her!

***

In the New York Helmsley Hotel, I knocked on Victor's door and forced myself not to smash it to matchsticks. I heard footsteps approach, and then a click of the lock. The door creaked open. Victor stood in front of me, a glass of red wine...

I hope that's red wine.

... in his left hand.

"Olivia! Please come in."

"Don't call me Olivia," I growled, entering his room. A quick glance assured me that I had arrived before Katrina. "My name is Gem."

"Of course." He closed the door and faced me. "Gem, it is then." His eyes roved over my body like feasting leaches. I was dressed to impress in my tight black gym suit.

I give the saying dressed to kill *a higher meaning!*

"You truly are the most wondrous beauty," he whispered.

"What a shame. This beauty is going to kill you." I battled to ensure that my teeth didn't bury themselves into his throat, just yet.

He didn't seem the least bit worried. "It was in this very room that I lost you." His voice carried a melancholy tone of dismay and regret.

I glanced around, not recognising the décor from my Mjölnir-induced vision, of course, eighty years had passed since I was here last.

He handed me a glass of wine. "I did not know you would forget who you were, I swear, and when you forgot me, I was shocked by my mistake." He tapped his wine glass against mine. "But now, here we are, together again." He sipped his wine as if he were at a party in Paris.

I wanted to hear more of his story before I silenced his voice forever. "Where have you been all this time?" I set the wine down on the table to keep my hands free if I had to go for my gun.

"My darling Olivia, you fled from me that night, yet I watched over you from afar as you stood in front of Tiffany's until dawn was nearly upon you. I feared you would burn up in the sun, but instinct guided you to the shadows. I knew you would survive, so with a broken heart, I left New York, never to return...or so I thought."

His voice was hypnotic. I could see why Olivia Martin had fallen so deeply entranced by him. Even I, Gem, had trouble resisting the allure of his lips.

"But the Mjölnir has drawn me back. I heard its vibrations calling out, sounds only a vampire can here, and I find you, Olivia. The Mjölnir has great power, which I wish to possess."

"I don't see any good coming from you being a Daywalker."

"Perhaps not, but if you give it to me, I will leave you to your life with Katrina."

I staggered back. "You know about Katrina?"

He smiled that devastating smile. "You have something I want." His gaze dropped to the floor then came up in a fierce stare. "And now I have something you want." He produced a gun as evidence, the gun Katrina had kept in the lock box.

I gasped.

He does have Katrina!

"Where is she?"

"Give me the Mjölnir or I will turn her into a vampire." His voice came out steady and firm. "And she will forget you, forever."

A fate worse than death.

I showed him my fangs.

He showed me his. "If you should be so lucky to kill me, you will never find her before she starves to death."

Everything I had worked so hard to protect was on the line. If I fought him and won, then she would die. If I fought him and lost, she would die anyway. And then what would become of Angel if we weren't around? Maria could hide her again, but how long would that last? She'd been found before. And Bradley's empire was on the verge of collapse. I'd be unemployed. I was about to lose everything.

I have no choice.

Gem

I brought my hand up to my throat and the zip of my jacket. With my eyes on Victor, I zipped it open, sensual as a Las Vegas stripper.

His face beamed like a child at Christmas...

Angel, I will always protect you.

...ready to claim his finest present...

I opened my jacket.

His eyes were drawn to my neck...

Katrina, I will always love you!

...where the Mjölnir hung on its golden chain.

Victor's mouth dropped open in wonder. I wasn't wearing a bra.

"The Mjölnir is yours." I removed the pendant from around my neck and closed my jacket without zipping it up.

A frown crinkled his gorgeous forehead. "No tricks?"

I held it out for him to take, my hand shaking.

No fear!

GEM – No More

No Choices

I pushed back the fear swelling in my stomach. The walls of Victor Kyle's hotel room closed in around me; the air pulsed with a tension I could taste, acidic and bitter. Vampire pheromones swirled musky rank in my nostrils. My fangs itched to break free of my gums. Raw, sinewy nerves stretched to the breaking point as his steady hand reached for the Mjölnir that I held out to him, dangling from the thin chain wrapped around my index finger. I stared into his dark eyes, but my concentration was on the gun just beneath my unzipped leather jacket. Silver bullets to end his undead life...before he ended mine.

This scene could have been a standoff in an old Western movie, less the tumbleweeds and blowing dust, and accompanied by a Sergio Leone soundtrack. The good guy, *that's me,* the bad guy, *my sire,* facing off in a battle to the death.

Over the pendant and a girl.

Katrina.

Victor held her captive now, a pawn in his plot to take possession of the Mjölnir, the Hammer of Thor pendant that had given Nótt the power of the *un-light* and allowed the Goddess of Darkness to walk in the sunshine. Just the sight of the pendant made Victor's jaw drop and his mouth drool. I expected to see tears of joy spill down his impeccably chiselled cheeks.

Normally I have that impact on men!

But of course, Victor Kyle was no ordinary man. He was my former lover in my former life. The Mjölnir had

~190~

revealed our history to me, and worse, that he was also the vampire who had made me what I am today.

Now I am Gem. Hit woman for the mob. Sexy and deadly in one hot package. Okay, so I turned out to be a little more than he could handle.

He had made me a denizen of the night and left me to fend for myself. Now he was back, and he wanted something only I could give him, this pendant, the artefact that would make him a Daywalker and the most powerful vampire in the world.

Nothing good could come of that.

His fingers neared the swaying pendant and trembled a tiny bit. He was probably leery from the last time he'd touched it, when it was around my neck and gave his hand a nasty burn. He'd learned the legend was true the hard way. He couldn't have the pendant unless I gave it to him willingly.

But I couldn't let him take it without a fight. I had too much to lose. The pendant meant more to me than power. Despite its brutal delivery of headaches and visions of my past, it was the only thing that could give me a normal life with my family: Maria. Angel. Katrina.

Katrina.

She had set out to kill Victor, to save me from another myth, that if I killed my sire, I'd revert to my human form. That wouldn't have been so bad if I wasn't over eighty years old.

But she messed up and tipped the balance of power in Victor's favour. I may have been holding the Mjölnir, but he was holding Katrina.

His greedy fingers began to close around the pendant.

I yanked it back from his expectant grasp. "Not until I see Katrina."

His pallid face reddened with rage. "Don't press your luck, Olivia."

"My name is Gem."

"Your name is dead vampire bitch if you don't hand it over."

I sucked in a breath of courage. He would drain me without as much as a tear for my passing. His heart wasn't only dead, it was cold. "I want to see her standing right here in front of me."

He hissed through extended fangs. "I could kill you right now and strip the pendant from your dead fist."

"Not if I don't let you have it of my own free will."

He flexed his fingers, all healed from the last time he'd grabbed it. "When you're dead, that doesn't count."

"You know that for sure? If you're wrong you'll never be able to touch it. Ever."

He stepped back, and for the first time I saw doubt creep across his face, dark as a passing shadow.

I showed him stern lips. "Now let me see Katrina."

"Give me the pendant first."

We were at a stale mate. I had to up the ante. "How about I give you this first?" I drew my gun from the slat in my black leather jacket and pointed it at his face. "Silver bullets with your name on them."

The last thing I expected was for him to laugh.

"Kill me and you'll never find your girlfriend, what's her name, Katrina? I've got her hidden so deep she'll starve to death in that lonely dark hole I put her in. So think real hard before you pull that trigger."

The luxurious room seemed stuffy as a coffin I didn't belong in. If what he said was true, I didn't dare kill him, not until I knew Katrina was safe.

And there's my selfish reason too! I could blow a hole through his heart in an instant, but then my sire would be dead and I'd become an old lady, my vampire powers gone.

I'm not ready to give them up!

Calling his bluff seemed the best course of action. I aimed the gun at his chest. "I can always get another girlfriend, but you've got only one undead life. You choose."

He looked down the gun barrel at me and grinned. "Oh, Olivia, I'm not afraid of your stupid little bullets."

My throat threatened to close off my windpipe. I hadn't considered the possibility that Victor may have been more powerful than silver bullets. They'd put the hurt on me a time or two.

Or maybe he is bluffing.

He showed me his fangs. "How did you expect this to pan out? We make the swap here tonight, and then you hunt me down and take back the Mjölnir?" He tilted his head to emphasise his question.

I made no reply or gesture but met his piercing eyes with a stare that could have stopped time. He was right about me hunting him down. I lowered the gun to his crotch and let my raised eyebrows say the rest. The arrogance on his face faded to fear.

Your move, jerk off.

He raised his hands in surrender. "I figured you would not be easily convinced to give up the pendant. With a rival such as you, I have taken precautions." He indicated a door behind him. "May I?"

What's in there? Maybe he'd say Katrina, but I doubted it. My acute vampire senses would have picked up on her presence, her luscious scent, her sensual breathing, her—

I stopped myself before I got all worked up. With a flick of the gun barrel, I gave him permission to move to the door.

He broke my stare, strode across the suite, flung open the door, and with a flourish of his hand invited me to look inside.

I stepped to the doorway and peeked into an antechamber. A coffin, basic, rudimentary, lay on the floor. A pine box at best. It looked like he'd brought it to the hotel in pieces and cobbled it together here. Sawdust and nails were still strewn about.

"Come back before sunrise," he said. "I will have Katrina with me to exchange for the Mjölnir. As sunlight brightens the room, this coffin will protect you while I make my daytime escape through the city."

"What makes you think I won't shoot you before then?"

A sudden force yanked the gun from my hand, breaking a fingernail. It happened so fast, so violently, I barely caught a glimpse of the gun flying to Victor's outstretched fingers.

I've never been able to do that!

My stomach clenched even as my hand reached out and grabbed at thin air. "Give it back."

"I'll even put out the *Do Not Disturb* sign on the door."

"How considerate of you." I shook the pain from my hand and bit at the broken fingernail.

"When nightfall returns, you will be free to go, oh, and be sure to pay the hotel bill before you leave. And be sure to tip big."

He's a thoroughly cheap sucker, but slick.

He closed the anteroom door and took a seat on the edge of the bed.

It required all of my self control not to rip out his throat before his tight butt made a dent in the mattress.

He examined my gun as if it were some department store curio.

"Simple as that?" I asked, unable to disguise the venom in my voice. "I get Katrina back, unharmed."

"Unless you make it complicated. But you really do not want to do that. Just a few more hours and you'll have her in your arms again. Take no chances, Olivia. If you follow me to my lair, she dies. I know your support network. The Mobster, John Bradley."

My boss. To think he wanted me to ask Victor to join

him in his fight against the British drug gang, The Gods, seemed ludicrous at this point. Desperation made for desperate acts. The Gods were taking over New York City, Bradley's territories, and bringing in a new drug they called Puritan. It would take more than a couple vampires to bring those bad boys down.

"Your maid, Maria, and that darling little girl, Angel."

Their names sounded like poison on his tongue. "You leave my family out of this."

"I have people watching them."

He's lying... I hope, but just in case, I'd better do as I'm told.

I pursed my lips and stood in that sassy pose that Katrina loved so much. She should see me now: one foot out in front of me, one hand on a hip, prominent chin pushed forward, eyes slightly creased in concentration. "I don't take chances with the ones I love. Not like you did with me."

Judging by the pained expression on his face, my barbed comment had hit a tender spot. He'd taken a chance by turning me into a vampire; he thought we'd be together forever, but instead, I'd forgotten him...and my old self, Olivia. The recorded memory of my past was rubbed clean as a chalkboard at the end of class. We became strangers, and now enemies. "You shouldn't have turned me, Victor."

"I turned you because I loved you."

"Save it for someone who gives a damn." I slipped the Mjölnir chain back around my neck. "I'll see you before dawn's first light, and I hope for your sake it's the last time we ever lay eyes on each other."

Victor gently lobbed my handgun to me. "Take your pea shooter," he said, his voice filled with vile arrogance.

I jammed it back into its shoulder holster and zipped my jacket closed.

He may get a taste of these silver bullets yet.

I turned to the door. The thought of never seeing him

again, of losing this link to my past and the person I was before I became undead, hurt my heart, pulled tears from my eyes, and let loose a tremor in my jaw. We had something back then, something special, but he ruined our love with his obsession for control over me, all wrapped up in his sweet-talking charm. Now I just wanted to pop his skull off his spine and spit down his neck. Easier said than done while he held Katrina captive. I would take no chances with her life.

I'd never felt weaker.

***

As dawn approached, I stepped inside the New York Helmsley Hotel and into the empty elevator. The door slid shut, and the carriage began its ascent. I slipped my gun out of my jacket and checked the clip, just to pass the time, and it's a cool thing to do.

I exhaled slowly, calming myself.

An ordinary life with Katrina and Angel, that's all I want at the end of the day.

The number of each floor illuminated briefly as the lift rose. I slid my gun back into place.

It was ready. I was ready.

Because I am Gem!

A 'ping' signalled I'd reached Victor's floor, and the doors drew back. I left the zip of my jacket open so his focus would be drawn to the Mjölnir and my ample cleavage.

I set my shoulders back and strode toward his hotel room. The door stood ajar. A note had been pinned to the wood. My heart pounded hard. A sheen of sweat slicked my palms, so I wiped them on my jeans to ensure nothing would slip through my fingers.

Not my gun, not the Mjölnir, and not Victor Kyle.

I stopped in front of the door and read the note:

Enter, close the door. Sit on the bed.

Gem

What game was this? Charades? My lips peeled back in a venomous sneer, allowing my fangs to poke out of my gums.

Once Katrina is safe, I'll show him how the game is really played!

The Mjölnir's power struck me with an icy headache and robbed me of my rage. I doubled over, and only my hands braced on my knees halted my slump to the lavish carpet. The fugue lasted mere seconds, but in that time my fangs receded, and the tension eased. I straightened and pursed my lips, now feeling resilient.

The Mjölnir was trying to help me, keep me calm, keep me focused.

I pushed the door open and stepped through the entrance.

Maybe the Mjölnir prefers to stay with me and not go with Victor.

I closed the door. The room appeared empty, but I sensed that I was not alone. Two hearts beat nearby, one dead cold, the other filled with anxiety. Katrina's heart. I glided to the bed. The curtains were pulled wide open, revealing a city warmed by dawn's first sunbeams. While I wore the pendant, I had no fear.

But once I give it to Victor, I will be turned to dust and ash.

I sat on the bed, and once the well-used bed springs calmed their squeaky cacophony, I heard shuffling from the bathroom.

Be calm, be ice.

The bathroom door opened, and Victor's gruff voice called out to me. "Olivia, you're right on time."

And I'm ready.

"Victor, how many times do I have to tell you my name is Gem."

"Olivia," he insisted. "Stand and face me."

I stood and faced him. He held Katrina in front of

him. Duct tape covered her mouth. Her hair looked greasy and wild, her eyes puffy from crying, and a shiner bruised one perfect cheekbone. From the looks of her, she'd put up one hell of a fight.

Victor crooked his left arm around her neck.

She's been to hell and back... Again! Because of me.

Katrina winked, a signal she was all right.

If she could see herself in a mirror, she wouldn't be winking.

When this is over, I'm going to give her the spa vacation of her life.

"I'm sorry," I told her.

"Don't bother with the pleasantries." Victor sneered, pointing the index finger of his free hand at the Mjölnir. "You have *that*, I have *this*."

"I've played by your rules, Victor." My eyes never left Katrina's. "Let her go."

He wiggled his finger at me like a school teacher telling a naughty primary school pupil 'no, no, no.' "For now she is my human shield. Take the chain from around your neck."

"Let her go first."

"How about I just choke her to death right now?" He jerked his elbow, tightening his squeeze on her neck.

Katrina squealed.

"Easy, Victor. Don't get your panties in a wad." As I looped the chain off around my head, I flicked my eyes down to where my gun was stashed under my jacket. Katrina blinked, showing me that she understood my signal.

Victor was too interested in stretching his paw towards the pendant to notice the communication techniques we'd practiced just in case a situation like this ever arose.

Heat on my back told me the sun had risen above the horizon, its blistering rays bombarding the room through giant picture windows. Without the pendant's protection, I'd have only seconds to dive into the next room. I was sure he had the window curtains full open in there as well, so I'd have to scramble into the coffin—

"Throw it to me. Do not try anything stupid, or I will snap her neck."

I tossed the Mjölnir across the gap between us, making sure his eyes were drawn up away from me as he traced its arc. In the moment his focus was fully on the pendant, I bumped my thumb off my chest and bobbed at the knees, telling Katrina to drop low when I gave the signal. Even if he'd had his eyes on me, he'd have had no idea what I'd meant, but Katrina did. A wink meant all right.

Victor snatched the Mjölnir out of the air and dragged the chain over his head. The look of wonderment on his face was instant. He let out a shrill cry of victory that chilled me despite the burn I felt on my neck. The morning sun was no longer my friend. I was running out of time. "Now get your hands off her."

Victor grinned wickedly. "I was going to push her towards you and disappear while you climbed into the coffin, but I think you will come after me. The Mjölnir may have bonded to you, and it will call to you. Nowhere will I be safe. So instead..." His head reared back, and his mouth opened, exposing his massive fangs.

Katrina stiffened in his arm as if she understood the impending danger.

In that moment, I saw a vision of his plan.

He would bite her neck, turn her into a vampire so she'd forget me, what we'd meant to each other, and she'd attack me to protect her sire. I'd be forced to fight her, tear her to shreds or be torn to shreds while he slipped out the door to safety.

How could I possibly know this was his plan?

The Mjölnir, of course. It had bonded to me, and now,

around Victor's neck, its power warned me of what he was thinking.

"Now," I shouted.

Katrina bent her knees and dropped low enough to expose Victor's heart to my gun, which I'd grabbed from my jacket so quickly a human eye would've missed the motion. I squeezed the trigger. An eardrum-busting bang unleashed a silver bullet.

But Victor's eyes did not miss what I had done. With equal speed, he yanked Katrina back up and directly into the path of the bullet.

The slug tore into her, made a splat sound, like a slab of meat hitting a butcher's block.

She screamed.

I wished I could have taken it back, undo what I had done, but the bullet was on a mission of its own now. It exited Katrina's body and bore straight into Victor's heart with a *thunk* like metal striking wood. His eyes bulged, and his wide-open mouth suddenly clamped shut. His head exploded into a cloud of dust.

The Mjölnir clattered to the floor.

Katrina, spurting blood from her chest, crumpled on top of Victor's immaculate but now empty wardrobe, crumpled and covered in vampire dust.

"No, Katrina, no!"

I sprang across the room towards her. My hair burst into flames. Either the sun had struck its deadly blow, or I was about to pay the price for killing my sire. Death by fire. Death by dust. Death by old age. I didn't know what fate awaited me. Terror took root in my heart, an emotion I wasn't accustomed to, sharp as a blade stabbing my chest. I holstered my gun and slapped at the fire, but continued rushing toward Katrina as she lay bleeding on Victor's pile of clothes.

"Katrina, don't die on me."

She ripped the tape from her mouth, leaving a smear

Gem

of blood across her face. "You need this." She threw the Mjölnir at me.

I caught the pendant in midair and slid the chain around my neck. Immediately, the flames extinguished. I no longer felt the sun's heat. But fearing I'd still be struck down for killing Victor, I tried to prepare myself for anything. I applied palm pressure to Katrina's wound. She was covered with Victor's gritty remains.

"I'm bleeding to death."

"Not if I can help it." I lifted her in my arms and carried her to the bathroom. After tearing her blouse open around the bullet wound, I grabbed a towel from the rack.

"It went right through me." Katrina pointed at her shoulder where blood spurted from a flesh wound the size of a dime, just below her collar bone, through muscle but not lung.

I tore a strip off the towel and rolled it onto a pad. "Keep pressure on that."

She held the towel-bandage against her chest. "I'm going to pass out."

"Don't you dare." I scrambled through the medicine cabinet, scrounged some tape and gauze. With a water cup from the sink, I collected vampire ash from her clothes then added a few drops of water, and using my shaky fingertip, the one with the broken nail, I stirred the concoction into a paste.

"What are you doing?" She wheezed.

Already her towel was soaked red. "Saving your life." I lifted the pad from the spurting wound and slapped on a glob of paste. The bleeding stopped.

"It doesn't hurt anymore," she said with a laugh in her voice.

I secured the gauze over the healing wound with tape. "Tomorrow this will have been like a bad dream."

Shouts, screams, and panicked footfalls came from the hallway. Banging on the door. "Are you all right in there?"

someone shouted.

And people had said New Yorkers didn't give a damn about their neighbours.

I need to get Katrina out of here, right away.

One more thing troubled me. I was still here. Still Gem. Was the myth just a myth? I'd killed my sire, but I was still young, still beautiful, still a vampire. I stepped to the mirror to see for myself, touched my vibrant cheeks, my plush lips.

"What's the matter?" Katrina whispered.

"I'm still alive."

"Undead," she corrected me, her face stern and pale. "The bullet that killed him...had my blood on it, maybe that insulated you from the consequences of killing your sire."

"If that's true, you saved my life."

"You saved mine first."

We both giggled like school girls.

She fainted. A side-effect of vampire dust medicine or the loss of blood? I didn't know which. This was new territory for me. I'd made the paste out of instinct, not direct know-how or experience, even surprised myself at how well it had worked. But now I'd have to carry her out of here.

I lugged her to the front door but hesitated opening it. Her arms and legs hung limp. Her blouse dripped blood. Anyone seeing us would think I'd just killed her. And I had a ready-made audience in the hallway, with everyone speculating on what they had heard.

"It was a gunshot, I tell ya," a man's voice said.

"The manager is coming with a key," said another.

"I'm calling the police."

"Call 911. I always wanted to say that."

"Someone in there has a gun," a woman shouted. "I'm not going near that door."

"Anyone in there?"

More pounding.

Gem

I rushed to the window and the fire escape outside. No way did I want to be around to explain the pile of clothes and dust on the floor. Vampire hunting would become a national pastime.

Climbing from the window with Katrina in my arms, we'd be long gone before anyone could muster a key. I leaped to the rooftop next door, hoping beyond hope that I wouldn't be seen.

No Fear

Katrina slept on the sofa. I stood vigil. She'd wake up with a headache from hell, but her wound would be healing, another wound inflicted because of me. How much more could she endure?

The Mjölnir was now calm against my skin under my jacket. I'd not changed or washed. I must have smelled like a quarterback at the end of a match. I'd not even removed my gun and holster. The heat of the sun that entered through our living room window merely warmed me instead of lighting me into flames. I pinched the seared strands of my hair between my fingertips and examined them for a moment, curled and stinky.

We are definitely going for a week at a spa.

Katrina moaned in her sleep, her left hand swatting at something in her dreams. The bruise on her cheek looked more colourful than the autumnal trees in Central Park.

Make that two weeks! With a built-in shopping trip.

I glanced up at the wall clock: seven thirty in the morning. Everything had happened so quickly since dawn. Angel and Maria would be up soon, getting ready for school, making breakfast. I had to get Katrina to her room or risk explaining the bandage and why she was out cold.

Wait a second! They should be up by now!

Victor's mention of them echoed through my mind. Had he kidnapped them, or worse? I dashed towards the back of the apartment, reached Angel's room and paused outside, terrified of what I might find, or not find, inside. I put my hand on the door handle, and as I began to turn it I remembered:

It's Saturday. Angel doesn't have school today.

I had been holding my breath, and I released it in one quick rush. My forehead made contact with her door. A dull thud resonated around the hallway. I detected a startled heartbeat behind the door.

"Maria?" a sleepy child's voice called out. "Katrina? Are you up yet?"

It broke my heart that she didn't think to ask for me in the morning, that she was so used to me being 'out at work' even before she'd brushed her teeth.

I opened the door and slipped inside. "Good morning." I smiled for Angel's sake, to mask my alarm and fatigue. Princesses and prancing ponies patterned the pink walls. Toys lined her shelves, and not a misplaced item of clothing ruined the magazine photo that was Angel's room.

"Gem!" she chirped. Her smile warmed my heart. Blonde curls framed her face, immaculate even though she'd just lifted her head off the pillow.

"Did you sleep well, honey?" I sat on the edge of her bed.

"Are you staying home from work today?"

My hand drifted towards the Mjölnir, fully aware of the new life this artefact had given me, but instead of touching it, I held hands with the little cherub. "Yes, I am. But to do that, I need to get something done this morning. Would you mind staying in bed for a little while longer...until I finish?"

I hated lying to her, but it was better than her seeing Katrina unconscious on the sofa, bruised, and bandaged.

I'd need to buy Katrina a hockey goalie's kit to protect her!

"Okay," Angel said.

I tucked the duvet under her chin, kissed her on the

forehead, and walked out of her room. As soon as I closed her door, two heavy knocks reverberated from the living room. I rushed in with real purpose in my step, pulling the handgun out from under my jacket.

More knocking on the door.

Katrina sat up on the sofa. Her eyes were wide, but her face was hangover white, and she cringed from the pain she was obviously feeling in her head.

With my vampire stealth, I approached the door, but before I could sneak a peek through the security spy hole, a heavy fist pounded again. And then came a voice that Katrina and I knew well.

"Gem, are you in there?"

John Bradley!

I unlocked the deadbolt. Bradley, all twitchy and nervy, sprang into our apartment. He was not the John Bradley we had come to know. Gone was the designer suit, replaced by denim jeans that looked to be stained with motor oil or dried blood. He wore a pair of old Nikes, clearly clocked up on mileage. His white t-shirt, tight over his muscular upper body, was blood-stained, and the leather jacket he wore was scuffed at the elbows and torn at one cuff. A black baseball cap and a carpet of not-so-designer chin stubble completed the look. His bloodshot eyes told me he'd gotten little sleep.

Maybe this is what his drug addicted brother would have looked like, if he had one!

I placed my gun on the side table. "What are you doing here?"

He stalked across the room to the window and peered down to the street. The curtains shook in the grip of his fingers. Sweat shined his cheeks. I saw a desperate man, afraid of his own shadow.

"What's wrong?"

He turned terrified eyes to me, and then realisation must've struck him hard enough to sideline his own fears.

"Why aren't you in your coffin? It's daytime."

"Keep your voice down, Bradley." The Mjölnir tingled against my skin. "We've got our own problems."

He looked down at Katrina and couldn't miss the blood-spatter on her clothes, the sprinkling of dust, or the white bandage taped on her shoulder. "What happened to her?"

"We've had a rough night."

He looked back to me. "I need your help more than ever. Did you sign up that other vampire?"

"No. I killed him."

"That was stupid, Gem."

"It was necessary."

"The Gods have assassinated my entire organization. They fire-bombed my apartment. I'm on the run for my life. I needed two of you to stop them. They're everywhere."

Katrina's face turned harsh, a mix of fear and rage. "And you came here? What if they followed you?"

"Where else am I to go? I'm sorry if I'm fucking up your fantasy family lifestyle, but Gem has to protect me."

And now he's gone too far!

"My family comes first, Bradley."

He shook his head. "And when the Gods kick your door in, is that what you're going to tell them?"

"If you've led them here..." Katrina struggled to her feet, an index finger pointed at his face. "...to our home, where Angel lives, too, I'll choke you to death myself."

"You won't have time for that," he growled out. "You'll be dead. Angel will be dead. Maria will be dead, and Gem, there's nothing you can do to stop them, not without help, and you just killed the only vampire who could have saved you."

My ire exploded. Not only did he bring danger to our door and tell me I was powerless against his enemies, but he spoke of my family like I couldn't protect them. My fangs yearned for his blood and split my gums. With a single hand I plucked him off the floor by his throat and banged his back against the wall.

"Don't ever—"

"Gem, no." Katrina lunged forward but tripped over her own feet, still tipsy on vampire dust. Her knees hit the side table, which sent my gun skittering across the floor. It came to a halt in front of a pair of slipper-clad feet.

Maria's feet.

Shock gouged deep lines in her face. I could see how this looked to her: a handgun on the floor, Katrina battered and bandaged, Bradley pinned against the wall by my sinewy arm, his feet dangling inches off the floor, not to mention I'd grown the most vicious fangs ever seen on a beautiful woman's face. She slapped both hands to her chest then crumpled to the floor.

Maria!

"Heart attack," Bradley said.

I shoved him to the door. "Get out!"

He didn't question me, just ran out of the apartment, baseball cap tumbling off his head. The Gods were less of a threat to him than my loosed temper.

I sprinted to Maria and checked her pulse. As I slid my fingers along her neck, desperately hoping that there would be at least a murmur, I called to Katrina. "Get the phone."

"Got it." She already held the handset and was punching in 9-1-1.

I found Maria's pulse. Weak, yes. Sporadic. But there. I grabbed a cushion from the sofa and placed it under her head.

Katrina gave our address to the dispatcher.

I adjusted Maria's night clothes to protect her dignity. What a mess I'd made of my family.

Katrina stood wobbly on her feet.

Maria lay on the floor, dying.

And Angel was still in her room. My vampire senses told me she was too terrified to come out.

The ambulance was on its way, but I couldn't see beyond the darkness that was engulfing our family, threatening to extinguish all our vital signs. Forever.

I may still be a vampire, but my time with Victor has changed me.

I'd tried so hard to keep a protective barrier around those who I loved, and yet it seemed that, time and time again, I had failed.

Maybe they'd all be better off without me.

Katrina fell back onto the couch, pale and visibly sapped of all her vigour.

Pull yourself together, Gem! You've got people relying on you!

Maria moaned. Her eyelids fluttered. I fetched a glass of water from the kitchen and crouched over her. She parted her lips, and I carefully dripped a few drops into her mouth.

"Aspirin," she muttered.

Katrina dragged herself off the couch. "I'll get it."

I should have remembered. An aspirin tablet under the tongue could save a heart attack victim. "I'm so sorry," I whispered. For the first time since I had known her, Maria looked frail.

I've done this to her.

She had never asked any questions or probed into my activities. She was never aware that I had a secret identity, like Batman, and that my name struck fear into the heart of the criminal underworld. But I didn't need rubber suits and fancy gadgets to get my job done.

Although a rubber suit would have been cool!

And now she knew exactly what I was because she had walked in on me doing what I did best, but doing it in the wrong place and at the wrong time. I had sworn that my work life and home life would never collide, but I had lied to myself.

Bradley had become a constant visitor. And Katrina was, not that long ago, a target for my assassin skills. I squeezed my eyes shut as my thoughts turned to Angel and how she had come into my care.

A man I'd been paid to kill shot her mother while he attempted a desperate escape...from me.

All this time, I thought I was using my powers to protect my family, these three people I would die for, but behind the façade, all I had done was bring them harm.

Katrina returned with the aspirin and put one in Maria's mouth.

The Mjölnir trembled against my skin. It felt warm, life affirming. And as if I'd just ran a marathon, a wave of endorphins coursed through my veins.

If we get through this alive, it's over. I don't need to be the vampire bitch anymore, the hit woman for one lesser criminal over another—

"Gem," Maria said in a voice quieter than a whisper. I looked down at her and stroked her face gently.

Sirens wailed in the distance.

"Just rest," I told her. "I'm so sorry."

"Gem, you think I don't know you are different?" The tremble in her voice told me it hurt her to talk, to drag breath down into her lungs, but her strong gaze affirmed she would not be silenced. "I love you for all that you are because I know that you are good."

Stinging tears streamed from my eyes, and when I looked across to Katrina, I saw her sobbing, as well.

"I love you too, Maria."

She coughed. "You are in danger again, yes?"

"Nothing I can't handle." I lied.

The guilt in my eyes must've betrayed me.

"Then Angel is in danger." Maria inhaled a raspy breath. "In the top drawer of my dresser is my sister's address. Take Angel there until the danger is passed." She closed her eyes and sucked in a slow, deep breath that hissed through her teeth.

The ambulance was now very close.

"Hold on, Maria, they're—"

"It will take more than this to kill me."

The siren shrieked right outside our window.

Katrina staggered to the front door and wrestled it open. The elevator dinged its arrival. Footsteps charged down the hallway.

"In here," Katrina said. "Hurry."

Two paramedics rushed into our living room. One headed directly to Maria. "We'll take it from here, miss."

I scrambled out of the way.

Katrina collapsed on the floor, every bit of energy gone.

The taller paramedic knelt beside her and popped open his medical kit. "What's her name?"

"Katrina."

He bent over her. "Katrina, can you hear me?"

"I'm all right," she moaned, ever the fighter.

The other paramedic strapped a blood pressure cuff on Maria's arm. "And what's your name?"

"M-Maria," she stammered.

He squeezed the cuff pump bulb. "As soon as we are sure you are stable, we'll get you to the hospital."

Katrina showed her mental strength despite her body's current state of weakness. "Take Maria first."

Within minutes, she was in the back of the ambulance and another had been called to transport Katrina. I sat on the sofa with my arm around her. "Maria will be okay."

"I don't need to go to the hospital." Katrina pouted.

"This time you'll do what you're told," I said firmly, thinking how last time she didn't listen to me, she'd ended up as Victor's hostage.

"Gem! I'm not hurt that bad, I…"

The paramedic approached. "Look, I've got to be

straight with you, Katrina. You're splattered with blood, and I believe that bandage might be covering a gunshot wound. I need to inform the cops."

"It's nothing, really," Katrina said.

"You don't need to involve the police," I added.

When they find out I'm a vampire, that I used vampire dust on Katrina's wound, I'm going to lose Angel!

While the rest of my world turned to shit, I knew that as long as I had that little sweetheart to focus on, then everything else would fall into place.

He reached for Katrina's loose bandage. She batted his hand away. "This is an old injury that's nearly healed. This morning I fell and got a bloody nose..." she pointed out the blood spatter on her clothes then indicated her cheek, "and a nasty bruise."

"You look like you've been beaten, miss."

Katrina signed one of her Oscar-winning sighs. "I'm careless, clumsy. Give me a break!"

"I don't need to know what went on here, but the cops will. I'm sorry, ladies."

"Ask the neighbours," Katrina added. "See if they heard any gunshots. Check with the hospital. They'll have my records. I was shot while in the park two weeks ago."

She had me convinced, but he pulled out his mobile phone and turned his back to us.

I raised my eyebrows at her.

She shrugged, and I knew that she hadn't thought this lie through entirely, that she had just reacted.

I love you, Katrina.

The conversation was brief. The paramedic hung up and turned to us. "The hospital confirmed you were treated for a bullet wound, Katrina, so I'm not going to call the cops. But I insist that you come with us."

"No, I'm fine. You can't make me—"

"She'll go with you," I said just as the second ambulance arrived.

"I thought you were on my side," Katrina said.

"They'll find out you're okay, and that'll be the end of it." I hoped anyway. "I'll get Angel settled at Maria's sister's and check on you both afterwards."

She knew better than to argue against me, and after a gentle kiss on her cheek, she let herself be escorted out of the front door and to her ambulance. For the second time that morning I walked to Angel's room with a heart full of trepidation and tension.

How do I explain all that has happened to her?

No Secrets

Maria's sister, Gloria, lived over the river in Queens with her husband Dean. I'd packed an overnight bag for Angel, and she grabbed a couple of her favourite toys before we headed over the bridge in the Porsche. Angel had not exactly been silent on the journey but certainly more quiet than usual. John Bradley had been calling my cell phone continuously, so I'd finally relented and switched the damn thing off.

My family comes first from now on, Bradley. First, second, and third.

Dean stood on the front stoop and looked at us with a sceptical crook on his brow, me, a sleek sexy woman whose bite *was* worse than her bark, and Angel, a little five-year-old packed for an indefinite sleepover. "Of course, we are happy to look after her," he said, his smile guarded.

"Who are you?" Angel asked him.

He glanced at me as if to say *I'll handle this*. "I'm your uncle Dean, young lady. Maria is my wife's sister."

Angel retreated behind my leg.

"I have some ice cream treats," he added. "If you like ice cream, that is."

She nodded.

He held out his hand to her. "I'll show you how many

flavours we have."

"Bubblegum?" she asked, barely loud enough to hear.

"Let's go see."

Cautiously, she took his hand, and the pair headed off towards the kitchen.

Gloria invited me in. "I see in your face that you worry about Maria, but she is one tough cookie." Gloria reached for my hand, but when she touched it, she instinctively pulled away as though she'd suddenly realized how cold it was. "And she thinks the world of Angel. And Katrina too. She talks about them all the time. But she tells me nothing of your life, Miss Gem. It's like she doesn't even know you."

"I work a lot." Lame, but a quick answer, and I smiled, despite the ache in my heart for the perilous impact my lifestyle has had on those closest to me. "I just want Maria to be okay."

"Of course you do, and she knows that. She never married, and she has no children, so she has taken you all to her heart."

I found myself reminiscing about all the things she had done for us, and I hoped that I would have the chance to do something special for her.

"But she is getting older now," Gloria said. "I think that maybe she needs to slow down now. Do you understand what I'm suggesting? We don't want her to have another heart attack."

I understood. She wanted Maria to quit working for me.

"Maria needs a life of her own."

And so do I.

Dean brought Angel back into the room, toting an ice cream cone.

"I got chocolate!" She beamed.

"Fresh out of bubblegum," he said.

I felt pleased that she finally had a happy expression

on her face, as well as chocolate smears.

"Are you going to be okay for tonight?" I asked her.

"Sure...but..." She turned solemn. "I'll miss Maria reading me a bedtime story." Tears filled her eyes and threatened to spill over. Her shoulders shuddered and her bottom lip curled. Ice cream melted across the back of her hand.

"We'll be just fine," Dean said. "How about I read to you tonight?" He dropped to his knees and looped an arm around her shoulders. "We should let Gem go now, to make sure Maria and Katrina are okay."

Angel agreed, and after planting a kiss on her forehead, I exited the house and strode back towards my parked car. The realization that Maria didn't really know me hurt like a chest full of broken glass. It was nearly midday, and the sun beat down on the road and my Porsche. The Mjölnir hung from my neck but had no adverse effect on me. No headaches. No visions. I hoped that it had, as Victor suggested, bonded with me. I needed its strength more than ever.

A male voice called out to me. "Gem! Wait up a minute, would you?"

I turned to see Dean jogging down the footpath towards me.

My throat tightened with angst. "Dean? Is Angel okay? What's wrong?"

"Angel is fine, but I'm worried about you and Katrina. Look, it's none of my business, but now my family is involved with your family. I just want to know that whatever trouble you're in you can sort it out. Assure me that my family isn't in danger, or this arrangement isn't going to work out."

I appreciated his honesty and his desire to protect his family. "It's nothing I can't handle, Dean."

"Really? Gloria tells me Katrina has been shot twice in two weeks. Your housekeeper has a heart attack." His voice was calm, not accusatory. "You have to hand Angel over to us, relative strangers."

"Your family is our family." I hoped he'd understand that.

"Oh yeah? Then tell me, Gem, when was the last time you were over for dinner?"

Never. I suck blood, but I can't tell him—

"Did you ever send Gloria a birthday card?"

What was it they said, truth hurts? His point struck sharp as a dagger to the heart. As much as I touted the importance of family, I wasn't much of a family participant, not like real family members were. Truth was, I didn't know how to insert myself any deeper than the superficial *Aunt Gem*, always working.

"You got anything to say about that?"

"I'm sorry," was all I would tell him. The truth about me being a vampire couldn't possibly help him understand.

"I see the way you look at Angel. You love her. That's clear, Gem. So do what you have to do and get back here so you can look after her properly. That's all." He shrugged and began to walk back to his house.

"Dean," I called. "I will take care of Angel. I promise."

He stopped and turned back to me. "It's not me you have to convince, my dear. I think the one who needs convincing is you." He walked away.

I got into my car and watched him trudge, head down, back to Gloria and Angel waving goodbye to me on the stoop. New tears blurred my vision, but I cleared my thoughts and drove off. I had no right to endanger their lives. The dark cloud over my head rained on everyone around me.

And that has to change...before someone I love gets killed.

***

After a brief stop at a sporting goods store to buy a heavy-duty rucksack and leather holdall, I visited four separate banks and emptied all of my accounts. The tellers were helpful, but the managers looked like they were going to cry.

And I thought I was the emotional one!

Carrying nearly ten million in cash and banker's bonds stashed in my Porsche's trunk and divided evenly between the rucksack and holdall, I arrived at my lawyer's office in mid-town Manhattan.

I made my wishes about the deeds to my apartment clear to my sixty-year-old brief, Andrew Kirby.

His mouth dropped open in exasperation. "You're not kidding, are you?"

"I'm not."

He fiddled with his tie while shaking his head no as if he was trying to send me a subliminal message to stop the nonsense.

"Prepare the papers for me as soon as possible."

"If you insist, Gem. I can have everything drawn up for you by seven thirty tonight. Shall I have them couriered over to you?"

"I'll pick them up myself."

His professional demeanour, usually so unflappable, took over again. "May I ask you a question, Gem?"

"Depends."

"Am I to assume that this ends our working relationship?"

"I'm afraid so, Mister Kirby." This was a big step for me to take. "Thank you for the discretion you have shown to me over the years."

He put his hand out to me.

I met it and we shook.

"Seven thirty then," he said. "You can sign the documents. My assistant will be your witness."

I left his office, my body filled with a warm glow that

had little to do with the sun.

I'm taking the sun for granted already.

Before I got to my car, I took a moment to sit on a nearby bench. I had watched New York City from the rooftops after dark for so long, it felt soulful to sit and watch it thrive all around me in daylight. The city held so many memories for me, and so many of them were bad. Clare's death. Victor Kyle. Clayton nearly raping me. Maloney nearly killing me. But the good memories were the ones I would hold close to my heart:

Angel. Katrina. Maria.

One name was missing from both lists, good or bad.

John Bradley.

The last time I saw him, he was begging me to help him, and in spite of everything he'd done for me over the years, I'd kicked him out, decreeing family over job. I'd used family as weapon against my responsibility to him. How betrayed and abandoned he must have felt as the door slammed behind him, I could only imagine. It was time for me to step up and do what I had to do.

I fished my cell phone out of my jacket and powered it up. It beeped to tell me I had a message. I called my service.

"Gem, it's John. John Bradley."

He sounds scared.

"I'm at the Plaza. Ask for me at reception. The God's might know I'm here. They're close. Gem. I need your help. Please... please."

The message ended. I hung up, dialled his number. It rang and went to voicemail. "Leave a message."

I groaned. Phone tag. I hung up. The Plaza was a huge luxury hotel uptown. He'd be safe there, for now. The Gods would have to breach security to get to him. Not an easy task at the Plaza. The drug-pushing British Gods had become a nasty loose end I'd have to tie up before I could leave New York. Otherwise, the city would become a cesspool of Puritan-addicted citizens. I decided to see Bradley after I'd picked up my documents from Andrew Kirby's office.

I'm going to settle things with my family...just in case I don't live through a confrontation with The Gods.

***

Maria was much better, stable but lightly sedated to ensure she rested. I sat in her room for half an hour, holding her hand and listening to her breathe and the monitors beep. The soft throb of the Mjölnir matched Maria's pulse and had a relaxing effect on me, but the insanity of the last few days kept me on edge, like a shark's fin cutting through calm water.

I blinked once, twice, my eyelids heavy with fatigue. I closed them, inhaled, and searched for safer seas.

This feels good.

A gentle squeeze on my hand brought me back to full alert. Maria's eyes were open, gazing at me, slightly glazed, but they still burnt with her contagious energy.

"Hi." I tried not to alarm her with any hint of concern in my expression.

"I will be okay, Gem," she whispered, her voice rough in her throat like she'd swallowed stones. "Do what you must for Angel. And do it now."

She fell back asleep, still holding my hand, and I wondered for a moment if I'd dreamt her words.

Or perhaps the Mjölnir had revealed them to me.

Either way, her sentiment was right. I drew the back of her hand up to my mouth and gently kissed each knuckle. "I'm on it, Maria. It'll all be over tonight, and then we'll be free." I placed her hand gently down on the sheet and left.

Katrina lay in a room just down the corridor. Her hard expression told me she was not happy about staying the night.

"I'm all right, Gem, I don't need to be here."

"It's safer here." I looked into her eyes in a way that I hoped conveyed my sincerity. "I've decided to help Bradley deal with The Gods."

"Gem," she gasped out, "you're not serious."

"I can't just cut him adrift."

"But The Gods, you can't take them on by yourself."She kicked a sleek leg over the edge of the bed. "I could help you."

Grabbing her ankle stopped from getting up. "You're more use to me here, looking after Maria. I'll come back for you after I sort things out."

I didn't want to alarm her with details or alert her to the difference between *sort things out* and do another *hit* for Bradley, especially when this hit would be the toughest hit of all.

No Loose Ends

I left Kirby's office at ten past seven that evening. The deeds were signed and witnessed. He'd placed them inside a plain envelope. I trotted down the steps and stuffed the envelope safely inside my knee-length black leather coat.

One more job done. One more loose end tied up.

The meter I'd parked the car in front of still had plenty of time to run, and because Bradley's hideout at the Plaza was just across Central Park, I decided to walk rather than try to secure another parking space. The sun was about to set.

This may be my last chance to see New York at night.

That was the romantic notion in me, of course. There was also the hardened professional in me that heard the fear in Bradley's voice, that he was certain The Gods were hot on his tail. I didn't want them to see my car in a Plaza parking spot. I wanted all possible exit routes open to me. A couple of popped tyres or a shotgun blast through my Porsche's engine block wouldn't help matters any.

That would be more annoying than a split nail!

The setting sun cast long shadows across the Park and illuminated the autumn trees in a spectacular palette of colours, striking in contrast to the deep green lawns. Romantic couples, old and young, breezed through the early evening hand-in-hand, smiles, laughter, love, all filling the air with an aura of true happiness. While I was able to appreciate the sweetness of the moment, I was also rendered deeply saddened by the scene.

I'd never have this with Katrina, not here in New York like we'd planned.

But then it struck me that the setting of our lives wasn't the important thing. My finger tips gently brushed the Mjölnir, and I was warmed with the freedom it offered us. In New York City there would always be a Maloney, a Clayton, a John Bradley.

In New York City I would always be Gem. Killer. Assassin. Hit-woman. Always putting my family in danger.

With steely determination, I exited the Park opposite The Plaza where the horse-drawn carriages were parked. As usual, the horses whinnied and backed away from me, but I ignored them. The light changed to *walk*, and I crossed the street.

At The Plaza's main entrance, the concierge swung the door open for me. I slipped a twenty into his free hand and swaggered, full of confidence, up to the reception desk.

The lady on duty greeted me with a smile. "Good evening, madam."

"My colleague John Bradley is staying here. Which room is he in, please?"

Her smile didn't falter as she referenced the computer screen in front of her. "If you would tell me your name, I'll check to see if you are on his approved contact list."

Good boy, Bradley.

"Gem," I said.

"Just Gem?" Again professionally spoken. That smile

would not have given away there was anything out of the ordinary going on had the conversation been overheard by an unwanted third party.

"Just Gem," I repeated.

"Room 937. Use the elevator to your right." She waved her left hand in the direction I should go. "Ninth floor."

"Is anyone up there with him?"

"Not that I know of."

"Thank you." I turned and walked towards the elevator, confident The Gods had not yet made their entrance.

The elevator carried me upwards, and the doors slid back on the ninth floor. I walked briskly to Bradley's room. Listened through the door. Nothing. I rapped gently, my vampire senses permeating the room beyond. A sudden tide of tension washed back over me.

"Come in," a male voice called. A male voice that did not belong to John Bradley.

This is not good.

My fangs burst from my gums, and my heartbeat threatened to shatter my ribcage. Not knowing what I was walking into, I could only picture the worst: Bradley trussed up like a turkey on the floor, Gods armed to the teeth all gunning for me.

Just my kind of party. I turned the handle and stepped in, eyes scanning the room for danger.

No one waited at the floor-to-ceiling windows that overlooked 5th Avenue. Deep, comfortable couches sat empty in front of a dark flat-screen TV. Bar stools stood vacant. But someone was here. I heard breathing, around a corner, in the dining area, and down the hallway from the entry vestibule: two bedrooms, at least one person in each room. I smelled their nervous sweat. And I sensed a faint hint of Bradley's presence, somehow muffled and exuding the aroma of blood.

Is he dead or alive?

Somehow The Gods had gotten in past security. Maybe they were gods...or ghosts. My fangs quivered in my gums.

Staying close to the wall, I slinked to the corner, peered around. A crystal chandelier hung above a thick wooden table with six chairs, one occupied: a blond man, his back to me, shoulders broad enough to support a bulldozer. He wore a tight-fitting white t-shirt, jeans, and a leather shoulder holster. A handgun sat on the table. A Nike holdall slumped at his feet.

Jeeze, it's Bruce Willis on steroids.

He turned in his chair and looked me up and down like I was fresh beef on the butcher's hook. "So you're Gem. Not exactly what I expected."

I had a flashback to the first time I met Maloney. He didn't expect what he'd seen either, a sexy woman, hot from head to toe. "You'll find I'm full of surprises. Where's Bradley?"

"Close by."

They've got him tied up in one of the rooms!

"If you bring him out here now, we'll leave nice and quiet like, and I'll forget I ever saw you."

"Oh no you won't." His forehead creased in anger. "You killed my brother." Spittle flew from his lips.

I didn't know which member of his gang he was referring to; I'd killed so many of them. "He probably had it coming."

"You're the last bitch standing in Bradley's drug-free empire, a super efficient assassin, I hear. We had to torture Bradley before he told us that you're a..." *Vampire?* "trained sniper. Ex-military." He leaned over and wrapped his fingers around the handle of the sports bag at his feet. "Sorry, gorgeous, but you're not going to shoot your way out of this one."

Bradley hadn't told them what I really was.

~222~

Gem

He stood, clutching the bag, and as if on queue, the bedroom doors opened, both at once. Four more blond Gods stepped out. They brandished silenced handguns, big calibre, one in each hand.

As the boss God placed the bag on the table and started to unzip it, eight gun barrels were levelled on me.

They have no idea what they are dealing with.

I cast them all a sly smile. "I'll give you one last chance to tell me where Bradley is."

Boss God reached his hand into the bag. "Right here." He yanked the contents from the bag and tossed it at me.

John Bradley's head tumbled through the air towards me, his dead eyes cold and blank, his mouth contorted and frozen as if he'd died with a painful scream on his lips. His neck hadn't been severed cleanly. Ragged strands of sinew, muscle, and veins told me his head had been brutally hacked off.

And he hadn't told them the truth about me, loyal to the end.

I ducked Bradley's head, and as it bounced off the carpet, The Gods opened fire. Slugs whistled into my body with perfect accuracy. I twitched to the left, to the right, but kept my balance. My blood splattered for metres, my leather coat was peppered to shreds, but I didn't go down. Bradley hadn't ratted me out as a vampire, so they were plugging me full of regular lead bullets. They stung a bit, and ruined my expensive coat, but they had no more affect on me than mosquito bites.

When their clips were empty, the dumbfounded looks on their faces was priceless.

"What the fuck?" Boss God shouted.

I grabbed up the severed head and threw it at him with all my vampire strength. They met, forehead to forehead with a bony crack, and the giant dropped to the floor, taking a chair with him.

"Shit," a God said behind me.

I turned quickly and tore out his throat. Blood spray painted the walls a macabre maroon. The other three stepped back from me and tripped over each other's feet as they scrambled to get into the bathroom.

"You're next." I lunged at them. With quick kicks, I caved in one guy's ribs, burst another's heart with my heel, and in a shower of gore, I sliced the last God's throat with my index fingernail. Instinct took over. I opened my mouth and clamped my teeth on the wound. His life-giving blood slipped down my throat, warm and luscious as steaming coco on a winter's day. I wanted to roar in victory but two more goons appeared from out of nowhere.

With a swipe of my hand so fast it was impossible to see with human eyes, I snatched the gun from the nearest God and turned it on them both.

Terror clouded their faces. The unarmed God raised his hands in surrender. The still-armed goon appeared to be weighing his chances of getting off a shot before I did. I must have looked like every nightmare these fuckers had ever seen all rolled into one. With two quick pumps of the trigger, they joined the rest of their merry band in hell.

Well, not all of them.

Boss God isn't dead. Yet.

I turned back to the dining room where Bradley's dead eyes looked up at me from the floor. The hulking Brit I expected to see lying prone next to Bradley's head was gone, and the door to the balcony and fire exit beyond stood open.

Damn it!

I didn't like leaving loose ends, but I had no choice. There was one lucky God running on the streets of New York tonight. I just hoped he had the common sense to keep running.

***

Wearing a man's trench coat I'd found on one of the

beds, I left the Plaza fifteen minutes later. My hair was wet from the quick shower I'd taken to remove the blood, both mine and the goons' who'd called themselves Gods. I felt nourished and energised. The envelope that I'd gotten from Kirby, complete with a couple newly acquired bullet holes, was now relocated to a pocket in my newly acquired coat.

I kept my head up as I walked, scanning the crowd for oversized blond baboons but none crossed my field of vision. Keeping to the busy streets, I made it back to my car without incident. Despite the number of deaths in room 937, the actual action was over in seconds and had drawn no unwanted attention.

I feel sorry for maid when she finds that mess in the morning.

I reached my car and pressed the alarm fob while glancing back where I had come from to make sure I didn't have a tail. I doubted Boss God would want to play any more games with me tonight, but I would be stupid to think he would let this lie.

All clear.

I checked the trunk to see the rucksack and holdall were still safely in place. With Bradley dead and his empire in ruins, I was suddenly unemployed, as I'd intended all along, just not this brutally.

At least now I don't have to write an uncomfortable resignation letter.

If Bradley's murder had happened just a few short weeks ago, I may have felt differently. His vision of a New York City free of drugs was a hope that I fully supported, but as my family became more and more at risk, the decision to quit was made easier for me.

Who am I kidding?

I was the one who chose the path of my undead life. I could try to deflect the blame onto Bradley as much as I liked, but at the end of the day, the blame was mine, and mine alone.

At the end of the day.

It seemed fitting that the last throes of my New York life would play out under the watchful eye of the moon rather than under the glow of the midday sun. I opened the car and rummaged around in the glove box until I found my mobile phone. I made my call to the airport and checked my watch. I had three hours. My next stop was the hospital.

***

Katrina lay in her hospital bed, eyes wide in shock and surprise. I sat in the only seat, a holdall full of money at my feet. In the stark fluorescent light, I told Katrina everything. Almost.

She doesn't need to know that John Bradley had his head hacked from his neck.

"The town may be crawling with drug Gods, so I can't stay long. I want you to get a cab, collect Angel, and go to the airport." I reached down, unzipped the holdall, and pulled out a wad of dollars. "This should be enough to cover the private jet I chartered."

"Where are we going?"

"As far from New York City as possible."

"What about Maria?" Katrina was already looking stronger, ready for a fight, but I needed to keep her out of this one.

"She's too weak to travel right now. Besides, it's time she enjoyed her retirement." I tipped my head to the bag. "I've got her retirement fund right here."

Katrina grinned. "And she could still come and see us, see Angel?"

"I hope so."

Katrina got up and started getting dressed.

I'd love to stay and watch...but...

"I'm going to see Maria. Be safe."

"You too."

I picked up the holdall and walked to Maria's room,

pulling the envelope from the coat pocket as I went. Maria's room was dark, and I could hear her breathing. I took a seat next to her bed and held her hand. Her eyelids fluttered open.

"Gem," she whispered, a small relief in her voice, and then drifted back to sleep. I was glad. It would be easier this way. I found a pen tucked inside a puzzle book and wrote Maria a note on the envelope I had brought from Kirby's office.

#

Dearest Maria,

Katrina, Angel and I must leave New York immediately. We will be in touch, and you will see us again someday. (skip over the bullet hole) The money in the holdall is for your retirement, a small compensation for everything you have done for us. Inside this envelope are the deeds to the apartment. It is yours now. Thank you for being our dear sweet Maria. You were the closest thing to a mother hen these three chicks ever had.

Love always,

(bullet hole) Gem.

#

By the time I finished writing, tears dripped off my face. One struck my signature and smudged it a little. I placed the pen and the envelope on Maria's bedside table, kissed her softly on the forehead, and left before my heartache convinced me to stay. If Boss God had managed to tail me, then I needed to lead him away from here to ensure Katrina had safe passage. I just had one more hit to do. Then get to the airport on time.

***

I pulled the Porsche away from the curb and picked up on a tail instantly. A chunky Mercedes SUV followed never more than one car behind me. As I'd learned from experience, The Gods never travelled alone, but in packs, some in the forefront, others in the shadows for backup.

Sneaky bastards.

I had a full tank of gas, so I weaved my way through Manhattan, doubling back on myself time and time again. I didn't do any rash manoeuvres or try to lose them in hopes I would flush out a second car.

That was the one I was more worried about.

I could deal with The Gods in the SUV on my tail.

For I am Gem, the most powerful vampire in the world. The Daywalker!

But as close to invincible as anyone could possibly be, I could be powerless against the hordes of bad guys Boss God would surely send after me. Silver bullets. Wooden stakes. Holy water. I could bet on Victor's dust that they'd send everything in a vampire hunter's arsenal against me. The battle had to be waged here tonight, before I left town for good.

After forty five minutes of playing kiss chase with the SUV hanging back the entire time, I decided I had just the one tail and cut across mid-town to the airport expressway. The approach road was clear, and I accelerated up the ramp, eyes on the rear-view mirror. The SUV fell in behind me.

They're about to make their move!

My fangs itched to pierce my gums and the bad guys' throats.

I merged onto the expressway and changed lanes to the left

The SUV signalled to follow me.

A sports car cut across the lane in front of it, forcing the SUV to swerve heavily.

Here's my chance!

I accelerated hard across three lanes to the exit, dodging cars, except one, another black Mercedes that careened into the front left side of the Porsche.

Shit! There's the backup!

Gem

The impact collapsed my left front suspension and catapulted the Porsche into a violent rollover: once, twice, three times. Red tail lights, skyscraper windows aglow, star-streaked heavens, red tail lights, white windows, stars, all spinning in a blur like an out-of-focus kaleidoscope. Industrial volume punches rained on the car's chassis every time it impacted the roadway, and I was jammed and jarred in my safety belt. Glass compressed and shattered, pummelling me with sharp shards.

No human could survive this crash!

The car stopped spiralling and slid sideways on its roof, sparks flying as the body work was stripped bare of its expensive paint job. I brace myself for impact with the central barrier, had a moment to consider how lucky I'd been that nothing else had struck me, and then with a bump, a grind, and a lurch, the Porsche hit the wall and flipped back upright on its flattened tires, officially dead on the road.

I quickly checked that the Mjölnir was still in place.

No!

It was gone, now part of the wreckage strewn across the highway. I didn't need it right now, not while the moon was in the sky, but I'd have to find it once I'd dealt with The Gods. I had them right where I wanted them.

Popping my seat belt, I tumbled out through the broken windscreen. Glass crunched under my feet. Blood dripped down into my left eye.

Not for long.

I focussed my vampire healing powers on the gash in my forehead, but the blood kept flowing.

What's wrong with me?

I looked back along the highway. The two SUVs had blocked off the road, and now eight Gods were advancing on me. The fuckers multiplied like rabbits.

One remained at the road block, Boss God, battered and bruised from his earlier encounter with me. My heightened hearing detected him telling the other drivers to stay in their cars, as this was an undercover bust going down. Cars travelling the opposite direction slowed, and morose faces stared out at me as they went by.

The hulking Gods drew their handguns. Horns blared. Voices rose with warnings and screams, "Run, lady, run."

But I still had one advantage over the killers.

I am Gem!

Their arms straightened in unison, guns aiming towards me, Gods approaching like a wall of death. One ordered the others to hold their fire until they got closer.

They don't know who the fuck they're dealing with!

I sucked in a deep breath.

But they will in a moment!

I tensed every muscle in my body.

Soon everyone will know what has been living amongst them. I can't keep what I am a secret any longer.

I leapt, and as I broke gravity's laws, my fangs poked through my gums. But something had changed. Instead of euphoric, orgasmic pleasure, I felt piercing pain. My gums suddenly hurt. And as my muscles grew buff, they ached like I needed a few hours in a sauna. What the hell? My fingernails extended into talons. Ingrown talons? I may have looked like every Twilight nerds' wet dream, but my undead senses felt tingly numb instead of sparkly alert.

I heard piss release from the nearest God's bladder just a half second before I jumped in front of him and snapped his neck. As he fell to the roadway, I jammed a foot into the chin of another steroid-using fool. His head flicked back with a crack, and he joined his fellow goon on the deck.

Two down six to go! Why am I out of breath?

One ran at me, and I twisted him into a head lock just as his friends finally found their balls and opened fire. I turned towards the firing squad and used their buddy as a shield. It was a waste of good blood, but better I spill his than any more of mine. I needed all my energy to finish this fight.

I threw his bullet riddled, blood splattered, lifeless corpse at the line of goons, and they tumbled over like bowling pins. Five skull stomps later, it was over for them. Despite their delusions of grandeur, eight Gods now had their blood spilt all over the freeway.

And I'm ready for a nap!

Traffic in the other lane sped away, as if the drivers were in fear for their lives, and a series of minor bumps and scrapes gave me the chance to make my exit. I got ready to jump for the nearest skyscraper but suddenly remembered the rucksack.

My multi-million dollar retirement fund!

And of course, the Mjölnir.

My key to a normal life with Angel and Katrina.

I advanced on my crumpled Porsche, my heart heavy for having to say goodbye to the sports car. The trunk was intact. In fact, it was jammed tight in the wreck. I took hold of the metal and prepared to tear the trunk lid loose, but I didn't have enough strength left to open a can of sardines.

"You've not forgotten about me, have you?" a familiar voice asked from behind me.

I spun around. Boss God stood ten yards away from me, pointing a rocket propelled grenade launcher straight at my chest.

He grinned.

His index finger squeezed the trigger. A burst of flame sent the missile screeching towards me. I had no time to move so I braced myself for the impact. No matter how hard this thing hit me, I'd bounce right back up and tear the fool's head from his neck.

Karma for what he did to Bradley! Payback by the vampire bitch is a bitch!

His aim was not very good. The missile ricocheted off my shoulder, knocking me to the ground. It struck what was left of my car and exploded, hurling debris into the air. Shrapnel fell all around me, bouncing on the road like hailstones. The steering wheel, bent all out of shape, rolled a manic arc around me. One of the headrests hit me in the thigh and the rucksack full of money, smouldering from one corner, landed not far from my feet, next to the trunk lid. My hair and long trench coat were peppered with tiny specks of hot metal.

I tried to sit up, but the base of my spine screamed out in pain. I tried again, this time using my hands to push myself up.

My hands!

I couldn't believe what I saw. My fingers were twig thin and wormy with veins and bumpy with warts.

Old!

I slumped back down amongst the wreckage. Grey hair hung across my face.

Grey hair? No! Anything but grey hair!

Every muscle in my body ached. Every joint. My front teeth fell out. I was suddenly an eighty-year-old woman.

Mortal again.

For killing Victor, my sire.

How could I have been so wrong? Katrina's blood on the bullet hadn't protected me from the consequences of killing him. The myth wasn't true, after all.

The Mjölnir!

It had kept my physique youthful as the day Victor had turned me into a vampire. And now the pendant was gone, lost somewhere amongst all this scrap iron. That allowed the ageing process to play a wretched game of catch up.

Not now, not now. I had to see Angel one last time, I wanted to see Kat—

"You think I'm stupid?" Boss God's voice dragged me from my thoughts. He stood over me, gun in one hand,

Gem

shit-eating grin across his smug face. "I knew you were a vampire the second our bullets didn't take you down. That's why I made silver slugs for this." He wiggled his handgun. "And I coated my RPG with silver, too."

So this is how it ends.

"I'm an old woman now..."

Just an ugly crone!

"...I could never stop you."

He snorted. "Sorry, sweetheart. Never trust a vampire. Puritan is going to rule this city. You've interfered in my plans for the last time." He aimed the gun at my face.

I wished I could stare down the barrel, but I didn't want him to see me cry. I wasn't afraid to die. I'd done that once before. I was sad to say goodbye to the life I'd come so close to living.

I turned my head to the side. Tears spilled down my cheek and onto the asphalt, the wrecked pieces of my car a blur to my eyes. Smoldering. Dying. Like me.

"You would have made a great ally, Gem," Boss God said, standing above me, my executioner.

"I'd rather die."

"As you wish."

I heard the *click-click* from his gun as he chambered a round, a silver bullet with my name on it. But I was mortal now. Any old lead slug would have done the trick.

Six inches from my face something pulsed, emitting a weak but pure light. My old eyes weren't as sharp as they had been, but I was able to make out the source of this strange phenomenon.

The Mjölnir!

It had bonded with me, after all, necklace chain broken but still calling out to me for a desperate reprieve.

One chance!

A quick glance to Boss God aiming his gun, and then I reached out a decrepit, liver-spotted hand and snatched the pendant.

Nótt, save me!

The highway swirled around. My senses expanded like a bubble of energy. I smelled the sweat on Boss God's skin, heard the slosh of blood in his veins and the muscles in his forearm contract as he began to squeeze the trigger. My heart surged with powerful pumps, my muscles became bear-trap strong, and my body recoiled like shotgun blast.

With all my strength, I sprang to my feet and threw a roundhouse kick that knocked the gun from Boss God's hand. It skittered across the ground, no use to him now. I followed up with a second kick to his chest that sent him staggering backwards.

"No!" he screamed and drew two semi-automatic pistols from his coat pockets.

With two short steps, I bounded to the dislodged trunk lid of my car, scooped it up, and threw it at Boss God like a plastic Frisbee. It struck him just above the hips, sliced him in two halves, and screech-landed twenty yards down the highway. Involuntary muscles contractions gripped his fingers. His guns fired bullets into the ground.

Bam, bam, bam-bam.

I enjoyed the look of surprise plastered on his face just before his guts sloshed out and his torso toppled to the ground, followed by his legs. The Gods had been vanquished, and royally so.

I opened my fist. The Mjölnir glowed with one final pulse, and then dimmed, as if my humanness had sapped its power. I brought it to my lips, broken chain drooping, and kissed its ancient carved surface. "Thank you, Nótt."

The goddess of the *un-light*. My redeemer.

I slipped the pendant into my coat pocket, a memento of my short time as a Daywalker.

"Hey, lady," someone shouted. "Are you all right?"

Time to go.

I stamped out the flames on the rucksack of cash that lay in the road. Lifting it by the handles, I must have been a

Gem

sight for all the rubberneckers and lookie-loos, an old lady in a long coat emerging from the highway rubble, hunched over and shuffling off into the darkness.

No More

The taxi driver didn't ask any questions, but I knew he could hear my sobs from the back seat. His eyes were drawn to his rear-view mirror.

Not so long ago, he'd be trying to catch a glimpse of my cleavage.

I sought my own mirror, my compact, and my stiff fingers slowly opened it. What I saw looking back at me struck terror in my heart like a wooden stake to the chest.

Wrinkles!

A million wrinkles, and those crow's feet gouges at the corners of my vein-webbed eyes. No amount of eye shadow and mascara would ever hide this damage. I'd retained my high cheek bones that had once made me such hot property, though they now reminded me of Lurch on the Addams Family. The sudden change in my hair colour upset my stomach. Long and black was now scraggly and thinning grey. The gasp that escaped my lungs drew words from my driver.

"Are you all right, ma'am?"

"I should be dead."

"Do you want me to take you to a hospital?"

I watched my lips, recently plump and sumptuous, now thin and emaciated, reply, "The morgue would be better."

"Nah. You're too young to die."

That'll earn him a big tip.

"And you're too kind, sir." I ditched the traitorous compact on the floor and kicked it under the seat. "The airport will be fine. Please."

At least my voice was still one I recognised as my own...

For I am Gem!

... and that only made my fate harder to accept. My breath hitched in my chest. I was about to lose control of my emotions. Like my best friend had died. My closest lover. My beauty deserved a proper burial. Oh Katrina. How could she love me when I look like this?

Pull yourself together, Gem.

But I didn't know how I could exist in this decrepit old body. The future I'd dreamt of with Katrina and Angel had been stolen away. As Victor had stolen my human life, in the end he'd stolen the undead life he'd given me. And now I was condemned to die like every other human being on this planet. After all I had done, all I had endured, I'd lost the things that made immortality and bloodsucking worth all the trouble: my body, my beauty, my sexy charm, fuel for my insatiable vanity. All gone now. Forever. The most unstoppable of life's challenges had finally caught up with me, and my biggest fear was that I'd lose Katrina and have to face *old age* alone.

At the airfield gate, I showed a security guard my identification.

He looked at it, looked at me, back and forth a couple times. "You need to get your picture updated, ma'am."

"I was a beauty in my younger days, don't you think?"

"Still are, ma'am." He waved my taxi through.

The driver followed the road out to the private tarmac. A Cessna Sovereign sat under floodlights, the white fuselage aglow under the industrial-sized arc bulbs, its passenger door open with a short set of steps pulled down.

I hope Katrina made it here with Angel all right.

They were going to be shocked to see me. Angel would never understand how this had happened. She wouldn't know me. I'd be a total stranger to her. And Katrina, I couldn't expect her to live with an old hag like me. She deserved someone younger, virile, hot...

I should have told the driver to turn around, drive

away as fast as he could, but even in the face of total rejection, I had the bag of money they would need to start a new life, even if it was without me.

Victor had ruined everything. The Mjölnir was the only reason I hadn't turned old as soon as I'd shot him. It had protected me up to the very end. I pulled the pendant from my pocket, felt its warmth in my doughy palm. I wrapped the broken chain around a gnarly finger, the chain that had kept Nótt close to my heart...

The cab neared the plane. A female shadow formed in the doorway, and then it bounded down the steps.

...Close to my heart. Where it had protected me. I cupped the Mjölnir in my hands and brought them to my chest. Lovingly.

The pendant began to vibrate. I held it tighter.

Slowing, the cab swung around, putting the jet on my side where Katrina's silhouette waited...to open my door...to see what's become of me. To fall back in shock. To run away screaming.

The Mjölnir pulsed and glowed. I drew it away from my chest. The pendant dimmed.

It remembers me, where it belongs, close to my heart!

It wanted me to wear it. I had to put it on. I had to do it quickly.

Feeble fingers fumbled the broken ends of the chain. I slipped them around to the back of my neck. The pendant vibrated wildly, excited as my fingers that clumsily looped the chain into a half knot. It slipped. I caught the loose end. Looped it again. First half-knot.

The cab stopped.

I looped it again. Second half-knot.

Katrina's silhouette approached the door.

I pulled the ends tight. The Mjölnir hummed. I tucked it inside my coat. It felt warm against my skin.

She pulled on the door handle. I turned my face away from her, raised a hand in front of my eyes. The dome light flashed on, revealing the white smooth skin of my hand, perfectly manicured fingernails.

"You're late," Katrina barked.

I wanted to scream with joy. The Mjölnir had saved me again. Saved my life. Saved my future with Katriana and Angel. But I didn't scream; I kept my head low and slipped the driver a wad of cash from the bag at my feet. If he noticed anything different about my hand, he didn't say, probably all choked up over the big tip he'd earned.

"The pilot is waiting," Katrina said.

Now I turned to her and smiled. I wanted to drag her into the back seat with me and have my way with her, but I didn't do that either. Business first. Pleasure later. "Is Angel all right?"

"She's excited about flying. Her first time. So let's go."

I hefted the money bag up and handed it to her. "Then help me with this."

Her eyes were saucers aglow in the airport lights. "How much?"

"Enough." I slid out and inhaled fresh air. With a flip of my head, I whipped my long black hair over my right shoulder.

I hope Katrina noticed.

We stood by the jet wing and watched the cab fade into the distance. She looked me up and down. "You look like road kill."

She should have seen me two minutes ago. I'd looked like death warmed over. I hadn't realized my trench coat had been tattered and torn in the crash.

"What happened to you?"

"I had a little accident on the way to the airport."

The pilot appeared in the doorway. "I'm ready to fire up the engines, ladies. I think you'd better get onboard now."

Katrina swung the bag of cash round and led me to the

jet's door. I followed her up the steps and into a luxurious cabin. Soft lighting. Beige leather. "Business class. Nice."

Angel popped up from behind an executive seatback. "Gem. Gem." She hopped down and ran straight to me, wrapping her arms around my waist. "I missed you!"

I knelt to her and gathered her up in a massive hug. "And I missed you too, Angel." I tried not to let the emotion of the moment overcome me, but when I saw Katrina over Angel's shoulder, the tears came without restraint. My family was safe. We had a future together, after all. Katrina joined our huddle, and we held each other as close as we could.

"What's in the bag?" Angel asked Katrina, ever the curious one.

"Grown up stuff."

"Where are all my toys?"

"We'll buy you new ones."

The jet engines revved to a high-pitched whine, and the pilot asked us to take our seats and buckle up. "Arizona is nice this time of year," he said. "Enjoy the flight."

"We're going to be okay," Katrina whispered and scooted the singed rucksack under the seat.

"I know." I stood, lifting Angel with me. "No more running scared."

"I'm not scared." Angel hugged my neck.

"Of course you're not."

"I want to sit by the window."

"Okay." I put her down in a window seat and sat next to her, but when I tried to help her buckle her safety belt she shooed me away.

"I can do it myself."

"Sure you can. Silly me." I buckled myself in.

Katrina settled in the chair opposite mine, crossed her legs at her knees. Those beautiful knees. I wondered if she would have left me if I was still an old woman. Or would love and loyalty have prevailed? I decided on the latter.

Maybe one day I would show her what I really looked like, take off the pendant...no. She would never see me that way.

"Are you all right?" Katrina asked me. "You look like you've seen a ghost."

I had. "I'm ready to start a new life." After being unable to live a normal life for so long, I was ready to live life the way life was meant to be lived, without all the killing and chaos of the New York City underworld.

Katrina sighed, her eyes moist and shiny. "I'm ready too, Gem."

Gem. My name didn't sound right anymore, didn't fit my new persona of mother and family matriarch. "I think that name has to go."

Concern washed over Katrina's face. "Do you think someone will come looking for you?"

"Don't worry. I didn't leave any loose ends. But I did learn my real name before I became Gem."

"Oh?" Her eyebrows tweaked with curiosity. "What was it?"

"Olivia."

"Olivia?" She smiled. "Yes. I think that suits you."

Angel took my hand. "Olivia is a nice name. I like it."

"Then it's settled. I am Gem no more."

"Can I be Gem?"

"No. You're an Angel. Not a rock."

Katrina chuckled.

The jet rumbled at full power and roared into the night sky. Through the oval windows, the lights of New York City twinkled as if they were waving me goodbye.

About the Author

Originally from South Wales, I have held a wide range of jobs from tennis player to gym manager to health service worker. I turned 40 in October, am married to Claire, and we have an insane ginger cat called Wookie. I went to school with Catherine Zeta-Jones, have played tennis with Jamie Redknapp, and coached Great Britain's first ever World Number One tennis player.

I have always loved horror stories, having grown up with Jason Voorhees and his slasher friends, and I love writing them even more. The thought of taking normal people and putting them in terrifying situations gives me a fantastic buzz. I hope to convey that buzz to my readers in every story I write.

https://www.twbpress.com

**Science Fiction, Supernatural, Horror, Thrillers,
Romance, and more**